OUR SECRET SUMMER

Our Secret Summer

HARPER BLISS

CHAPTER 1

Raffo parked the car in front of the garage and cut the engine, silencing the music she'd been belting along to. She inhaled deeply and examined the house in front of her. Connor wasn't the kind of person who understated things—quite the opposite —but that's exactly what her best friend had done with this property. It looked vast and luxurious from the outside, more like a year-round home than a weekend getaway place.

She got out of the car and stretched her limbs. Raffo hadn't stopped on the road from Los Angeles to Big Bear Lake. It was only a two-hour drive and she just wanted to go-go-go. Away from LA and Mia and their open relationship that had failed so spectacularly, it might be funny if it didn't hurt so damn much. The temperature dropped several degrees at this elevation, a welcome relief from LA's smoggy summer heat.

Raffo grabbed her backpack from the car. She'd fetch her suitcases and painting materials after she'd explored the inside of this swanky house she'd be occupying for a while. It was up in the air exactly how long—as long as it took, she guessed— but Connor had told her she could stay as long as she wanted. The property belonged to his mother who was on a spiritual

'Eat-Pray-Love journey'—Connor's words—through Europe and she wouldn't be using it this summer.

Raffo walked to the front door and put the key in the lock. As soon as she opened the door, her gaze was drawn to the massive windows overlooking the lake. Oh yes, this would do nicely. Raffo might have to go on her very own spiritual journey to get her groove back, but she didn't have to travel all the way to Europe for it. A two-hour drive might be all it took.

When she was able to look away from the magnificent view, she scanned the living area. There was a half-full glass of water on the coffee table and the couch cushions were propped together at one side, as though someone had recently rested their head on them. And was that a used coffee cup on the kitchen counter?

"Hello?" Raffo shouted. Was Connor playing a prank on her? He was supposed to be on the way to New York to visit his long-distance boyfriend, but maybe it had just been a ruse. But why would Connor want to stay here with her when Raffo had been sleeping in his spare room for the past month?

No answer came. Still, it was becoming glaringly obvious that someone was staying here. Maybe there had been a mix-up. Maybe Connor's mother had rented the place out for the summer while she was in Europe. Surely Connor had checked with her whether Raffo could stay here?

Raffo advanced farther into the house.

"Anyone here?" she yelled, a little louder this time.

She headed toward the stairs and listened carefully for any noise coming from the second floor. She thought she heard something, but couldn't quite make out what. Or maybe she was just imagining sounds now. She ascended the stairs, trying to make as much noise as possible, continuing to announce herself until her repeated hellos felt too silly and awkward.

She cast her gaze around the landing. The door to the bathroom was open. So was the door to the master bedroom. Raffo's eyes were drawn to a shape on the bed. She froze. Her heart hammered in her chest. She definitely wasn't alone. She felt like an intruder—she *was* an intruder. What should she do? Call Connor or approach the stranger? Raffo wasn't someone who scared easily and her curiosity quickly got the better of her. She peered into the bedroom. *Oh, damn.* Raffo withdrew. Not only was that person a naked woman with the sheets thrown off her chest, but that was also Connor's mother. What the hell was going on? Raffo did panic now. Because why wasn't Connor's mother responding to her calls?

Raffo tried to remember her name, but it escaped her. She'd only met Connor's mother a few times at the gallery. Was she really sleeping so soundly that she hadn't heard Raffo's many hellos?

Raffo didn't want to, but she looked a little closer. She did her utmost to ignore her best friend's mother's bare breasts and focus on her ears to check for ear plugs, but they were covered with her tousled, honey-blond hair.

Raffo stopped thinking and shot into action mode. She knocked on the half-open door while trying to remember if, perhaps, Connor's mother was hearing-impaired.

All of a sudden, two bright blue eyes stared right back at her. Connor's mother inhaled sharply as she sat up, covering herself. Then she removed a pair of stark-white AirPods from her ears.

"Raffo?" she said, her face a mask of confusion. "Is that you?"

"Mrs., um, Hart." Raffo still didn't know where to look, even though Connor's mom had wrapped as much of the sheet around her chest as possible.

She shook her head. "Hart is Connor's father's last name. I'm Dylan French." Somehow, she managed to send Raffo a zestful smile. Maybe she'd just had an ultra-rejuvenating nap. Or what she'd been listening to through those AirPods was something extra special.

"I'm so sorry, Mrs. French," Raffo mumbled. "Did you not know I was coming here? Did Connor not tell you?"

Connor's mom expelled a deep sigh. "It's complicated," she said. "And please call me Dylan."

"Why don't I wait for you downstairs?" Raffo needed to get her bearings as well, and she was sure Dylan could do with some time to regroup—and put some clothes on.

Dylan nodded. "Pour us a glass of that chablis in the fridge, will you?"

CHAPTER 2

Dylan crashed back onto the mattress. That her son's best friend had just walked in on her half-naked was the very least of her worries. She had a lot of explaining to do, most of all to Connor, but she would have to start with Raffo—and hope that Raffo could keep a secret.

She took a breath and hopped out of bed. She found her discarded clothes from earlier and quickly slipped into a pair of jeans and light-blue T-shirt. She must have fallen asleep while listening to her podcast. Dylan ran her fingers through her hair, decided not to consult a mirror—Raffo had seen her asleep and half-naked already—and hurried down the stairs for a conversation she wasn't ready to have—about the very reason why she was here without anyone knowing.

Raffo was gazing out of the window. Behind her on the kitchen countertop stood two glasses of wine. She turned around as Dylan approached.

"It's so gorgeous here," Raffo said.

Dylan took her in. Connor talked about Raffo a lot, so Dylan felt like she knew her better than she should—she doubted her son talked as much about his mother to his best friend. Raffo was tall and broad-shouldered and exuded an intriguing energy with her long, black hair but decidedly masculine clothes. Dylan had also witnessed firsthand what Connor had been saying all along: Raffo Shah was the Connor Hart Gallery's most extraordinary talent to date.

"Yeah. I'm so lucky." For now, Dylan thought.

"I did as you asked." Raffo nodded at the generously filled wine glasses. "It's the least I can do after walking in on you like that. Again, I'm so sorry."

"It's not your fault." Dylan grabbed the glasses and handed one to Raffo. "Shall we sit on the deck?" Difficult conversations were always made easier by sitting shoulder-to-shoulder over-looking the water.

They sat in two sun-bleached Adirondack chairs. Dylan took a sip of wine, swallowed slowly, then said, "Connor doesn't know I'm here. He thinks I'm on a silent retreat in a Swiss forest, unreachable by phone or email." Lying to her son had been more awful than the reason for the lie—her own stupidity. "I can't tell him the truth yet. I came here to work up to it, to get myself ready."

"Are you okay?" Raffo fixed her coal-black eyes on Dylan. "Physically, I mean?"

"Physically, I couldn't be better. Well, for a fifty-nine-year-old woman, at least." Dylan chuckled despite herself, to lighten the mood. "I did something really stupid and I've been so mortified, I haven't been able to tell Connor about it. I haven't told anyone. I lost… a lot of money and I came to Big Bear to hide out. I can't afford a trip to Europe any longer." Dylan tried to un-hunch her shoulders, but they remained glued to her ears. "I'll have to sell this place." She shook her head. "It's all a big mess."

"I'm so sorry." Raffo shot Dylan a gentle smile. "You must feel really bad if you didn't tell Con. Surely, you know he thinks the absolute world of you."

Warmth blossomed in Dylan's chest at Raffo's words—so

6

Connor did talk about her to his friends?—but it was quickly obliterated by a sharp pang of guilt.

"Thanks for saying that. That's really kind of you." Dylan huffed out some air. "I hate to keep a secret from him. It's horrible to be hiding out here, lying to my son about where I am." Since she'd arrived in Big Bear two weeks ago, Dylan had picked up her phone to call Connor several times every single day, but she couldn't bring herself to do it. Then, as time passed, and the lie she'd told her son had stretched and stretched, it only became harder to come clean.

"He's going to be such a drama queen when he finds out," Raffo said so matter-of-factly, it made Dylan burst into an inadvertent chuckle.

"Yeah," Dylan agreed. "He gets that from me."

Panic seized her as a thought jumped into Dylan's head. "He's not going to show up here, is he? To meet you?"

Raffo shook her head. "He's in New York with Murray until next week."

Dylan's shoulders loosened a fraction. She hadn't talked to her son in two whole weeks, which was the greatest agony of all.

"He'll probably call me, though," Raffo said.

"Oh, fuck." Dylan couldn't ask Raffo to lie to her best friend.

"It's okay. I'll text him to let him know I've arrived safe and well and my cell service is spotty or something like that," Raffo said.

"Thank you."

Raffo shuffled in her seat. "I should probably also come up with a reason why I can't stay here after all."

"Oh, no, no. You can stay. Really. You're very welcome here." Dylan was relieved to have someone to talk to. To get out of her head. To stop spiraling and succumbing to doom scenarios. "If you want to. You probably didn't come here to spend time with a woman in crisis. I get that. But you should at least stay the night. Let me make you dinner. Sleep on it." She tilted her head. "Why did you come here, if I may ask?" Dylan rolled her eyes at herself. "I'm sorry. I'm just rambling now. I'm just…" Dylan didn't continue because she didn't know what else to say.

"It's okay. It's a lot." Raffo had a very calm, soothing voice. "I'll stay the night. We'll see in the morning." She didn't elaborate on her reason for coming to Big Bear. She probably wanted to escape LA for a bit. Have some time to herself. That's why Dylan had bought this place.

"I'll make up the other room for you and get you some towels." Dylan pushed herself up.

"You don't have to do that. Especially if you're already making me dinner." Raffo slowly nodded at the chair Dylan had been sitting in. "Just relax. Isn't that why people come here?"

Raffo had such a quietly commanding quality about her, Dylan sank back into her chair as though someone was pulling her down. She reached for her glass of wine, took a long swig, and gazed into the soothing water of the lake. She'd been doing that since she arrived, but she still felt like the least intelligent person on the planet—a sensation Dylan was decidedly not used to.

CHAPTER 3

Raffo had made her bed and taken a long, hot shower, letting the steaming water wash away the dust from the drive. She headed down the stairs, her stomach rumbling as she followed the delicious smells emanating from the kitchen.

So far, coming to Big Bear had been the opposite of what she'd expected—solitude and all the space she needed to just *be* —but life could be funny that way. Like when Mia had suggested they open up their relationship in order to make it more robust, as if the solution to their problems was to invite others into their bed.

Dylan was clearly going through some things—and Connor would have a fit once he found out about this—but she hadn't seemed too thrown by, firstly, Raffo showing up out of the blue and, secondly, walking in on her asleep and half-naked, all sun-kissed skin and tousled hair.

Dylan was humming along to a Fleetwood Mac song, looking far more relaxed than earlier, her hips swaying slightly to the beat as she stirred something aromatic on the stove.

Raffo caught herself admiring Dylan's shapely, jeans-clad rear for a tantalizing split second before saying, "I hope you have enough for two of whatever smells so good." Raffo had planned to get settled and then head into town for some grocery shopping, but this day was not going according to plan at all.

Dylan turned around with a crooked grin on her lips. Her hair caught the light of the evening sun as she moved. Objectively speaking, and for a woman on the cusp of sixty, she was rather stunning. Raffo stopped her train of thought and only managed a strained smile in response. Yet, it was far better than her brain being suffused with images of Mia all the damn time.

"There's plenty for unexpected guests," Dylan said. "I hope you're hungry."

"What's cooking?" Raffo settled at the kitchen island opposite the stove.

"Pasta primavera," Dylan said, her attention back on the task at hand. "Ready in two minutes."

"Lucky me," Raffo joked. "If Connor had told me this house came with a private chef, I would have come up a lot sooner."

It was a true delight to see Dylan's shoulders shake as she laughed.

———

Raffo and Dylan sat opposite each other at the weathered wooden table on the deck by the lake. The view was gorgeous, the air was just the right amount of crisp without being chilly, and that chablis was not half bad either.

"I should have seen it coming from a mile away. The distance growing between us, the silences that stretched too long, the way her eyes stopped lighting up when I entered the room. But I had my head too far up my own ass to notice until it was too late."

"I'm sorry," Dylan said, her voice soft with understanding. "Is that why you came out here? To get away, clear your head?"

Raffo nodded, not trusting herself to speak around the lump growing in her throat. She took a fortifying sip of wine before continuing. "She didn't just break my heart, she also stole my

10

mojo. It's like I can't paint anymore. I still go through the motions, but that thing that makes it special, that makes it feel like the most *me* I can ever be, is just… gone. And without my mojo, without my art, I only feel like half a person."

"What you're feeling is perfectly normal," Dylan reassured her. "You're grieving the loss of a relationship, a huge part of your life. You need time to heal."

"I'm just so scared that she broke something vital in me, something that can never be fixed and that, as a result, I'll never paint a great work again." The words poured out of Raffo in a torrent, the anxiety that had been gnawing at her, growing with each failed attempt at painting, with each frustrating day spent staring at a maddeningly mediocre canvas. Raffo had sat on Connor's couch so paralyzed with this particular fear, he'd practically pushed her into her car in the direction of Big Bear.

"How long were you and Mia together?" Dylan asked gently.

"Ten years," Raffo said. "Well, minus two months and a handful of agonizing days that felt like an eternity."

Dylan whistled through her teeth. "Damn. A decade is a long time."

"Yeah," Raffo said on a ragged sigh. "God, I loved her. Still do." She swallowed something out of her throat. "I still think she's the greatest person in the world." She scoffed. "Certainly not the nicest or the kindest or the most considerate, but just one of those irresistible larger-than-life characters, you know? Someone who only has to take one step into any room to have all eyes on her." Raffo shook her head. "Not that she isn't also nice and kind and all those things. At least, she used to be, but… she fell out of love. Like, it didn't match anymore." A fat tear slid down Raffo's cheek, but she made no move to wipe it away. "The love I felt for her and the love she had for me, they stopped matching up. It became completely lopsided, uneven, and it's the most excruciating feeling in the world when the person you love the most, the one you can't imagine life without, stops loving you back the same way."

"Oh, Raffo. Oh, sweetheart." Unlike Mia over the past few months, Dylan was plenty kind. "Here." She slipped Raffo a clean napkin from a stack on the table.

"I just want to fucking paint again." Raffo dabbed at the tear on her cheek. "I'm, like, at least fifty percent happier if I can do some painting. It fills me up, gives my life such meaning and joy, but I can't. I'm totally blocked. It's driving me insane."

"It will come back. Your talent is an intrinsic part of who you are. It hasn't gone anywhere, even if it feels out of reach right now. You just need some time, and some peace, to rediscover it." Dylan smiled sweetly. "There's no doubt in my mind about that."

Raffo shrugged, then peered at the lake. "Maybe a few good swims will do the trick."

"That lake can be somewhat of a miracle worker." Dylan sounded wistful. "I hope you stay long enough to experience its magic."

"Magic?" Raffo looked at Dylan. "Has it magically solved your problem?"

"My problem is a little different than yours," was all Dylan said—and rightly so.

Raffo hadn't meant to sound so sharp. "Look at us," she said. "In this gorgeous spot, feeling so miserable."

"That's just life, though." Dylan inhaled deeply. "That's just how life can fuck with you." Connor's mother certainly liked to swear—and Raffo was rather fond of a woman who knew her way around an expletive.

CHAPTER 4

Who was this Mia who had dumped the likes of Raffo Shah? Dylan didn't get it. Then again, she wouldn't. Connor was always raving about Raffo and now that Dylan had spent a few hours in her company, apart from devastated about her break-up, Dylan found Raffo to be incredibly down-to-earth and unexpectedly captivating. She could see why a drama queen like her son would have someone so cool and collected as his best friend. Even the way Raffo spoke was thoughtful and measured—even when she talked about how she got dumped. Even when she shed a tear, she did so with an incongruous kind of dignity.

Dylan must have crossed paths with larger-than-life-Mia the same way she had with Raffo, but she hadn't paid any attention at the time—Mia's room-filling charisma must have failed to reach her.

Dylan had many questions—and she hadn't had a proper conversation with another human being in two long weeks—but she decided it was best to further avoid the topic of Raffo's ex tonight.

"I had my trip to Europe all planned and booked. I'd been looking forward to it for the past year," Dylan confessed. "Then the cryptocurrency I invested most of my savings in crashed, and here I am." Saying it to Raffo's serene, kind face somehow made it easier to speak these wretched words aloud.

"Fuck." Raffo's voice was deep and low and perfectly matched how she looked. "How much did you lose?"

Dylan was taken aback by her directness, but part of her also appreciated it. She took a sip of wine, gathering the courage to declare the amount.

"Half a million dollars."

"Oh, damn." Raffo's voice wasn't so evenly deep any longer. "Oh, fuck, I'm so sorry."

"It was my own fault. I got greedy. I invested too much and I just kept going, ignoring the warning signs." She cast her gaze over the deck, then let it land on the soothing water. "Apart from taking a long vacation, I had big plans for that money. I quit my job and I wanted one last hurrah for my career. One last adventure before retiring." She turned her palms upwards. "I'm going to have to sell this place to make up for what I lost."

"Fuck. I really am sorry, Dylan. But, um, you may have put your money into it, but you didn't cause the currency to crash."

"That's irrelevant." Dylan found it impossible to show herself kindness when it came to this. "I got dollar signs in my eyes and was convinced I could make some easy money. I couldn't have been more wrong. That's all on me."

"This might irk you under the circumstances," Raffo said. "But in the end, it's just money. You're healthy. Your son is healthy and happy. And you're a good-looking woman. I mean, things could be worse."

Dylan broke into a chuckle, despite how she felt about herself. "I could be ugly?" she joked.

"For instance." Raffo shot her the kind of goofy smile that obviously didn't come natural to her. "When I met Mia, I'd only just found the courage to start painting. I had nothing. I worked three minimum-wage jobs just to keep afloat." She briefly pursed her lips. "My paintings sell for six figures now, thanks to

Connor. My point is that money comes and goes, but what difference does it even make when the rest of your life is falling apart?"

"It makes a big difference when you've just lost half a million. I've always made good money, but five hundred thousand bucks is a hell of a lot to no longer have in your account." Dylan huffed out some air. "But it's not just the money. It's the shame. I'm so ashamed of what happened. Of how I let myself get carried away. How I, basically, lost my sanity. That's the biggest reason I haven't told Connor yet. I won't be able to bear the look on his face."

"So you're hiding out here." Raffo nodded thoughtfully. "I'm sorry if I sounded flippant earlier. That was not my intention. My relationship with money is very up and down and I should know that everyone relates to it in their own weird, special way. I get why you haven't told Con. You don't want him to think any less of you."

Dylan managed a small smile. "It's a relief that I don't have to worry about Connor's money situation, what with his gallery representing you and your paintings selling for such big amounts." It certainly hadn't always been this way and Dylan had loaned her only child plenty of money when he'd just started his gallery.

"The art world is all about capitalism now," Raffo said, the tone of her voice betraying her ambivalence about that.

"Congratulations, by the way. I love your work. Connor gave me one of the paintings from your first show at his gallery. It's so incredibly joyful. It doesn't surprise me in the least that your work achieves higher and higher prices."

"Thanks," Raffo all but mumbled.

It surprised Dylan that Raffo found it so hard to take a compliment. Her star had been on the rise for several years— surely she must be used to it by now. But, of course, Raffo had lost her mojo.

"No pressure, okay." Dylan pointed at a spot beneath the

porch that got great light during the day. "But you can set up your things over there, if you want. I'll give you all the privacy you need."

"Thanks." There was a note of something deeper in her voice. "If I decide to stay." Raffo waggled her eyebrows.

"If you decide to stay." This dinner with Raffo had been such a welcome change from Dylan being on her own all the time, she truly hoped Raffo would linger a while—even if it meant not telling her best friend about it. But maybe it was too much to ask.

"I'll stay a couple of days, anyway." Raffo gazed at the spot that Dylan had just indicated. "I just want to clear my head. Go on a few hikes. Have a couple of swims in this allegedly magical lake. Get a few nights of decent sleep."

"Anything you want."

"Well." Raffo painted on a devilish grin. "I was welcomed by a half-naked lady who then proceeded to cook me a delicious dinner, so I'm off to a wonderful, if slightly surprising start."

Dylan smiled, again, considering that she and Raffo could help each other put their respective issues into perspective. And that might—indeed—be wonderful, if slightly surprising.

CHAPTER 5

Raffo wanted to call Connor so badly. A couple of times, she picked up her cell and her finger hovered over his number. But she had agreed to keep Dylan's secret. Lovely, sweet Dylan. Raffo couldn't tell anyone that she had walked in on her best friend's mother half-naked, and had subsequently spent a lovely evening with her. Maybe it was for the best, even if she and Connor had the kind of relationship that didn't harbor many secrets—Raffo knew more about Murray, Connor's boyfriend, than she ever wanted to know. In return, Connor knew all the details of Raffo's failed open relationship with Mia —not that Raffo had taken much advantage of the opening up part of their decade-long affair.

As she brushed her teeth, and looked at herself in the mirror, she concluded it might be easier to hide out in Big Bear to keep Dylan's secret than to go back to Los Angeles, where she actually had to face Connor and would actively have to lie to him until his mother told him where she really was. Staying here protected her from doing that—and she still had to get her mojo back.

On top of all that, if you could judge such a thing by one evening spent together, Dylan was wonderful company.

Although that shouldn't come as a surprise to Raffo. Connor only ever spoke highly of his mother. They were thick as thieves, which is why it surprised Raffo that Dylan would keep such a big thing from Connor.

She texted Connor that she had arrived safely at his mother's house in Big Bear Lake, but wouldn't be able to speak to him on the phone due to spotty cell and internet service. She added, to cover her tracks more, that she was happy to be off the grid for a while—perhaps it would enable her to paint again quicker—and thanked him for the opportunity to stay at his mother's house. It didn't feel totally right—of course it didn't—but Raffo was here with Dylan, so she had to follow her rules.

As she got into bed, she did hope that Dylan would come to her senses and tell her son sooner rather than later. Maybe she could talk to her about it tomorrow, after she'd told her that she had decided to stay a while. To take things easy and enjoy a slow, unhurried, stress-free pace of life. With Dylan as unexpected but pleasant company.

For the first time in a long while, Raffo fell asleep almost as soon as she closed her eyes. Yet another reason to stay.

———

"I'm truly thrilled." Dylan's lips seemed to have taken on a life of their own and were fixed in a permanent smile. What was that all about? Sure, she was glad for the companionship because it got her out of her own head, where she'd been spending too much time, but it couldn't just be that. Dylan glanced at Raffo, who looked brooding yet radiant in the morning light, and realized that she was looking forward to helping Raffo feel better about herself. To see her come into her own again. To watch her paint. It would be such an honor to witness Raffo Shah put paint to canvas. "Please, stay as long as you like."

"I do have an issue with not telling Connor." Raffo was nothing if not straightforward. "I get it, but I hate lying to him."

"I know." In the grand scheme of things, and in the hierarchies of white lies—if there even was such a thing—Dylan didn't think this particular lie, this omission of the truth more like, was that bad. She just needed a little more time to lick her wounds before facing Connor who, she knew very well, would ultimately be understanding, but not before making a big drama out of it. A drama she could do without at this stage. And she had already set the lie in motion when she had supposedly left for Europe, where she was meant to stay for two months. "Can you give me a little more time, please?" Dylan looked into Raffo's dark eyes.

"He's my best friend, not just my gallerist." Raffo sounded earnest.

Dylan nodded. There wasn't much else she could do.

"Also, um…" The hesitation in Raffo's words didn't show in her face when she looked at Dylan. "Given your circumstances, I want to pay rent for staying here. It's only fair."

"You don't have to pay to stay here, Raffo." Dylan shook her head. "I'm not destitute."

In response, Raffo just arched up her thick, black eyebrows.

"Okay, look." Dylan placed her elbows on the kitchen island and leaned toward Raffo. "I'll make you a deal."

Raffo tilted her head, a small smile playing on her lips. "Yes?"

"Paint something for me. You don't have to give me the work. But if you want to pay me some kind of rent for staying, then get your mojo back while you're here. That would mean a lot to me."

Raffo frowned. "But getting my mojo back is a reward for me. I don't get how that translates into paying you."

"You getting your mojo back is a reward for everyone, including me." Last night, Dylan had explored Raffo's website and had marveled at her work. At its colors and its exuberant

19

spirit. Even though she'd seen a lot of her paintings before, they looked different after spending an evening with the artist.

"But no pressure?" Raffo grinned.

"It's not meant as pressure. Simply appreciation and an unshakable belief that you'll be creating genius art again in no time."

"Genius?" Raffo scoffed, then shook her head. "How about I buy all the groceries and take you out for a meal whenever you want?" She scratched the side of her head. "I'd offer to cook, but then I think you'll want me to leave as soon as possible."

"Deal." Dylan stretched out her hand.

Raffo looked at it, then shook it.

"Your cooking is that bad?" Dylan asked.

"It's not so much that I can't cook," Raffo said. "It's more that I have such an aversion to it that you can taste it in the food I make."

"Really?" Dylan was more intrigued by Raffo with every minute she spent with her. "Why is that?"

"It's a long story."

"Good thing we'll be here for a while." Dylan couldn't shake the feeling that, ever since Raffo had arrived, things had started looking up for her—despite her bank account not having been magically replenished overnight.

Raffo chuckled low in her throat. "How about you make me a shopping list and I go to the store first?"

CHAPTER 6

Raffo floated on her back in the lake and gazed up at the bright blue sky. The water was cool but not cold and as clear as the sky overhead. Little had she known that when Connor had pushed her into her car, she'd end up in this little slice of paradise.

Her head was still too full of thoughts of Mia—and her new girlfriend who, mercifully, Raffo hadn't met—but those thoughts were more bearable out here, away from the city she shared with her ex. Away from her everyday life that hadn't felt like hers any longer. Her heart was still broken into a million pieces, but Raffo had found an excellent distraction in Dylan.

It was easy enough to forget she was Connor's mother—nor did it matter when it came to considering how fine her behind looked in a pair of jeans shorts. How she had the kind of hair that caught the sunlight in a way that made you feel like summer was simply an inextricable part of her. How her deep blue eyes sparkled when Raffo said something that surprised her. None of it meant anything. It was just the flimsiest of balms for Raffo's ruptured soul. She was just taking whatever morsel of joy she could find, and sneaking peeks at Dylan brought her a tiny burst of joy every time.

Maybe it was because Dylan could not look more the opposite of Mia with her sharp body angles and jet-black hair. Dylan was much softer around the edges and the frivolous smattering of ginger freckles on her nose a sight for sore eyes as well as hearts. Raffo simply enjoyed looking at Dylan. She was hot—and kind and empathetic and a great listener—but that's where it ended. It felt a bit like going on a wellness retreat and finding it came with a private chef/therapist who was also very easy on the eye. Like a win-win when all she'd been doing lately was losing.

Raffo tilted her body upward and gazed in the direction of the house. Dylan was standing on the deck, waving at her. Raffo swam closer.

"Lunch is ready." Dylan threw in a wide smile as well. God, what a woman. Connor might be pissed off when he found out Dylan had lied about her trip, but he should still thank his lucky stars every single day for having a parent like Dylan. Raffo knew from experience that not every kid got that lucky.

———

"I might get my painting materials out later," Raffo said. She'd been studying the spot Dylan had designated for that purpose all throughout lunch, and its appeal was increasing.

"Already?"

"Just to set up." Raffo looked into Dylan's kind eyes. "And don't worry. I brought plenty of protective sheeting."

"I'm not worried," Dylan said. "The way I see it, any paint spatters left by Raffo Shah can only increase the value of this house."

Raffo ignored Dylan's comment. A paint stain on the porch was still a paint stain, no matter whose hand had left it there.

"Can that spot be screened off?" Raffo asked. "I can't leave my paints and brushes exposed to the elements." Raffo wasn't too worried yet about any work she might produce, but she'd need a location for safekeeping that as well—later.

22

"Yep, that's why I think it's such an ideal place for you to work." Dylan sent her a smile. "No pressure of course."

Something went soft inside Raffo at the sight of another one of Dylan's gentle, friendly smiles.

"Let me take you out tonight. To thank you." Raffo smiled back.

"You don't have to. Seriously. I should be thanking you for not telling Connor about me being here." Dylan's smile faded. "Besides, I don't feel comfortable going out as long as I haven't told Con. You never know who I might run into. News has a habit of traveling fast in places like this."

"Fair enough. But I can at least pick us up a pizza or something. Please don't feel as though you have to cook for me all the time."

"That's not how I feel." The skin around Dylan's eyes crinkled as she smiled. "Whether I make food just for myself or for both of us really doesn't make a difference."

"Okay." Raffo nodded. "Thank you."

"You're very welcome." Dylan held a hand in front of her mouth as she suppressed a yawn. "Being here on my own the past two weeks has made me accustomed to an after-lunch nap."

"A topless after-lunch nap, if I remember correctly." And how could I ever forget, Raffo didn't say out loud. While she deemed it appropriate to admire Dylan's supreme physique from a safe distance, brazen flirting was far from proper behavior. She'd probably already said too much, although it was just a joke and it was such a pleasure to see Dylan break out into a chuckle like that in response.

"You got me," Dylan said.

"I won't walk in on you this time. I promise."

"Good to know." Dylan didn't make to get up.

"It goes without saying that I'll take care of the dishes and your kitchen will be spotless when you come down from your nap." Raffo wasn't too fond of doing dishes either—of any housework, really—but cleaning up after Dylan cooking for her hardly felt like a chore.

"Thank you." Dylan rose from her chair.

Raffo's gaze was immediately drawn to the smooth curve of her thighs, which were now at table level. She quickly cast her eyes upward. "Have an excellent nap."

As Dylan walked inside the house, Raffo considered that just being able to think of Dylan as a smoking hot lady was infinitely better than the coldness that had settled inside her heart since Mia had dumped her. Moreover, it was perfectly innocent, just a little indulgence which, really, was to be enjoyed as much as possible just for the sheer miracle of it existing at all.

She cleared the table while trying very hard not to think of Dylan sleeping upstairs with her breasts bared to the crisp Big Bear air.

CHAPTER 7

For the past weeks, Dylan had been listening to financial advice podcasts, hoping to pick up some sort of miraculous tip that could help her make up for the money she'd lost. All these podcasts had accomplished, however, was to put her swiftly to sleep. As though her brain rejected any talk of money and chose to switch off at the sound of it.

As she crawled into bed, her AirPods already in her ears out of habit, she remembered an ad she'd seen recently—she couldn't recall where—for steamy audiobooks read by big-name actors. She'd wondered at the time, perhaps prudishly, what times they were living in that this was now a thing. She can't have been that uptight about it, however, because she had promptly downloaded the app, although she hadn't listened to anything on it yet. She opened it on her phone and scrolled through the options.

Those really were some big names. Elisa Fox. Stella Flack. Brian Walsh and ooh, Ida Burton. For the life of her, Dylan could not resist Ida Burton. There had definitely been a time in her life when she'd wished she was Ida Burton, although, like every other person on the planet, Dylan hadn't known that the magnificent Ida Burton had locked herself into a big, old Hollywood closet all that time. But none of that mattered anymore. Ida Burton was out and proud now and married to Faye Fleming. Dylan downloaded the story read by Ida Burton hoping for some sultry sapphic content to accompany her nap. Neither the app, nor the story, and least of all Ida, let her down.

Dylan didn't sleep a wink—how could she with Ida Burton whispering sentences like that straight into her ears? She'd need to dive straight into the lake to cool off. She slipped into her bikini and headed downstairs.

What she saw there was even better than Ida's sensual crooning in her ears.

Raffo stood in front of a canvas that was decidedly not blank. She was staring at it intently, paintbrush in hand. Dylan didn't want to disturb her, but she also didn't want to spy on her. Either way, she couldn't look away if she tried.

She cleared her throat to announce herself.

Raffo turned around and gave her a funny look, before not-so-subtly raking her gaze from Dylan's bare feet to her bikini-covered breasts.

"Sorry." Raffo blinked, as though shaking something off her. "I didn't hear you. I wasn't expecting, um, yeah, this." Her eyes raked over Dylan's body.

"A swimsuit in a lake house?" Dylan wasn't born yesterday —and Raffo had already declared her 'good-looking' the day before. "Or are you disappointed I'm not topless?" She followed up with a wide smile, conveying she was just joking. Although, after the story she'd just listened to, Dylan was feeling perhaps a touch too brazen. She immediately felt sorry for Raffo, who was nursing a severely broken heart.

"I hope you don't feel you need to wear a top just because I'm here." Raffo had, obviously, quickly regrouped. "Far be it for me to cramp your style."

"You're painting." Dylan pointed out the obvious to deflect attention from the blush creeping up her cheeks.

"Not really." Raffo turned to the canvas she'd been working

on. "This is not painting, just noodling. Just greasing the wheels."

"Whatever you say." Dylan headed farther onto the deck. "I'm going for a swim." She couldn't help swaying her hips a little as she walked to the pier that stuck out from the deck. She dove straight into the water, hoping it would do its job of tamping down the Ida-Burton-created heat beneath her skin.

―――――

Raffo had just been feeling her way through the familiar motions of painting. She didn't have a specific idea for a new work yet—it was too soon for that. She'd painted what could pass for a body of water, because the lake was omnipresent around her. But now, in said lake, Dylan was swimming in what could only be called a very skimpy bikini. Raffo inwardly chastised herself for not keeping her roving gaze in check earlier. *Jesus.* Luckily, Dylan had made light of it—as she did. Maybe that was the thing about Dylan. Despite the investment mistake she'd made, and the shame it saddled her with, she walked through life, at least life in her gorgeous lake house at Big Bear, with an infectious lightness—an airiness that Raffo craved for herself. Of course, now her glance was irresistibly drawn to the water again—and to the person swimming in it. Dylan swam away from the shore with long, strong strokes, heading deeper into the lake.

Then, out of nowhere, the image popped up in Raffo's brain. The image she wanted to paint. The only image she could possibly paint right now. Unfortunately, it was also an image she couldn't possibly paint. Not with her canvas out in the open like this, for Dylan to walk past twenty times every day. *Argh.* Raffo had been waiting, fruitlessly, for a moment like this for months now. For that magical flash of inspiration, that hell-yeah moment when she just knew—no doubt about it—that this was what she would paint next. It was an integral, indispensable part of her process.

She looked out into the water. Dylan was just a bobbing wet head of blond hair far away—she really was going for that swim. Maybe if Raffo asked for her permission, but still… She closed her eyes, took a breath, and the colors exploded onto the backs of her eyelids. *Oh, fuck*. This was wholly unexpected but so incredibly sweet and joyful. Just like that, it had come back to her. With every breath she took, her precious mojo rushed through her. Just like that, she knew, with every single fiber of her being, that she wanted to paint Dylan.

Topless.

Fuck.

She took another breath. Maybe she could paint her in that skimpy bikini—it would lend itself well to some adventurous color-blending. As though asking permission from her muse, which was a concept Raffo didn't rationally believe in, except when she was in the throes of something exactly like this. She took another breath and closed her eyes in order to see what she had to see. Nope. No bikini, no matter how skimpy, in sight.

Raffo exhaled deeply as she braced herself for an awkward conversation over dinner later.

CHAPTER 8

Dylan was marinating the vegetables she'd cook on the grill later. The silence in the house suddenly struck her. She always listened to music when preparing a meal, but somehow she'd forgotten. She blamed Ida Burton.

She connected her phone to the sound system that had speakers in the kitchen as well as on the deck. Raffo had put away her painting materials and her canvas was stowed away for the day, everything safely ensconced behind the wooden porch screen that Dylan only used when she shored up the house for winter.

Ida Burton's voice came over the speakers.

"Please, lick my clit," Ida said.

Oh no. The steamy story app was still open on Dylan's phone and the story she'd been listening to had just continued playing. Damn it. Dylan lunged for her phone, frantically jabbing at the screen. It was too late, though. Raffo popped her head into the kitchen, a devilish grin on her lips.

"Everything okay here?" she asked, eyebrows all the way up to her hairline.

Dylan swallowed her embarrassment down and leaned into

the moment. "I told Ida Burton to stop calling me, but she just won't leave me alone."

"That's what Ida Burton says when she calls you against your will?" Raffo's eyes sparkled with mischief. "If you don't want to take her call, please forward it to me."

Dylan burst out laughing. "Small IT mishap. It's common at my age."

"It happens to the best of us." Raffo walked into the kitchen. "How about I open some of that rosé I bought this morning? It must be nice and cool by now."

"That would be amazing," Dylan said, grateful for the swift —and gracious—change of subject. "Meanwhile, I'll do my best to put on some actual music." The flush in her cheeks retreated as she swiped away her guilty-pleasure app, and put on some Lady Kings instead, although, when you really listened to the lyrics of some of their songs, it wasn't all that much better.

———

Dylan held her hand on top of her wine glass, indicating she'd had enough. She watched Raffo as she topped up her own glass, emptying the bottle. As had been the case throughout dinner, Dylan couldn't shake the feeling that something was bothering Raffo.

"Are you—" Dylan started to say.

"I need to—" Raffo said at the same time.

"You go," Dylan said.

Raffo shuffled in her seat. "I need to ask you something that will make us both uncomfortable, so how about I start a fire first? We can sit by the fire pit."

"Sure." Dylan watched Raffo as she went to work. Her long, black hair was pulled back into a ponytail and that denim shirt looked so exactly right on her. She clearly knew how to build a fire and five minutes later they sat looking into the flames, the lake shimmering darkly behind it.

Raffo took a sip of wine, swallowed hard—worrying Dylan slightly over what was to come—then said, "I think that, um, my mojo has already made a rather unexpected return."

Dylan couldn't help herself. She turned to Raffo and beamed her a wide smile. "That's amazing. I'm so happy for you."

"The thing about my process is that not always, but sometimes, I get this image in my head. A fully formed, crystal clear image that… well, let's just say that I have no choice but to paint it, or at least try." She scoffed lightly. "I'm sorry if this sounds woo-woo. It's a hard thing to explain."

"It's very interesting and I'm all ears." Dylan made sure there was nothing but encouragement in her voice.

In response, Raffo took another sip of wine. If she was tipsy at all, it didn't show, but Dylan hoped it gave her the liquid courage she so obviously craved to ask Dylan this 'uncomfortable' question.

"This afternoon, an image… came to me."

Dylan nodded in silence instead of expressing her elation. For some reason, Raffo was finding this very hard to articulate and she wanted to respect that—even if she didn't fully get it.

"It doesn't help me to be bashful about this and it's going to be weird and awkward either way." Raffo turned to her, then rolled her eyes—presumably at herself. "The image was of you, Dylan. I don't know why, although it's hardly rocket science. Ever since I've arrived here you've been so incredibly nice and lovely and, well, I mean, I walked in on you and my subconscious must have somehow latched onto that particular image and now I just can't let it go. It's selfish of me to even mention it to you, what with me invoking my muse and all that." Raffo scoffed again. "You should really, um, tell me not to do it, but —" She puffed out some air. "I'd like your permission to paint you. Topless." She gave a weird chuckle. "Oh, fuck. I'm so sorry. I think the air here is messing with my head."

Dylan fought to keep her jaw from dropping. This was what Raffo had been working up the nerve to ask her all evening?

31

There was no doubt this was a serious question—that Raffo wasn't playing some prank on her.

"Of course, you can paint me." Admittedly, Dylan was taken aback by the fact that she would be topless in this painting, yet part of her already couldn't wait to see it. Because it would be Raffo Shah, all mojo-ed up again, creating it.

"Argh." Raffo put her wine to the side and buried her face in her hands. "This is excruciating."

"No, Raffo, this is absolutely nothing short of excellent news. You want to paint again. You know exactly *what* you want to paint. You've barely been here a day."

"I don't get it either," Raffo said. "All I can tell you is that it just came to me this afternoon and it's one of those images that I feel…" She let her hands fall away from her face and put one on her belly. "I feel it burn inside here. But I'm also well aware that it can be misinterpreted and I know I'm putting you on the spot and it's…"

"It's fine. I would be honored. You didn't even have to ask me." Although, Dylan thought, it was adorable and sweet that Raffo had gone through the trouble—because it really did look like an ordeal to her—to do so. And it would have been difficult for Raffo to hide what she was painting. "Honestly, I couldn't be more thrilled."

"For real?" Raffo found the courage to look Dylan in the eyes ever so briefly.

"Who am I to stand in the way of your art?" Dylan shook her head. "It's why Connor sent you here."

Raffo burst into a chuckle. "It's probably not what he had in mind, though."

"No." Dylan laughed along, even though it reminded her of lying to her son. But it was easy enough to focus on Raffo—and her new-found desire to paint. "So, um, do you need me to pose, or…"

Raffo shook her head. "Oh, no. The image is in here." She tapped a fingertip against her forehead.

"An image of my breasts?" This too, Dylan couldn't help.

"Yes, but…" Raffo took a beat. "I know how this sounds, but that's not what it is."

"That you can't get that image of my breasts out of your head?" Dylan was enjoying this a bit too much, but what was not to enjoy about this moment? It was both a little ludicrous and utterly delightful.

"Yeah, but the image has already completely transformed into something else. Into… art."

"If you say so." Dylan grinned at Raffo.

"No, Dylan, seriously." Raffo pivoted in her chair and looked at Dylan with a grave expression on her face. "I suppose it can only sound as though I'm objectifying you, but that's not what this is. A painting is something entirely different to me." Agitated Raffo still sounded cool; her voice as smooth as the unruffled water of the lake at night. "I would be equally mortified if this made you think that I'm trying something on with you. I swear to you, hand on my heart"— Raffo actually made the gesture—"that is not the case. That's not why I'm here and, well, also lots of other reasons, obviously."

Dylan wouldn't mind hearing those reasons for not trying it on with her, although she could probably guess a fair few, but now—and possibly never—was not the time to ask.

"It's all good, Raffo. Really." Dylan supposed she wouldn't have to bare her breasts to Raffo again any time soon. "If anything, I take it as a huge compliment."

"Thank you for being so chill about this." Raffo finished the last of her wine.

"No problem at all." If only all life's surprises were this much fun.

"To be clear, this work will be just for me. You can have it when I'm done—if I manage to finish it, that is."

"Let's see what happens." Dylan relaxed into her chair. These two evenings with Raffo had been a gazillion times more pleasant than the ones she'd spent on this deck alone, fretting over her mistakes and how to go back to real life.

CHAPTER 9

It was almost laughable how little Raffo had to try. As though last night's conversation, awkward though it was, had freed her from whatever obstacles lingered in her subconscious that had kept her from painting.

She had awoken with the first light and sneaked downstairs like a child on Christmas morning, all glee and bubbly anticipation. She had prepared a new canvas, mixed her colors as though she hadn't also lost the ability to create unique color combinations that gave her paintings that special Raffo-edge—her most prized quality in every review of her work. After Mia had left, her life and also her art had lost its luster, draining away the spectacular colors she was known for into mere shades of gray.

Of course, it was utterly ridiculous that Raffo had been in Big Bear less than forty-eight hours before she felt like herself—like an actual painter—again.

Maybe she really did just have to get out of the city, away from her neighborhood, and her studio, and everything else that made up her life—and made her think of Mia. Maybe Connor had divined this. Or maybe he'd been desperate and had suggested it as just another viable option, which it was.

Who wouldn't want to retreat to a gorgeous, empty lake house in Big Bear? Except, of course, that the house wasn't empty.

It also wasn't rocket science to Raffo that Dylan being Connor's mother, or just being a mother, filled a fraction of the massive mother-shaped hole in her own life.

Raffo went to work and to her delight—and the biggest relief she'd felt in months—she could access that place inside herself where she went to produce her best work effortlessly. Painting itself was never effortless. It was always that very peculiar combination of hard and not-so-hard-because-it's-what-she-did. It always left her exhausted, but only in the best kind of way. It always took a lot from her, but not without giving back double to her in joy and pride and artistic satisfaction.

Raffo wished every single person in the universe could know the special joy of creating art, of making something that couldn't exist without you being there to make it. The piece she was working on now was such a perfect example of how creation, how making something brand-new, was the sum of so many different things. It was the perfect illustration of cause and consequence in a life that was never always good, but, at the very least, always surprising.

Mia breaking up with her, in hindsight, wasn't that much of a surprise, yet it had still shocked her—stunned her into the most dreadful listlessness. And although she was angry with Mia for how she had handled their break-up—with the charade of an open relationship—Raffo stood here, in Big Bear, in front of a canvas, sketching the first lines of Dylan's breasts. How was that for surprising? How was that for the incredible healing powers of art?

She couldn't help a chuckle as she made her first attempt at Dylan's nipple. Obviously, accuracy wasn't very important. She'd only seen Dylan's breasts for a split second. This wasn't an anatomically correct drawing. Yet, Raffo had seen enough. And it wasn't just Dylan's breasts she was using as inspiration.

It was her face, with those impossible blue eyes and that always-kind smile and those infuriatingly cute freckles around her nose that she wanted to paint as well.

Raffo focused on the sketch that would be the basis for her painting. She lost track of time as the contours of the image that burned so brightly in her mind made their way onto her canvas. She had no idea what time it was when she emerged from her state of utter focus to the sound of her stomach rumbling as though she hadn't eaten in days. Complete concentration always made her extra hungry. She downed her tools and went into the kitchen in search of something to eat.

Dylan sat smiling brightly at the kitchen island and a wave of something warm engulfed Raffo. The simple truth was that Raffo really liked Dylan. As far as she could tell, there was nothing to dislike about her—even though Raffo had to lie to Connor for her, but that was almost too easy to forget under the circumstances. Both of them had fled real life and had quickly found themselves in this sunny bubble on the shore of Big Bear Lake. And Raffo was already painting again—Connor would never be able to object to that.

"Morning." Dylan hadn't bothered combing her hair and her golden locks looked deliciously tousled. "I didn't dare disturb you. You looked so… into it."

"Oh, Dylan, please. This is your house. You should be able to go wherever you want whenever you want. I don't mind if you come out when I'm painting. Truth be told, I might not even notice." Raffo settled at the island opposite Dylan. "Promise me that you won't let me stop you. I'd hate to be a nuisance."

"You're anything but a nuisance to me."

Raffo tilted her head, trying to gauge the meaning behind Dylan's words, but maybe there just wasn't anything deeper behind them.

"It's such a joy to have you here. I wasn't sitting here smiling into my morning coffee like this before you arrived, I can tell you that." Dylan shot her an actual wink. "To come downstairs and see you paint on my deck is such an enormous treat."

"You say that now." Raffo didn't really know how to respond to that wink. "But you might get sick of it after a couple of days."

"Not a chance in hell." It felt as though Dylan couldn't keep her eyes off Raffo. "How did it go?"

"Really well." The words burst from her with unexpected brightness, her hands animated as she spoke.

"I can tell. You're like a different person this morning. Your energy is… I don't know how to describe it, but it's very special."

"That's because, for me, painting is the most powerful drug on the planet." Raffo's stomach grumbled again.

They both burst into a giggle at the sound.

Dylan slid off her stool. "Let me get you some breakfast."

"Dylan, no. I can get my own breakfast."

Dylan rested her hypnotic blue gaze on Raffo. "I know that you can, but I want to get it for you. I take care of the meals. You take care of the groceries and the masterful painting."

Raffo didn't know why she was arguing about this—because this was like a dream, really—yet she couldn't stop herself. "Even if it makes me uncomfortable?"

"Why does it make you so uncomfortable to have someone take care of you?"

Raffo huffed out a funny kind of breath. "So many reasons. Too many to hash out when I'm starving." Her stomach emitted another loud growl.

"Pretend you're at a luxury artist retreat where everything is taken care of." Dylan headed to the fridge and took out a carton of eggs.

"But I'm not." This was the most fun kind of argument Raffo'd had in a long time—especially compared to the exhausting verbal fights she and Mia had gotten into without ever getting out of them again. "I'm at your house."

"You make my house a million times brighter with your presence," Dylan said with her back to Raffo. "Even more so now that you're painting again."

Raffo stopped arguing and, instead, poured herself some coffee from the pot Dylan had brewed, into the mug Dylan had set out for her.

Raffo wasn't used to someone taking care of her—and that was an understatement and a half.

She watched Dylan's easy, graceful movements as she scrambled eggs and put slices of bread in the toaster, and let her mind drift back to half an hour ago, when she'd applied the first touch of paint—of exquisite color—to Dylan's face on her canvas. This moment couldn't be more perfect if she'd tried to dream it up. She was painting again—she already looked forward to getting back to it—and one of the nicest women she'd ever met was preparing her breakfast. And, most importantly, Mia Rodriguez could not be further from her mind.

CHAPTER 10

Raffo's presence across the kitchen island was magnetic. She exuded a kind of confident, look-at-me-now energy that was still somehow understated and not arrogant in the least. The more Dylan tried to dissect Raffo's new vibe, the less she understood its paradoxical quality, but the more addictive it became to be around her. Raffo was in her element and Dylan, already, couldn't get enough of it. The least she could do was scramble a few eggs for her—mainly because getting sucked into Raffo's mojo was keeping her from getting lost in her own head. She would deal with her own problems later—tomorrow, or the day after or, perhaps, even the week after.

"There you go." Dylan put a plate in front of Raffo and looked her in the eyes. The fleck of sparkly yellow paint on her cheek was cute and strangely maddening at the same time. "Enjoy and it was my utmost pleasure."

Dylan couldn't wait to sneak a peek at Raffo's work later—after all, she was its subject.

"Thank you. I'm so hungry." Raffo tucked into her eggs immediately. "Hm." She hummed low in her throat. "I love this luxury artist retreat. I already want to book my next stay."

While it was a thrill to see Raffo like this, what she said

reminded Dylan of having to sell this place. But it was easy enough, once again, to push that thought to the side, because Raffo sat across from her, eating her breakfast with the same gusto as she had waltzed into the kitchen earlier.

Dylan vividly remembered Connor telling her, years ago, his voice thick with excitement and, perhaps, disbelief, that he had come across the most amazing artist. Her name was Raffo Shah and her use of color was out of this world. Her talent was vast and unmistakable and, "Be sure to remember her name, Mom, because you'll be hearing it for a long time to come."

Dylan knew that even if Raffo left tomorrow, making this just a fleeting three-day encounter, she'd never forget her name —not after last night's conversation that still lingered like honey on her tongue, not after witnessing this morning's transformation. There was something magnetic about watching someone step back into their power. Raffo's energy was contagious, and Dylan could swear some of it rubbed off on her. Watching her transform from a broken-hearted painter who couldn't paint to this reborn version of herself sparked something hopeful in Dylan too.

If Raffo could show up here like that and turn into this in less than three days, maybe there was hope for Dylan as well. She wasn't a painter, but she'd always had a creative profession, and maybe she could learn from Raffo by example, or absorb some of her special mojo just by being around her.

―――

Dylan had caught a quick glimpse of Raffo's painting before she'd put it away for the day, but she hadn't been able to see that much—probably because there wasn't much to see just yet.

After lunch, Raffo had gone out in search of more painting supplies, followed by a hike. For the first time since Raffo's arrival, Dylan found herself truly alone in the house.

She went through the motions of going upstairs for her daily post-lunch nap but hesitated when putting in her headphones. Dylan had only been briefly mortified when Ida Burton's voice had come over the speakers, thanks to Raffo's grace about it. But she couldn't help but wonder what Raffo really made of her. Was she her best friend's sad mother hiding out from the world at her lake house? Or her unexpected topless muse? Dylan saw herself more as the former but maybe Raffo saw her as both. To even be considered the latter was a humongous compliment.

Dylan threw the sheet off her upper body, baring her breasts —the unexpected inspiration for an artist rediscovering her craft—and pressed play on Ida's steamy story.

In no time, her skin was on fire and her clit pulsed like a second heart. Dylan was alone in the house and she used this time wisely—and the only way she knew how when she felt like this. She brought her hand between her legs and came hard. As she caught her breath, she, too, had an image in her head she couldn't shake—and it wasn't Ida Burton.

It was Raffo Shah, with that small, brazen smile she'd worn in the kitchen that morning. Dylan's hand shook slightly as she deleted the app from her phone. She couldn't risk these thoughts about her son's best friend taking root. That was simply unthinkable—no matter how much the memory of that smile lingered.

———

"I got us something special for tonight." Raffo wasn't exactly crowding Dylan in the kitchen—it was too spacious for that— but Dylan felt a little ill at ease—or was it agitated?—being so close to her. Raffo opened the fridge and took out the bottle of expensive champagne Dylan had spotted earlier. "To celebrate the extremely welcome return of my mojo."

Though pleased for Raffo, Dylan sighed inwardly. She'd hoped to abstain from alcohol tonight—to keep complete control over everything she said and did.

She acquiesced quickly nonetheless, because she wanted to celebrate with Raffo. She wanted to end another gorgeous day, with Raffo, in style.

They went onto the deck with their full glasses of Ruinart and settled in the Adirondack chairs where they'd already spent quite some time. Dylan pushed hers sideways a little so she could see more of Raffo's face—it was far more interesting than the lake.

"I'm so happy." Raffo lifted her glass. "I don't know what's in that water but, fuck, you were right. It's magical."

Dylan tilted her glass to Raffo's and they clinked rims. From what Raffo had told her, it wasn't so much the lake's water that had sparked something in her.

"I'm almost emotional because… I don't know what was worse, losing Mia or losing my mojo." Raffo cleared her throat. "I could learn to live without Mia." She shrugged. "I'll have to, regardless. But I could never live without painting." Her next breath was a little unsteady—a little ragged with emotion.

Raffo took a sip of her champagne and fell silent. Dylan studied her face. No matter what mood she was in, there was always something regal about Raffo's features. She carried herself with a gravitas that Dylan hadn't encountered in many people.

"I hope you'll stick around for a while longer, even though you've already got what you came for." Dylan wasn't sure how she would cope with Raffo leaving.

"I've only just started my first painting." Raffo shook her head. "I'm not going anywhere." She found Dylan's gaze. "As long as you'll have me."

Dylan just nodded. It didn't need repeating that Raffo was welcome to stay.

"But enough about me." Raffo grinned at her. "I feel like it's been about me all day."

You have no idea. Dylan remembered her 'nap'—although she hadn't slept a wink.

"I've been here all this time and apart from your financial mishap, I don't know all that much about you." Raffo peered at Dylan over the rim of her glass. "I'd like to know more. I know you're Connor's lovely mother; you're an excellent hostess; you are exceedingly kind and welcoming and, well—" She chuckled. "You have an extremely inspiring pair of…" She gestured at Dylan's chest.

"I'll drink to that." Dylan laughed, not just because the situation was funny, but because, in that moment, as she lifted the champagne flute to her lips, and looked into Raffo's dark eyes, she was genuinely happy. For the first time since she'd lost half a million dollars, she didn't feel like a complete loser. Raffo was saying all these beautiful things about her—and she was working on a topless painting of her. Although, admittedly, Raffo had also just claimed to know very little about Dylan.

"Well," Dylan said. "To start at the very beginning, when I was born, my parents gave me the name Diane. I changed it to Dylan as soon I was legally able to."

"No way?" Raffo widened her eyes in exaggerated fashion. "You're a Diane? That totally changes my perception of you."

"I've never felt like a Diane. Dylan is so much cooler."

"You're right. You're much more of a Dylan than a Diane." Raffo tipped her glass. "Thanks for sharing."

Dylan tried to think of another innocuous confession she could make, something frivolous, befitting of this lovely evening.

But Dylan had a bit of an issue with impulse control, especially after a few sips of delicious champagne.

"I'm one of those lazy bisexual women who only dates men because it's just so much easier."

Raffo nearly spit out the sip of champagne she'd just taken. She swallowed hard, then said, "I'm sorry. What was that?"

"I'm a bad bisexual because I give my kind a bad name." Dylan took too much glee in these things—she knew this about herself. It didn't feel dissimilar to buying more cryptocurrency, followed by

HARPER BLISS

even more. Just because she could. Because she liked to believe—
wrongly—that she was much smarter than anyone else.

"Please explain further." If Dylan admitting she was bi had
any effect on Raffo, she didn't show it—which was a real
bummer, because that's why she'd said it.

Dylan drank more champagne—so much for staying in
control.

Raffo was Connor's age, a full generation younger than
herself, and while Dylan considered herself plenty woke, she
had to tread carefully because she knew from experience with
Connor this was gaffe-prone territory. Because she was almost
sixty, and had a different life experience, and enjoyed a whole
other host of privileges than the generation that came after her.

"Even though I'm attracted to both men and women, I've
primarily dated men because there are simply many more
single straight men available than there are women who are
attracted to women. It's a numbers game more than anything
else, really."

"What's so bad about that?"

"Nothing. I just—I'd hate to be one of those seemingly
straight women saying I'm bi while enjoying all the privileges
of being perceived as heterosexual, all the while complaining
my sexual preference is so invisible."

"It's complicated," Raffo just said in that typical understated
way that Dylan had already gotten to know so well. "That
doesn't make you less bi."

Dylan had struggled on and off with this all her life, but she
hadn't spent a lot of time discussing it. She'd married a man—
Connor's father—whom she'd been perfectly happy with until
the marriage crumbled, like so many did, under the crushing
weight of everyday life, of growing apart while being together,
of failing to communicate what was bothering you because, one
day, you simply ran out of words to say it, and all that followed
was a painfully slow disintegration called divorce.

"I'll be sixty next year and I've only been with two women in my life." So much for innocuous conversation.

"You wish there had been more?" Raffo asked. Was that a hint of a blush on her cheeks? It was hard to tell—and it could be the effect of the champagne.

"I don't know. I haven't really given it that much thought." That much, at least, was true.

"You're not a bad bisexual just for living your life," Raffo said. "As far as I know, you haven't done anything wrong."

"I'm sorry for not asking you before, but… are you bi? I certainly didn't mean to offend you."

"I'm so gay." Raffo pointed two thumbs at herself. "Look at me. I've never been mistaken for straight in my life." She shrugged.

"Looks can be deceiving," Dylan said.

"Sure, but in my case, they're not. What you see is what you get."

An extremely hot butch, Dylan thought, but luckily didn't say out loud because she needed to brush up on the latest lingo to check if butch was still a thing. Probably not for some people and it was impossible to know if Raffo was one of them. Dylan didn't have the courage to ask in that moment. Besides, she wanted to ask Raffo something else.

"What about me?" Dylan put away her empty champagne glass, well aware of the speed she'd knocked it back with. "What do you see when you look at me?"

Raffo's features folded into a grin, and she held Dylan's gaze with an audacity that made Dylan's pulse quicken. "I've definitely been getting mixed vibes," Raffo said, her voice carrying a hint of something that made Dylan grip her glass tighter. "Although I was a lot less confused after the Ida-Burton-speaker incident."

"Oh, god." Dylan pressed two fingers against her forehead. "It's this app. I have to applaud the makers as well as the marketing team because I've found myself completely unable to resist it."

"I have it, too," Raffo said. "It's insane."

"I've had a crush on Ida Burton since her very first movie," Dylan admitted.

"And then, all of a sudden, as if it's the most normal thing in the world, she's whispering all of that into your ears." Raffo had the kind of knowing smile that could only come from having listened to the same story Dylan had enjoyed.

"Yeah. That's quite something."

They fell silent for a few minutes but it wasn't an awkward silence. That was the other thing about Raffo. She was an easy person to be quiet with.

Dylan wanted to stay in that chair a good while longer, but she had dinner to prepare, and maybe a little break from this conversation, and its unexpected intensity, was what she needed most of all.

CHAPTER 11

Could it be? Raffo gazed into her empty glass, as though the answer lay at the bottom of it. Was Connor's mother flirting with her? Even if she was—and it was a big if because Raffo could immediately think of about five arguments against it—Raffo wasn't open to flirting right now. Especially not with her best friend's mom. Not in a million years would Raffo even entertain the notion, although—admittedly—she might well have started it. It was all well and good to tell Dylan, as she had, that she wasn't trying anything on with her, but did that stand if her actions contradicted her words? If she spent the morning painting a topless picture of Dylan—and enjoying the hell out of it?

These things were so easily misconstrued and Dylan could be feeling vulnerable in a way that made her extra sensitive to the attention of another woman. She clearly admired Raffo as a painter, there was no mistaking that.

Granted, Raffo had been riding the high of her startling painting flow so hard, that she might have failed to pick up on some things. And she wasn't clueless enough that she couldn't see there was some chemistry between them. That they enjoyed each other's company in this dreamy location away from everything and everyone. A situation like this was the perfect breeding ground for heightened emotions, for feeling something inadvertent for another person that you wouldn't even consider in normal-life circumstances. Three days ago, they'd both been in crisis. To her surprise—and delight—Raffo was feeling so much better already, and she didn't know if it was just the surroundings, or the woman she'd been spending time with—and who took such great care of her—or a special combination of the two, but for Dylan nothing much had changed. Except for Raffo's arrival.

There were so many reasonable explanations for a touch of flirting over a glass of champagne. For coming out as bisexual—because, why not? Raffo had done her utmost to keep a poker face, to not give away her secret glee at what Dylan was saying about herself, because a reaction might have… Raffo didn't really know. Nor did she know what to do about this situation —this possible flirting vibe between them—so she decided to do nothing.

Moreover, it would be preposterous to assume that Dylan was flirting with her simply because she was bisexual. What was quite possible, however, was that Dylan flirted with her because Raffo had, on more than one occasion, expressed her appreciation for Dylan's physical appearance as well as her kind nature.

But none of that mattered, because not only was Dylan Connor's mother—and Raffo would never come between her best friend and his mother like that—but a fling was the last thing Raffo was looking for. Thoughts of Mia might have dimmed, pushed into the shadows of her mind after she'd started painting again, but Raffo's heart was still broken into too many pieces. All she wanted was a good, long break from women altogether, and to paint. That's why she'd come here, after all. Instead, she was living with an extremely easy on the eye middle-aged bisexual woman going through, Raffo guessed, something like a midlife crisis.

As soon as they sat down for dinner, Raffo would change the subject. With her history, she had plenty of other things to talk about that could not be misinterpreted and firmly closed the door to any flirting.

———

"Hot damn," Raffo said. "This is incredible."

"It's just a salad." Dylan's modest deflection belied the dish before them—tender roasted bell peppers that melted on the tongue, a dressing perfectly balanced between tart and sweet that Raffo could drink by the cupful.

"Do you want to know why I hate cooking so much?" It was high time for a swift gear change.

"I'd love to." Dylan refilled their water glasses—a wise switch from the earlier champagne.

"I don't know what Con has told you about me, but, um, my mom died when I was thirteen. Ovarian cancer."

"I'm so sorry." Dylan put down her cutlery.

"Yeah." Raffo had missed her mother every single day of the almost twenty years she'd been gone. "So, it was just me and my dad and my three brothers. Guess who had to do all the cooking at home from then onwards?"

"Oh, god." Dylan slanted her head.

"You will never meet a more staunch defender of the patriarchy than my father," Raffo said. "I was the only female left in the house, so I would do the cooking—and the cleaning, for that matter." She paused to take a quick sip of water. "I cooked when my mom was ill as well, but that was different. I did it for her. She'd taught me how to cook a few dishes by then and I did it to help her, but… after she died." Raffo shook her head. "I was so angry. All the Shahs are stubborn assholes, me included, and, well, there was a lot of fighting, which was, in the end, more an expression of our grief than anything else."

"Oh, Raffo. I'm so sorry that happened to you."

"I ran away from home when I just turned fifteen."

Dylan did a visible double take. This information was not part of Raffo's carefully curated artist biography, but she'd assumed Connor might have told his mother some things about her past. Either he hadn't, which Raffo appreciated, or Dylan had an excellent poker face.

"Where did you go?" Dylan asked.

"The Rainbow Shelter. I'd read about it online and it seemed like my only option at the time."

"The Rainbow Shelter? Why does that name ring such a bell?" Dylan knotted her shapely eyebrows together.

"They made a movie about it. About its founder, Justine Blackburn. *Gimme Shelter*. Did you see it?"

Dylan shook her head. "No, but I've heard about it."

"It's pretty safe to say Justine Blackburn saved my life." Raffo could give her all the paintings she wanted, but she'd never be able to repay Justine for what she'd done for her. But Justine was not the kind of person who needed—let alone accepted—payment for any of her actions. That's not why she did what she did.

"Jesus, Raffo. I'm stumped for words. I'm sorry about your mother dying so young and… your family not…"

"Being better?"

Dylan nodded. "What about your brothers? Didn't they help you?"

"No. Not really. They weren't allowed to. My dad… he went nuts after my mom died. He couldn't cope. He just could not cope."

"Is he still alive?" Dylan asked.

"Oh, yeah. He found himself a new wife-slash-servant, but we're not really in touch. He doesn't approve of my 'lifestyle' and that pertains to both my choice of partner and what I do for a living."

"And your brothers?"

"They come to my openings sometimes, but it's all very…

businesslike. We haven't been able to mend things between us. As a family, we didn't heal after my mom died. It just wasn't in the cards for us. It all just went to shit." Even though it had happened so long ago, Raffo had to swallow a lump out of her throat. "My youngest brother, Rishi… A sister knows—I just know he's gay, but he's married to a woman and has two kids." Raffo expelled a deep sigh. "I've always known, but now he's just another self-loathing homophobe. It's so sad."

How was that for not flirting? Dylan hadn't touched the delicious salad she'd made since Raffo had started talking—neither had Raffo.

"Jesus," Dylan muttered.

"I'm sorry for, um, bringing down the mood like that. I didn't mean to. I just wanted to explain…" Raffo took hold of her fork, more as a statement than anything else. "I'm fine now. Well, except for my girlfriend dumping me, but the rest of it all happened nearly twenty years ago."

"You're so strong." Dylan leaned back in her chair. "I'm in complete awe of you."

"Don't be. My life is like so many other people's. Ups and downs. Good things and bad things."

"No." Dylan shook her head vehemently. "You were thirteen, Raffo. And no one was there for you. That's not okay."

Raffo waved off Dylan's comment with her fork. "My mom made me promise her, on her deathbed, that I'd go to college. That I'd work hard in high school so I could get a degree. I would have left home earlier if I hadn't made her that promise, but I soon learned that I didn't have time to do my homework if I stayed. So I left before finishing high school. Justine made sure I got my diploma when I was at the shelter, but I never went to college. I broke that promise to my mother."

Dylan dabbed at her eye. "Any mother would be immensely proud of you."

Raffo would never know—could never know—but she still felt, in her heart, that her mother would be proud of the work

53

she did, despite her not going to college, and not becoming an engineer like Rishi, or a doctor, like her two older brothers.

"Thanks for saying that. I appreciate it." Another gear change—and a mood shift—was in order. "Just like I appreciate the hell out of this salad. Good thing it can't get cold."

"Forget the salad." Dylan looked at her, her eyes all moist and soft. "I just really want to give you a hug, unless you think that's inappropriate."

Raffo could do with a hug right about now. If only for all the motherly hugs she'd gone without since the tender age of thirteen. Because that's what this hug would be—motherly.

"Okay." She stood, closing the distance between them. Dylan's arms enveloped her, and Raffo allowed herself to soften, her own arms finding Dylan's waist. The embrace was kind and lovely and warm—just like Dylan—and exactly what the moment called for. Though part of her wanted to linger in that comfort, Raffo pulled back after a few seconds.

"I don't want pity," she said. "I just wanted you to understand why I hate cooking—where that deep dislike comes from." She offered Dylan a soft smile. "Now let's eat this gorgeous salad you made. It's the least I can do."

CHAPTER 12

And so the evening—and Dylan's clandestine stay in Big Bear—had taken another turn. Dylan couldn't help but feel compassion for thirteen-year-old Raffo. That's why she'd wanted to give her a hug. It was already excruciating to lose your mother to cancer at that age, but then to also have to deal with a father like that. To not have a parent capable of comforting her—of parenting her. It was infuriating. But it was also a miracle that Raffo sat opposite her—that this was who that girl had become. This beautiful, successful woman who, though heartbroken, seemed so at peace. Like a testament to the astounding resilience of humans—well, some humans.

"Every time I sell a painting, ten percent goes to the Rainbow Shelter." Raffo had started on her salad again, eating it with the same gusto as her eggs this morning. "But don't worry, I won't ask you to donate ten percent of what I think the painting of you will be worth." She chuckled and it was such a joy to hear the sound of Raffo's understated laughter again, after what she'd just confided in Dylan.

"I would if I could." Dylan's financial woes paled in comparison to Raffo's childhood trauma. "Back when I was still gainfully employed, I donated to a few queer charities. And I made sure whichever agency I was with took on campaigns for queer organizations, often free of charge."

"I'm sorry if I forgot," Raffo said, "but I'm not sure I know what it is you do."

"I'm in advertising." Dylan drank from her water. Maybe she should have talked about her job earlier, instead of professing her bisexuality. "I quit my job a few months ago to go on a sabbatical. For my 'Eat-Pray-Love journey' to Europe that never happened. After that, for my last professional hurrah, and with the money I made from my crypto-investment, I wanted to start a brand-new agency. A small start-up like the one that gave me my first job as a fresh-out-of-college copy-writer many years ago. Work with a bunch of young people on some exciting projects, like a sort of full circle moment for my career, before retiring."

"That sounds like it would have been an amazing plan."

"Yeah." Dylan glanced at her house, then at the lake. "I could still do it, but only if I sell this house."

"A place like this would go for how much?" Raffo pursed her lips. "A million?"

"Realistically, in today's market, around eight hundred." Dylan'd had the property valued already. "It's gorgeous, but not very big."

"So you have a choice to make."

Dylan nodded. "I could also go back to a more corporate role like the ones I've had the past decade. I was the CEO at a big agency for six years before I quit."

Raffo whistled through her teeth. "That sounds like it would bring in a bit of cash."

If it had been anyone else, and perhaps under different circumstances, Dylan would have been flummoxed, perhaps even annoyed, by this kind of directness, but after three days in Raffo's company, she already knew this was how she was.

Dylan nodded. "I lost a lot of money, but I'm not poor. I have my house in West Hollywood as well." Dylan cast her eyes downward. "Hiding out here is more of an ego thing, although losing all that money hurts a lot, and not just because of my ego."

"Would it be difficult to find a new job?" Raffo asked.

"No." Dylan had an inbox full of inquiries from head-hunters. She had forty years of experience in a cutthroat business and she was damn good at her job. "But being CEO for another five years, or however long I choose to work, doesn't appeal to me anymore. The hours. The stress. The endless meetings." And, as she had recently had the misfortune of finding out, her wayward handling of funds—not something Dylan had ever worried about before, but couldn't help but be conscious of now. She had to be.

"I'd love to see some of the campaigns you worked on before you became the big boss."

"That can be arranged." Dylan relaxed in her chair. "How about tomorrow?"

"Sounds like a plan." Raffo stretched her arms above her head. "That hike this afternoon really took it out of me." She rested her gaze on Dylan. "But I don't feel like going to bed yet. Shall I build a fire?"

"Why not?" Dylan rose. "How about another glass of champagne as a night cap?"

"Why not, indeed?" Raffo's wink caught the twilight as she made her way to the fire pit.

———

"I have a burning question," Raffo said, poking at a glowing log.

"About the fire?" Dylan's lips curved into a teasing smile.

"No," Raffo said matter-of-factly.

"Shoot." Dylan settled deeper into her chair.

"Who were the two women you've been with?"

Dylan huffed out a deep-throated chuckle. Raffo sure could

come up with a killer question. Although Dylan had left the door wide open for this particular one.

"Well." Dylan savored a sip of champagne, letting the memory surface. "The first one was in college—cliché of all clichés, I know. Her name was Alex. She was a TA, a few years older than me. Nowadays, what we did would be more than frowned upon, but I didn't mind one bit forty years ago." Dylan hadn't thought about Alex in decades, that's how far away the memory of her first time with a woman was stashed. "It ended when I graduated and moved to LA."

"How long were you and Alex together?" Raffo appeared relaxed, her ankle on her knee, her glass of champagne on the armrest of her chair, her body angled toward Dylan.

"About five months, if I remember correctly. God, it was so long ago."

"What was she like?" Raffo really wanted to know everything.

"So fucking hot." Dylan chuckled. "I know how shallow that sounds, but I was twenty and very horny."

"Can you describe her to me?" Raffo asked.

"You want me to describe my first girlfriend to you?"

"If you don't mind. You did say she was 'fucking hot'. I guess I'm curious what that means to you."

"Fair enough." Dylan could still easily picture Alex and she wondered what she would look like now—and what she was doing. "Short, dark hair. Brown eyes. Such a friendly face with a big smile. Not overly, um, feminine. She had this walk… I couldn't look away from it if I tried. I loved seeing her dash across campus. Alex Petrovski." Dylan made a mental note to Google her later, just out of curiosity.

"Was it hard to leave her behind?" Raffo was clearly enjoying this, judging by the smile playing on her lips. "Where did you go to college?"

"Boston." Dylan expelled some air while trying to remember the answer to Raffo's other question. "I guess it was hard at the time, but it's been forty years. I've been married since. I've had a son who's in his thirties now." Dylan met her future husband —Connor's father, Joe—not long after. He was a client at the first agency—the one in West Hollywood that she'd been hoping to emulate—she'd worked at.

"You gave birth to Connor and raised him." Raffo nodded. "That would make you forget about your first female lover." She held up her hand. "Your son is truly one of the best people I've ever met. I love Con to absolute pieces. And not just because of what he's done for my career. I mean as a friend. He's more than a friend. He's family."

"Aw. Thank you." Dylan's mother heart grew a size in her chest.

"If you could divulge some embarrassing moments from his childhood that I can drag out at his next dinner party, that would be amazing." Raffo grinned at Dylan.

"I really miss him," Dylan said. "We usually talk every day. I always know what's going on with him, but right now I don't even know if he's in LA or in New York with Murray."

"There's a pretty easy solution for that."

"Yeah." Dylan was aware that all she had to do was pick up the phone and call her son, but she couldn't bring herself to do it yet. "Soon."

"He's in New York with Murray. He will be until next Sunday."

"Yeah." Dylan nodded. "What do you think of Murray?"

"Murray is incredibly sweet. I like him a lot, although he just loves to talk and talk and talk. Oh my god, that guy cannot shut up. But it's okay. It's who he is and he has really interesting things to say. And, most importantly, he says them well." Raffo sat up a little. "Don't worry, I'm not telling you this behind Connor's back. I've told him the exact same thing."

This didn't surprise Dylan in the least. "And the long-distance thing? Do you think it's… viable long-term?"

"They've been doing it successfully for three years, so yes, I think it's very viable and it's already long-term. Not every couple wants to be together all the time."

"Connor hasn't mentioned moving to New York?" Dylan's heart shrank a size now.

"Ah, that's what you really want to know." Raffo sent her a gentle smile. "I told him he's not allowed to. Our interests are totally aligned here." Raffo shook her head. "Connor is such an LA boy and he's built his gallery in Los Angeles, which is such a huge part of his life, of who he is. Never say never, but I don't think he'll be moving to New York any time soon. He wouldn't be able to deal with the winters, for starters."

"I'm glad he has you as his friend." Dylan meant it from the bottom of her heart. If her son had friends like Raffo, she knew for certain that he was doing all right.

"So I tell him every time I see him." Raffo winked at Dylan, her eyes reflecting the flames of the fire. "But, um, I feel like my question is, once again, expertly being dodged." She tilted her head and gave Dylan a quizzical look. "Your second female lover?"

"I wasn't willfully dodging. The conversation just went off in another direction, as conversations tend to do."

"Okay, but now we're firmly back on topic." Raffo drank, then peered at Dylan over the rim of her glass.

Dylan's affair with Angie was much fresher in her memory.

"I met Angie a few months after my divorce from Joe. She was newly divorced as well and we bonded over that, at first. Then, it turned into something more."

"Just like that?"

"Yes and no. It was complicated." Dylan let her head fall back as the memories rushed over her. "It was certainly not straightforward. Even though I probably wasn't ready for something new yet, I felt myself falling for her, but… it was different for her. More like friendship with benefits than amorous. That's the word she used when she broke up with me. *Amorous.* I think I was more of an experiment to her, a welcome distraction after the devastation of her divorce—from a man. We had an on-and-off thing for about eight months or so, but it wasn't to be."

"I'm sorry it didn't work out." Raffo's voice exuded genuine warmth.

"That's okay. Some things are not meant to work out." Dylan briefly closed her eyes, picturing Angie. She was much less inclined to Google her than Alex. "After that, I took a long *amorous* break to properly process my divorce."

"Are you still friends with Connor's dad?"

Dylan nodded. "Yeah, I guess you could call us friends. At least, we've found a way to be amicable again. It took some time but, in the end, neither one of us wanted to be at war with the other parent of our child. Connor and his dad are very close. Joe invested a lot in the gallery." Dylan knew she was lucky. Even though the divorce had been harrowing—it had been difficult distancing herself from her twenty-five-year marriage—and the aftermath pretty brutal, it had ended fairly well. "At least once a month, the three of us go out to dinner. Sometimes the four of us, depending if Joe has a girlfriend or not. He usually doesn't. He really embraced the bachelor lifestyle after we split up. It makes me wonder sometimes."

"And no more women after Angie?" Raffo steered the conversation away from Joe.

"I was single for a few years, enjoying being alone again, doing whatever the fuck I wanted when I wanted. I've had a few relationships since, but none of them lasted very long—all of them with men." The last one, Dylan pondered, with the man who'd made her aware of the digital coin she had too heavily—and wrongly—invested in.

"I met your ex-husband a couple of times at the gallery. He struck me as a really nice guy," Raffo said.

"Joe's a good guy. And a great dad."

"Neither one of you batted an eyelid when Connor brought home his first boyfriend," Raffo mused. "He's told me the story many times."

"It just made complete and utter sense to me that, one day, he would bring a boy home. Then he did. It was great. I was so happy for him." Inadvertently, Dylan stretched out her hand to Raffo. "I'm sorry it wasn't like that for you."

Raffo stared at Dylan's outstretched hand with an unreadable expression. Dylan withdrew it quickly, the gesture hanging awkwardly between them in the firelight.

Raffo inhaled sharply, then slowly let out the breath. "Thank you for sharing all of that with me." She turned her head more toward Dylan. "Are you too tired for the story of the most ridiculous-slash-painful lesbian break-up of the year?"

"I'm absolutely wide awake for that," Dylan said.

CHAPTER 13

"Mia started floating the idea of an open relationship about a year ago. In her defense, suddenly, non-monogamy was everywhere. Newspapers, socials, documentaries. Some of our friends were trying it. The zeitgeist was just totally right for it." Raffo wished her glass of champagne would magically refill itself. "I wasn't exactly thrilled by the idea and I resisted for a long time. Maybe because, somehow, I knew it wasn't so much an open relationship she wanted. But that's all hindsight, so I don't really know." Raffo scoffed, but it came out as a weird snort. "I'm giving away the punch line to the most dreadful joke ever already, but long story short, Mia left me for the first woman she hooked up with when we opened up our relationship. It was love at first sight, apparently. Her name's Ophelia and she looks like a Scandinavian beach volleyball player. You know the type? Like she couldn't be more the opposite of me." The relative calm of the past few days crumbled as Raffo's sadness surged to the surface, raw and familiar.

"The way I see it, for some reason, because it's actually really unlike her, Mia didn't have the guts to simply break up with me. She needed the ruse of an open relationship and she convinced me it was what we needed in our lives and… Argh, the whole thing just makes me so angry." Raffo ignored the itching behind her eyes. "For all I know, she'd already met this Ophelia, but no one has been able to confirm that. Which doesn't mean that she couldn't have kept it a secret from every-one. I don't know. Maybe I'll never know. Either way, our break-up was not amicable in the least." Raffo rubbed at her eyes, trying to hold back the first tear—she knew from experi-ence that once she started to cry, it might be difficult to stop.

"If Mia didn't love me anymore, yes, that would have still hurt like hell, but there are definitely far more honorable ways to break up with the person you've been with for ten years than to stage an open relationship." Connor, who was friends with Mia too, had tried to convince Raffo that she was perhaps too paranoid about how things had gone down, and that Mia wasn't that calculated, but Raffo didn't believe him. She only believed what her own gut told her.

"That's not a very funny punch line," Dylan said.

"I know. My contributions to our conversation tonight have been really gloomy. Thank god for your two affairs with the ladies." Raffo had very much enjoyed observing Dylan as she talked about Alex and Angie.

"That must have been very painful, Raffo. Break-ups always are."

"Connor's been so great. He put me up in his guest room, took care of me, rubbed my back while I cried and cried." Raffo took a deep breath, hoping it would stave off the tears, but they were dangling from her lashes already. "It's a whole mess back home. I have to find a new place to live. We have to sell our house. But I can't talk to her right now. I just can't. The sight of her just… makes me want to cry," Raffo said, as the tears started spilling.

"Oh, Raffo." Dylan was out of her chair in an instant, and crouched beside her. Her warm hand found Raffo's back, her thumb tracing gentle circles against the nape of her neck. "Come here." Dylan pulled her close and then Raffo was crying on Connor's mother's shoulder as well, after having already shed so many tears on her son's shoulder. This family had caught more of her tears already than her own ever would.

Dylan's hand moved to her hair. Raffo tried to steel herself somehow, tried to stop this endless, stupid flood of tears, but it seemed impossible. Because she still loved Mia, had loved her for so long, had loved their life together—and now it was all just gone.

So she cried on Dylan's shoulder for a while longer, not caring who she was with. Her tears didn't care, either way, they just streamed and streamed, until all moisture seemed to have flowed from Raffo's body and she had nothing left to push through her tear ducts.

"I'm sorry. I'm really not a crybaby," she whispered into Dylan's wet hair. Yeah right. Although it was true. Raffo had barely cried since her mother had died, because nothing had ever come close to being that devastating again. Until this. She breathed in deeply and, reluctantly, pushed herself away from the comfort of Dylan's body. "It's like she broke something in me and now I can't seem to stop crying."

"She hurt you." Dylan's voice was a little unsteady as well. "Of course, it makes you cry."

Raffo was exhausted and she fell back into her chair.

"Let me get you some water." Dylan gave Raffo's shoulder a quick squeeze before fetching some water.

If only, Raffo thought, as she gazed up at the stars, she could find a way to stop loving Mia. Mia hurting her hadn't made the love stop—it was the other way around. It hurt so much because Raffo still loved Mia with all of her silly heart.

"Thanks." Raffo took a few greedy gulps of water, as though needing to rehydrate—she probably did. "I always kind of felt I was punching above my weight with Mia, that she was out of my league. Not only because she's drop dead gorgeous, which she is, but because of how she is. Everybody likes Mia. And she always had such faith in me. She believed in my painting long before I did. She was a really great girlfriend—until she wasn't."

Suddenly, all the talking and the crying took their toll, and Raffo could barely keep her eyes open. What a day it had been. From the elation of painting again to uncontrollable crying on Dylan's shoulder.

"Let's get you to bed," Dylan said as though, on top of everything else, she could also read Raffo's mind.

————

Raffo woke with her temples throbbing, not because she'd drunk too much champagne, but because of crying over Mia. Yesterday's joyful energy had evaporated, leaving her muscles leaden and uncooperative. All she wanted to do was curl up under a blanket in the couch and watch something on TV that didn't require any brain power to process.

For the first time since arriving, she regretted not having the house to herself—as Connor had promised her—so she could sulk in private. But then she remembered it was Dylan she was sharing the house with and a tiny flicker of energy coursed through her. Dylan was so easy to talk to, Raffo had told her everything. Dylan was also the subject of the painting she'd so enthusiastically embarked upon yesterday, but painting was out of the question today. She'd undo everything she'd accomplished the day before with the mood she was in today. With the freight train of grief crashing into her again and again, crushing her spirit—and her mojo.

Arriving here to meet Dylan had just been a temporary respite of dealing with her grief. Raffo knew a thing or two about dealing with grief, namely that the pain never fully went away, and that it could hit you all over again, with all its brutal force, when you least expected it. But Mia wasn't dead. She was probably in bed with Ophelia right now. Nausea arrowed through Raffo at the thought.

To escape thinking about Mia doing to Ophelia what she used to do to Raffo in the morning—peppering featherlight kisses onto her neck until she was fully awake and smiling so widely her cheeks hurt—Raffo fled the bed.

She didn't shower and just went downstairs unwashed, uncombed, and in the tank top and shorts she'd slept in.

Dylan was standing on the deck in her bikini, overlooking the lake. It was the perfect sight to replace the image in her brain of Mia and Ophelia. Raffo waited to see if Dylan would jump into the lake, but she didn't. As if she felt Raffo's eyes on her, she turned around and, through the window, shot Raffo one of her smiles.

Suddenly, Raffo didn't mind sharing the house any longer. She inwardly chuckled at how fickle she was, but then Dylan walked into the kitchen in that barely there bikini and Raffo found herself fighting to keep her eyes on Dylan's face—a battle she'd lost the day before.

"Morning." Dylan walked all the way up to Raffo and put a hand against Raffo's upper arm. "Did you get some sleep?"

Raffo could only nod. "Yeah. I was totally exhausted."

"I can imagine. Coffee?"

"Were you about to go for a swim?" Raffo asked.

Dylan poured her a cup of coffee regardless of Raffo not answering her question.

"I was contemplating it, but then I heard noise upstairs and I figured you were awake. I wanted to see how you were feeling."

"I feel exactly like someone who's been dumped by her girl-friend of ten years would." Raffo straightened her shoulders. "But I'm not that big a fan of self-pity, so I shall try to pull myself together."

"You don't have to do that on my account."

You make me want to pull myself together though, Raffo thought.

"You've been through a lot." Dylan handed Raffo a steaming mug of coffee.

"Thanks," Raffo said, both for the sentiment and the coffee. "I won't be painting today. There's no point."

"What would you like to do—if you want to do anything at all," Dylan asked.

"For starters, I don't want to keep you from your swim."

"My swim can wait, Raffo. I just, um, wanted to—"

Raffo's phone buzzed, startling them both. She'd told most people she was going off-grid for a while. Her stomach tightened as she checked the screen.

"Oh, fuck. It's Connor." She glared at her phone as though it was a ticking time bomb. "Should I ignore it?"

"Damn. Um, I don't know." Dylan looked all flustered.

Raffo's phone stopped ringing and then promptly started up again.

"He must have something really important to say. I'll go into my room and call him back."

Dylan nodded

Her phone chirping in her hand, Raffo hurried upstairs. Cell reception wasn't nearly as bad as she and Dylan had been pretending. She called Connor back and he picked up after the first ring.

"I'm sorry for interrupting your me time, Raff," Connor said. "But I figured you'd want to know this straightaway."

Did Mia and Ophelia split up? Raffo's heart started racing.

"Guess who's going to have a show at the Dolores Flemming Gallery in Chicago this fall?"

"Who?" Raffo said stupidly, her mind still stuck on Mia.

"This incredible artist called Raffo Shah. Surely, you've heard of her," Connor all but shouted down the line.

"What? No way. You got me into Dolores Flemming's Gallery?"

"I sure did, babe. I sure did."

Dolores Flemming's prestigious Chicago galleries were kingmakers in the art scene—a single show could launch an artist's career.

"To be honest," Connor said, "and you might want to sit for this. She called me. Dolores Flemming wants you, Raff. How's that?"

"That is amazing…" Raffo's voice caught. After weeks of emotional blows, here was some purely good news.

"I'm not calling to put pressure on you," Connor added quickly. "I just wanted you to know. We can absolutely put on a show without new work."

"Thanks so much for letting me know, Con. I so appreciate this."

"How are things in Big Bear? How are you holding up?"

"Good." This was excruciating. Connor was her best friend. Raffo couldn't lie to him, but she also couldn't break Dylan's confidence. "Better. I got my painting materials out yesterday." She would also never be able to show Connor the painting she'd started on—and Connor saw every little doodle that she drew. "It's early days, but still."

"That's so great. Ah, Raff. That makes me so happy."

"Yeah." Whereas Raffo never had an issue making conversation with Connor, she didn't know what to say next because she didn't want to say the wrong thing—she didn't want to betray Dylan.

"The house is okay? Up to your standards?"

"The house is absolutely wonderful. Thank you for sending me here and, um, letting me use it."

"It's not my house. Thank my mom when she gets back from Europe."

"You know what I mean." Raffo's hand got so clammy, she nearly dropped her phone.

"Sure. Look, I gotta go. I have a meeting." Sweet mercy. Raffo was too tongue-tied under these circumstances to enjoy this chat with her friend. "Congratulations. You're the bomb, Raffo. Love you."

She rang off and took a breath. With the tension of pretending to be alone in the house, she hadn't paid enough attention to the reason why Connor had called. Dolores Flemming was one of the most highly regarded gallerists in the country—and a very hot, power lesbian to boot—who could elevate an artist's career to the very top. Raffo's career was already on the up, but who knows where this might lead? Instinctively, the first thing she wanted to do was call Mia to share this wonderful news. Instead, she took another breath and rushed downstairs to do the next best thing. Share the news with Dylan.

CHAPTER 14

Raffo bounded down the stairs transformed, excitement replacing her earlier tension. Yet Dylan's own anxiety lingered because Connor's perfectly ordinary phone call had left her feeling like the worst mother on the planet.

"Good news?" Despite feeling guilty, Dylan couldn't help but mirror Raffo's smile.

"The best. I'm going to have a show in the number one art gallery in Chicago this fall. It's like a dream."

Dylan was so happy for Raffo to get some good news for a change. Yet, she stopped herself from getting up to hug her— she was barely wearing any clothes.

"That is so well-deserved. Congratulations."

Raffo pumped her fist. "Fuck, yeah. It's really great."

"How was Con?"

"Good, I think. I didn't really ask, to be honest. He was over the moon about the news. He wanted to call me as soon as he heard." A shadow crossed Raffo's face. "Don't worry. I didn't give away that you're here, but, um, I would really prefer if I didn't have to do that again. If I didn't have to pretend like that."

"I know, Raffo. I'm so sorry. Thank you for… keeping my secret."

"Why is it so difficult for you to tell him? Connor's a great guy with lots of empathy and it's not like you lost his money."

"As a parent, it's hard to admit a stupid mistake like that to your child. And I don't want him to worry about me." *Or lose respect for me.*

"Being a parent doesn't make you any less human, nor immune to making mistakes. Connor will be so much more upset that you lied to him about being in Europe than about you making a bad investment."

"I know but I just… need this time. Time for myself, without having to worry about Connor and what he thinks of me, but also about what I'm going to do next. I need time to decide and once I've made my decision, if I choose to sell, I need time to say goodbye to this house."

"It's not for me to push you, I know that," Raffo said. "Nor to question your reasons for being here and for not telling Con, but… Dylan, surely you know that he will not think any less of you. I've only just met you and I already know, in every cell of my body, that you are an amazing person. I can say that with confidence because I know Connor very well. That buys you some credit. You're not some shitty parent who never tried and never did anything right, only to lose a bunch of money on top of everything else. You raised a wonderful son who will understand this, because of how you brought him up."

Dylan was moved by Raffo's kind words, but guilt still gnawed at her. Losing half a million dollars wasn't just financially devastating—it had shaken her to her core. She might have two properties, but her savings account was empty. She had gambled, and lost—not only money, but a lot of self-esteem as well. It forced her to take stock of herself and of her life—and the decision to quit her job.

"Thanks," Dylan said, feeling rather inadequate again. "Let me get you some fresh coffee." Sometimes, going into automatic mom-mode was the easiest, most comforting, thing to do—even though her own son hadn't needed hands-on mothering in a long time.

"I'll get the coffee," Raffo said. "You sit. Take a load off." Raffo was still dressed in what passed for her pajamas, showing a lot of skin—although not nearly as much as Dylan, she realized. Dylan had been about to jump into the lake, to give her body a jolt of energy to start the day with, but she'd rather sit here drinking coffee with Raffo instead.

———

Dylan finally dove into the lake an hour later, after Raffo had left for another hike. She pushed through the water trying to burn off the restless energy that had arrived with her unexpected house guest. Dylan had taken to the lake every day since she'd arrived, but she hadn't felt this urge to move her body, to exhaust it, before Raffo had arrived.

She tried focusing on her stroke—the rhythm of her arms cutting through the water, the steady kick of her feet—but her thoughts kept circling back to Raffo. To Raffo's mother. To Mia and the open relationship and the new woman who looked like a Scandinavian beach volleyball player. To Raffo's question last night about the two women Dylan had been with. She'd Googled Alex this morning, before Raffo had gotten up. She was a professor at the University of Chicago—probably close to retirement age. Chicago made Dylan think about the news Raffo had received from Connor, and that started her brain up in the wrong direction again. Dylan hoped Raffo would only get good news from now on. Her tears last night had been heartbreaking. To see Raffo crumble like that had touched her deeply. Raffo had shed a tear on the first evening as well—Mia clearly had done a number on her—but last night's torrent had been different. Everything about last night had been different. The conversation deeper, the vibe more intense, the connection between them more profound—as though the two of them being in this house together worked as a pressure cooker for their emotions.

As Dylan swam back to the house, she figured it was only logical that her thoughts kept drifting back to Raffo because they were in this emotional pressure cooker together. They were each dealing with their own turmoil, but being able to share it with each other so unexpectedly, brought them closer together.

As she caught sight of the house, which would be very difficult for her to part with—especially after this particular stay, no matter its reasons—Dylan could only hope that Raffo would get her painting mojo back soon. She was absolutely dying to find out what that painting of her would look like. And every time she thought about Raffo, so deliciously awkwardly, asking her permission to paint a topless picture of Dylan, it brought a smile to her face—which was not ideal while swimming. Still smiling, Dylan coughed up some water, as she approached the pier of the house she would have to sell.

CHAPTER 15

Raffo hadn't cried in days, which was a relief. The news about the Dolores Flemming Gallery show had sparked her mojo back to life, and her painting of Dylan was progressing well. While it was still a topless image of her best friend's mother, for Raffo, it had transformed into something else. Even though she'd only painted in about ten percent of the colors, she could already see, in her mind's eye, what it might look like finished—when she'd applied all the colors that were bursting on her eyelids every time she closed her eyes.

Raffo got her drawing talent—her artistry—from her father, not that he'd ever told her that. The only reason she knew was because she'd found some of his drawings—beautifully refined portraits of her mother—between her mom's belongings after she'd died. Her sense of color, however, Raffo owed completely to her mother. Most people with a bit of flair for it could learn to draw and paint, but the way color worked inside of Raffo's brain was inherited. Color was in Raffo's DNA—as it had been in her mother's. She'd seen it in Rishi too when he was little, but now, probably as a way to protect himself, he only dressed in black and white. As though denying himself color could take away his truest desires.

Raffo, on the other hand, cherished her love of color. Her use of it was a tribute to her mother. It made her feel connected to her in a way that would otherwise not be possible. It was yet another reason why, without the ability to paint, Raffo only felt like half a person. Because her mother felt too dead to her when she wasn't working, whereas when she was painting, for brief moments, Raffo felt like her mother was somehow still alive inside her.

Just because Raffo could see what the painting might look like when it was done didn't mean that getting there was an easy process. Mixing the exact colors that she wanted, and applying them in the right spot, with the desired consistency and brush stroke on the canvas, was a slow undertaking with lots of trial and error. But it was all part of what she did. Besides, if it was easy, it wouldn't be special. Raffo didn't think of herself as special—ever—but it was impossible to be unaware of what her work meant to some people. Her work *was* special to certain people. She had accepted that. And now it was going to be on display in the best art gallery in Chicago. The news still made her stomach flutter.

A knock came from behind, pulling her from the reverie her mind drifted into when she was in the zone.

"Hey." Dylan was barely wearing any clothes again—just a spaghetti-strap tank top and the shortest pair of jeans shorts Raffo had ever seen. Raffo had been here over a week now and she didn't try as hard to look away anymore. Moreover, she couldn't shake the feeling that Dylan enjoyed it when Raffo's gaze lingered. "Dinner in about half an hour. Does that work?"

"Absolutely." Raffo shot Dylan a big smile—she deserved every last sprinkle of it. "Thank you."

As the days had passed, and Raffo had been spending more hours in her painting nook in the corner of the porch, Dylan had grown less hesitant about disturbing her.

As Raffo's gaze traveled down Dylan's smooth, tan thighs, Dylan studied Raffo's painting—not something Raffo could hold against her. Dylan never commented, though. She didn't nod or react, keeping her thoughts carefully hidden.

"I'm grilling some chicken and I want to time it right." Dylan's blue eyes glinted in the early evening sun that bathed everything, Raffo's work most of all, in a flattering, honeyed hue.

Goodness. This woman. Raffo wasn't sure she would ever want to leave Big Bear. What would she even be going back to? A life in ruins and no one to grill her the perfect piece of chicken, that's what.

"I'll put my stuff away and get cleaned up," Raffo said.

"Great. I've opened that bottle of white you bought, if you want some." With that, Dylan turned on her heel and, barefoot, her jeans shorts seemingly shrinking by the minute, sauntered off. Raffo couldn't look away if she tried.

––––––

"As promised," Dylan said after dinner. "I'll show you some of *my* work now."

Raffo knotted her eyebrows together. Had Dylan secretly been painting? Or taken up a craft like crocheting?

"Let me just get my laptop. It took a while for me to cobble it together." Dylan shot up, a wild kind of energy about her all of a sudden.

As Raffo cleared the dishes, it slowly came back to her. That long conversation they'd had a few days ago, when she'd basically told Dylan all about her past and present traumas. Dylan's work. Advertising campaigns.

When Raffo looked at Dylan, she didn't see a woman ready for retirement, although lounging in her Big Bear house seemed to agree with her. But for how long could a person, realistically, do that? It was probably different for everyone.

Raffo grabbed the bottle of wine from the fridge on her way back to the deck and generously refilled their glasses.

She enjoyed the silence of her surroundings as she waited, the lowering sun across the lake, and the general sense of peace that was impossible to find in Los Angeles. Unwittingly, her mind drifted to Mia. What was she doing? Making her divine tamales for Ophelia? Luckily, Dylan waltzed onto the deck, laptop in hand.

"We did a lot of movie promotion work, as you can imagine. My second agency had an exclusivity contract with one of the big studios. There were a few years when all I worked on were movies."

"Sounds thrilling." Raffo meant it. She'd grown up in Los Angeles and it was easy enough to be jaded about the movie business, and all it entailed, but Raffo had always thought it special. After her mother died, Raffo often fled to their neighborhood theater just to get away from the house and her demanding father and useless brothers.

"Especially when working on this." Dylan flipped open her laptop and showed Raffo the screen. On it was a poster for *Sweet Tomorrow* starring Ida Burton.

"Oh my god." This movie had been made long before Ida came out of the closet—when she'd still been fake-married to a gay male movie star—but Raffo had seen it many times nonetheless. "Did the ad agency people get to go to the premiere? Did you meet Ida?"

"I was in my late twenties when we did this. Maybe my boss got some perks, I don't remember, but I certainly didn't." Dylan sat there beaming, obviously proud of the work she'd once done.

She showed Raffo some more of the campaigns she'd worked on, some of which Raffo remembered seeing at the time of launch—especially a few of the queer-oriented ones.

They made Raffo think of the Rainbow Shelter. One day, if the weather in Big Bear turned, and they weren't subjected to this glorious—and, admittedly, somewhat sensuous—sunshine every day, they should watch *Gimme Shelter* together—the movie about Justine Blackburn and the Rainbow Shelter.

"I'm impressed," Raffo said, after Dylan's slideshow.

"Thank you." Unlike Raffo, Dylan had no problem accepting a compliment.

"I can't read your thoughts, obviously, but from where I'm sitting, and from what I can see, you're so not ready to retire."

"I'm not," Dylan confirmed. "I wasn't planning to, either. I just wanted to make a change. Be creative again instead of talking about business and pitches and financial projections all the time. Seeing my old work again only reinforces that."

"Maybe selling this place is a small price to pay for that." Raffo could say this with confidence because nothing was worth more to her than being creative—no material possession, no matter how lovely the house and the lake attached to it—could ever be.

"Maybe," Dylan said on a sigh.

"Alternatively, you could get a business loan," Raffo offered. "Or refinance your properties."

"No," Dylan stated firmly. "Either I finance my new agency with my own money or I don't do it. I'm not going into debt. Not after what happened."

Or I could give you a loan, Raffo thought, but quickly quashed the idea. Dylan hadn't even told her son about her bad investment, which probably didn't make her the type of person to accept a loan from her son's best friend. Besides, Raffo had to buy a house for herself—*by herself*—in LA's lethal real estate market.

"You'll figure it out, Raffo said instead. "Despite what happened, you're a smart woman."

"I don't feel so smart right now." Dylan's earlier confidence seemed to plummet.

"Smart people do dumb things all the time. It's called being human."

"What's the last dumb thing you did?" Dylan asked before taking a large sip of wine.

"Me?" Raffo shook her head. "Agree to an open relationship."

"No." Dylan's tone was firm. "That doesn't count. Mia broke up with you. That's not on you."

"That's not on me?" Raffo's eyes widened. "My girlfriend stopped loving me and that's not on me?"

"It's on her. It's got nothing to do with doing something really stupid. With getting so carried away with something you lose all common sense."

If only Raffo knew why Mia had stopped loving her—although what good would it do? She wouldn't be able to make Mia love her again, unless she changed into slender, blonde Ophelia, and that was impossible.

"Okay." Raffo easily acquiesced. "That was not a good example. But it doesn't matter, because we're not going down this route. You made a mistake and I understand it's a difficult thing to accept about yourself."

"For what it's worth…" Dylan leaned back in her chair and drew up one shapely leg. "I have no idea why Mia would stop loving you. You're so… talented and down-to-earth at the same time. You're extremely easy to be around and so incredibly interesting. Frankly, I can't get enough of your company."

The only response Raffo had to that was a slackening jaw.

"I don't mean in a romantic way, obviously," Dylan quickly added.

"In an *amorous* way, you mean?" Raffo quipped, now that she was able again.

"That's right." Dylan had no trouble meeting Raffo's gaze. Raffo was unable to look into Dylan's eyes for longer than a split second, though. "You know that's not what I mean, don't you?"

Did she? Raffo wasn't so sure, but maybe she was projecting. Although there wasn't anything amorous—her heart wasn't free for anything like that—about how she felt about Dylan, it was undeniable that Raffo found her attractive.

"Of course," Raffo said. For the first time, she felt a little uncomfortable in Dylan's company—not because of what Dylan had just said, but because of Raffo's own thoughts. "And thank you for saying those lovely things about me. That feels so nice after being dumped like that."

For a moment, Raffo considered what might happen if she continued down this road their conversation had taken—if she flirted with Dylan a little—but she soon thought better of it. Dylan was Connor's mother and that was the end of that.

She feigned a yawn. "I'm sorry. I seem to be rather tired. I got a lot of painting done today. So much for being on vacation." Once she'd got going, Raffo hadn't been able to stop. Because she'd felt like her full self again. "I might have an early night."

"I can imagine it's exhausting, being a genius and all that." Dylan rested her chin on her knee and gazed at Raffo.

Someone using the word genius to describe her always raised Raffo's hackles all the way up, but Dylan had a different effect on her when it came to many things. Raffo just made a mental note to address that wrong assumption about her—she didn't consider herself a genius in the least—later, and rose from her chair.

"Thank you so much for dinner, for the excellent company, and another lovely day in your house." As she walked past Dylan's chair, Raffo briefly touched a hand against Dylan's shoulder, before heading inside.

CHAPTER 16

Sleep proved elusive yet again. It was one of those restless nights that seemed to multiply as Dylan aged. Rather than fight it, she'd learned to prepare for these wakeful hours—a book within reach, the TV downstairs, or perhaps that steamy story app she'd deleted but hadn't quite forgotten.

Reaching for her water glass, Dylan found both it and the bottle beside it empty. She eyed the lesbian spy thriller on her nightstand—from the infamous *Underground* series by Charlie Cross—which, come to think of it, was quite steamy as well. But it was far less dangerous than having Ida Burton whisper naughty words in her ears.

Dylan padded downstairs for water, pausing at the kitchen window. The lake stretched before her like black glass, its surface as smooth and unruffled as she'd hoped to become by retreating here. The turmoil in Dylan's brain had been smoothed over a bit, but that was more down to Raffo's arrival than to Dylan being able to forgive herself for her mistake. Instead of letting her mind wander down the same old path of self-incrimination, which never conducive for sleep, she tried to remember what had been happening in the book she was reading. She quietly made her way back upstairs, looking forward to re-immersing herself in the thrilling life of a female spy.

When Dylan reached the landing, the door to Raffo's room swung open. Raffo emerged.

Their eyes locked, and the air crystallized between them. This wasn't Raffo's usual appreciative glance—this was something electric and unprecedented. In that suspended moment, Dylan recognized the inevitability of what would follow. Her pulse jumped, a Morse code of want beneath her skin.

She made the first move, reaching for Raffo's hand. She drew her near, walking them backward until her back pressed against the wall. She dropped the bottle of water to the floor and tried to read Raffo's face. Before she could draw any conclusions, Raffo's lips hovered a mere inch from hers. Raffo didn't say anything. She hadn't spoken at all since coming out of her room. All she did with her lips was touch them against Dylan's.

Dylan breathed heavily against Raffo's mouth, one hand still entwined with hers, the other clutching Raffo's T-shirt. She pulled her closer, her body communicating what words couldn't: yes, this was exactly what she wanted. Dylan's knees went soft as Raffo's tongue slipped into her mouth.

She knew she shouldn't be kissing Raffo like this, yet somehow, it felt exactly right. Their kiss was only tentative for a few moments before swiftly morphing into so much more. Into intention and red-hot lust burrowing its way to the surface of Dylan's skin.

Raffo kissed her and Dylan forgot about everything that bothered her. She stopped being the person who had lost half a million dollars. That was the one and only Raffo Shah kissing her. And there was no mistaking anything about this kiss. About Raffo's soft tongue against hers and how it made her feel. All Dylan could think, as she opened her mouth wider for Raffo, was more, more, more.

When they broke from their first, deliciously endless kiss,

without saying a word, Dylan pulled Raffo into her room. Speaking now would just break whatever spell they were under. Dylan did not want this spell to be broken. She didn't want Raffo to suddenly have a crisis of conscience. She just wanted Raffo's lips on her again, and then all over her body.

Dylan tugged at Raffo's top. In one swift move, Raffo pulled it off and tossed it aside. Dylan wanted to quickly follow suit, but Raffo didn't let her. She grabbed Dylan by the wrists, immobilizing her arms, before reaching for the hem of her tank top.

Dylan groaned low in her throat. She hadn't been this aroused in a very long time—not even by Ida Burton's voice in her ears.

Inch by inch, Raffo lifted Dylan's top away from her skin, starting a raging fire between her legs. Ever so slowly, Raffo revealed Dylan's breasts.

Dylan raised her hands above her head so Raffo could get that torturous tank top off her.

Raffo breathed heavily, her gaze locked on Dylan's breasts. She took her time taking in the sight—ogling Dylan some more. Dylan did the same to Raffo.

She'd been so entranced by Raffo undressing her, by how she'd clasped her fingers around her wrists earlier, that she hadn't fully absorbed the stunning sight before her: Raffo Shah, topless in her Big Bear bedroom. It was all so far from probable, yet it was happening. Raffo was as beautiful as Dylan had imagined her, but it wasn't so much the view of Raffo's bare breasts she was so profoundly drawn to. It was all of Raffo. It was how she stood there, looking at Dylan as though she was the most gorgeous human on the face of the earth, with all that lust lighting up her dark eyes, that made Dylan's knees go weak. She wanted to tumble onto the bed so badly, and pull Raffo on top of her, yet she waited. She waited for Raffo to come for her again. Time stretched like honey, sweet and slow.

Then Raffo did.

Like the most divine avalanche of soft skin and nimble body

parts, Raffo maneuvered them onto the bed. Dylan moved like water beneath Raffo, her body going with the flow, in whatever direction Raffo wanted her to go. It wasn't so much a matter of being in charge, perhaps—subconsciously—because Raffo had a lot more experience with women in the bedroom, but it was just how things unfolded, instinctively, between them. Raffo on top, Dylan beneath her, her body wild with lust, her whole being enthralled with whatever Raffo would do next—she hoped it would include taking off her shorts sooner rather than later.

Raffo moved Dylan's arms above her head while her knee slipped between Dylan's legs.

Then, Raffo smiled at her. A small, but very promising smile. And Dylan smiled back. Of course she did. She had everything to smile about. She might not be romantically—or amorously—interested in Raffo—that was impossible, anyway—but she sure was interested in *this*. It had been humming beneath her skin for a few days now. During daylight hours, Dylan had managed to suppress these desires, but this chance midnight encounter had shattered her carefully maintained restraint. Because Dylan was not alone in this.

She shared her desire for this with Raffo. She'd seen that as soon as she'd looked into Raffo's eyes earlier. She was curious to know what had made her emerge from her room at that precise moment, but there was plenty of time to ask that question later.

First, Raffo's knee pushed high between her legs, against the useless fabric of her shorts. Raffo's gaze was firmly fixed on Dylan's breasts—was she committing them to memory in order to paint them more accurately? Raffo didn't hide her work in progress and Dylan had seen it, but she couldn't draw any conclusions about it yet. That would be unfair to Raffo and to what the work would ultimately turn into. The biggest pleasure was to see Raffo work. When she was painting, Raffo was so in the moment, she probably had no idea how much time Dylan had spent just watching her—observing an artist at work.

Maybe that's what had moved her the most, along with all the things that Raffo had revealed about herself.

To Dylan, everything about Raffo was just about perfect. The degree to which she was mesmerizing, but not needlessly mysterious. How, in her appearance, she was both irresistibly masculine and beautifully feminine at the same time. How she could tie her hair so delicately, fling her ponytail about so girl-ishly one moment, and then sit with her legs wide apart, all abundant big dick energy, the next. How she came across as so stoic when you didn't know her, as unshakeable—her soul always strong and her heart impenetrable—but then she'd cried on Dylan's shoulder for a long time the other night. And perhaps most of all how, as a true artist, she had seen Dylan half-naked and had, even though it was challenging, not hesi-tated to ask Dylan if she could paint her, because it—very simply—was the one image she wanted to paint. Dylan couldn't get enough of Raffo. And she planned to get all that she could tonight.

Goose bumps bloomed across Dylan's skin as Raffo's lips found her nipple. The tenderness of that warm touch would have brought Dylan to her knees if she wasn't already lying down. She freely—gladly—gave herself up to all the sensations Raffo bestowed on her. She reveled in the soft touch of Raffo's lips as she trailed a moist path from Dylan's nipple, to the deli-cate skin of her neck, to Dylan's lips for another round of breathless kissing.

While she kissed her, Raffo's hand meandered down to her breast, capturing Dylan's hard nipple between her fingers. All the while, Dylan's clit thumped wildly—uncontrollably. She was so hot for Raffo, the sheer force of it astounded her.

Dylan's hands traced the planes of Raffo's back, fingers teasing beneath the waistband of those familiar pajama shorts—the ones that had tormented her for days. But Dylan could hardly hold that against Raffo. She, herself, was very skilled at walking around the house with the smallest amount of fabric

HARPER BLISS

covering her skin—knowing full well how Raffo couldn't look away when she did. Dylan had done so on purpose, but it was summer in Big Bear, and this was still her holiday home—for now—so she could wear as little as she damn well pleased.

When Raffo wrapped her lips around Dylan's nipple next, she broke the silence between them. Dylan couldn't help herself.

"Oh, Raffo," she moaned. "Oh, fuck. I want you so much."

Raffo didn't respond with words. She sucked Dylan's nipple deeper into her mouth and her hand floated downwards—exactly where Dylan wanted it. Raffo's fingertips dipped below her shorts and Dylan nearly exploded. What the hell was happening to her? But it wasn't only getting to know Raffo that sparked this madness in her flesh—this bottomless desire that had taken hold of her—it was the circumstances. It was the fact that another human being found Dylan worthy of her time, attention, and lust. That's how deep her self-esteem had plummeted after losing all that money. It wasn't just that, in Raffo's arms, she could temporarily forget. To Raffo, it didn't seem to matter all that much. It certainly hadn't stopped her from reciprocating to flirty banter, to touches that were perhaps meant as innocent but, in the end, had turned out to be so much more—and it hadn't stopped her from painting Dylan in all her topless glory.

It was all of that combined that drove Dylan right to the edge, that made her skin extra sensitive, and her lust peak outrageously, and her desire for Raffo so completely out of control. And she was still wearing those damned shorts.

Raffo's fingers ventured lower, a deliberate tease, while her mouth claimed Dylan's nipple with exquisite focus. Dylan dug her nails a little deeper into Raffo's skin as Raffo's tongue danced around her nipple. Then Raffo finally let Dylan's nipple slip from her mouth—and Dylan knew exactly where she wanted Raffo's tongue to go next.

"You're so fucking gorgeous." Raffo spoke for the first time

88

and her voice, low and gravelly, matched the vibe in Dylan's bedroom perfectly. It only made Dylan's clit thump more wildly.

Dylan swallowed hard. She was so turned on, she feared she might have temporarily lost the power of speech. She pulled Raffo to her again, even though it meant her clit would be pulsing uncontrollably for a while longer. But she wanted more of Raffo's kisses. She wanted the lips from which those lovely words had slipped against hers more than anything else. She wanted Raffo close. She wanted to feel her breasts against her own. That soft meeting of skin, Raffo's knee riding dangerously high again—their tongues again doing a delicious dance with each other.

Raffo ended the kiss and zigzagged a line of kisses along Dylan's neck, until Dylan felt Raffo's lips stretch against her ear.

"I'm going to make you come so hard," she whispered, and her audacious promise was nearly enough to make Dylan climax right there and then, without Raffo even touching her.

This, too, apparently, was who Raffo was. There were no limits to how special, how utterly extraordinary, Raffo Shah was. Dylan could only count her blessings that this was happening. That Raffo had shown up at her house and that Dylan had been here instead of where she thought she'd wanted to be—in Europe. There was absolutely nowhere else she'd rather be than right here in her bedroom in Big Bear with Raffo. This was far better than any spiritual journey could ever be.

At last, Raffo peeled Dylan's shorts off her legs. Then, Dylan spread wide for her—yet another deliriously sensual sensation. This whole thing was delirious, yet, somehow, it also made perfect sense. It was just another paradox of life, like being smart and dumb at the same time.

Raffo ran a fingertip from Dylan's knee to the apex of her thighs. Ever so lightly, her finger circled Dylan's clit. Oh, damn. Dylan had been so beside herself, and what was happening was so unexpected, that she'd forgotten to think about an essential element for any woman approaching sixty. But her throat was so constricted with lust, her mouth so dry, she couldn't even form the one short word. She'd have to, somehow, trust Raffo, who was in her early thirties and had perhaps never even considered lube because she had no use for it. Raffo, whose magic hands didn't just produce amazing works of art, but whose fingers were producing round after round of fireworks beneath Dylan's skin.

Then Raffo sent Dylan a smile that was so gentle and joyful, so perfectly adequate in conveying that Raffo, too, couldn't possibly dream of being anyplace better than here, that made trusting her easy. Because everything with Raffo was easy. Being around her. Sharing a house with her. Talking to her. Admitting to stupid mistakes. Even this, in this moment, wasn't complicated in the least. It was a simple matter of one and one equaling two. Of tension turning into lust, then turning into an inevitable midnight encounter. Spreading her legs for Raffo was one of the most logical things Dylan had ever done. It was effortless and easy and oh-so arousing.

Raffo's finger stopped moving and Dylan's breath stalled in her throat. Raffo shifted around until she kneeled between Dylan's legs. Some of her hair had come loose from her ponytail and fanned over her naked shoulders. Dylan couldn't think of a more beautiful sight.

Raffo angled forward and kissed her way up Dylan's inner thigh. Every single nerve ending in Dylan's body was buzzing. Raffo bent at the waist, her stray hair now tickling Dylan's skin, and she put a warm hand on Dylan's belly. Dylan covered it with hers as Raffo's hot breath tickled between her legs.

Dylan closed her eyes and reveled in this exquisite moment, because she knew, with absolute certainty, that what was to come would be even more exquisite—Raffo had promised her, after all. And Raffo didn't come across as someone who broke a promise easily—or ever.

Then, at last, Raffo's tongue touched against Dylan's clit. Gently, at first, but soon Raffo's warm lips closed around her. Her tongue swept hotly along her clit and Dylan, squeezing Raffo's hand on her belly tightly, gave herself up to the majestic sensation of it all. To the week she'd spent here with Raffo. To the pleasure of getting to know her. To all the little moments they'd shared that, perhaps, could have only led to this. To the earth-shattering orgasm rolling through her muscles, seizing her flesh and mending a little bit of that hole in her soul she'd come to Big Bear with.

CHAPTER 17

"I guess this makes me woman number three," Raffo joked, perhaps inappropriately—but this whole situation was rather inappropriate.

Luckily, Dylan chuckled, and pulled her close.

"And what a number three you are," Dylan breathed into Raffo's ear. "Fuck, Raffo."

"Yeah." Raffo had to laugh as well. It made it easier to ignore that Dylan was Connor's mother. Besides, it was a little late to focus on that now. She should have done that before bolting out of her room earlier, before letting Dylan grab her hand and pull her into her bedroom. Before that obliterating kiss against the wall. But Raffo couldn't stop herself. She'd lain awake, tossing and turning, after the conversation they'd had, and when she'd heard Dylan on the stairs, her body had taken over. Her feet had walked her to the door and her hand had swung it open and then Dylan had stood there, looking so fucking sexy and inviting. Then their eyes had met and now here they lay, naked in Dylan's bed.

Dylan's weight settled against her—leg draped over hers, head tucked into her shoulder, arm curved beneath her breasts. The press of skin against skin made Raffo's breath catch. She stroked Dylan's hair while, between her legs, her clit stood to attention. And Raffo was still wearing her pajama bottoms.

"For a moment there, I almost panicked because I didn't tell you where to find the lube." Dylan's body shook lightly against Raffo's as she giggled.

"No lube required." Raffo moved her hand downward from Dylan's hair to her back, until it came to rest on the swell of her behind. Dylan was so utterly gorgeous. Raffo had no idea what she was doing in bed with the likes of her dumped, sad self—although Dylan had said all those lovely things about Raffo tonight, greatly contributing to Raffo not being able to sleep. Either way, the pulse between her legs didn't allow for more questions in that vein. Because they *were* in bed together and Raffo had just made Dylan come and by the way Dylan's body had convulsed beneath her, Raffo had done a spectacular job. "Not this time," she said. "Maybe later."

"We'll see." Dylan pushed herself up and sent Raffo one of her smiles. She had one of the dreamiest, sexy smiles Raffo had ever seen. It wasn't just sunny and genuine; it did something to her face that made everything about her even more alluring. Raffo couldn't help but mirror it every time. Dylan made her smile. Maybe it was that simple. She'd made her smile from the minute Raffo had encountered her in the house, in this very room. She undid, with an easy stretching of her lips, the corners of her mouth lifting deliciously upward, the feeling that Raffo was a first-class loser after Mia leaving her.

"We will." Realistically, when they came back to their senses —although who knew when that might be?—they would need to limit this madness to one night only. In that case, and it was the only case possible, Raffo had every intention of making it a night she would never forget. And there was so much more she wanted to do to Dylan—things for which lube would most defi-nitely be required.

"First things first." Dylan locked her blue eyes on Raffo, then leaned in for a kiss. Raffo could kiss her forever. The softness of

Dylan's lips was a perfect extension of how gentle she was in life. The smiles she liked to intersperse their kisses with a perfect illustration of how lovely and caring she was as a person. There it was again. Raffo could feel Dylan's lips stretch against hers into one of her smiles. It blossomed on her face as she leaned back, as she slid her hand down Raffo's belly, inside her shorts. Dylan's smile faded when her fingers slipped between Raffo's legs.

"Oh, fuck," Dylan said on a sigh, as though she was the one being touched like that. "You're so wet."

Raffo swallowed slowly. Of course she was wet. This was one of the hottest moments of her life.

"Let's get these off." Dylan seemed to have come to her senses again and hooked her fingertips under the waistband of Raffo's pajama shorts. She quickly slid them off Raffo's legs and threw them over her shoulder.

Then Raffo lay fully naked in front of Dylan. Despite being in an open relationship, she hadn't been naked with anyone but Mia in ten years. Despite already having made Dylan come, Raffo felt vulnerable—just as naked on the inside as she was on the outside.

"Are you okay?" Dylan brought the back of her hand to Raffo's cheek and caressed it softly. A finger lingered on Raffo's lips and she trailed it along Raffo's bottom lip.

"Yeah," Raffo said as she tried to catch her breath. Yes, this was a vulnerable moment, but, because of the week they'd had together, and all those candid, fireside conversations, she felt completely safe with Dylan. In this house, Dylan took care of Raffo in a way that no one, not even Mia, had since before she was thirteen years old. It was only natural for Raffo to respond to that, as well as to all the other irresistible things that Dylan was. Endlessly kind, first of all. Someone who really listened when you told them something. Generous with her time and attention and the amount of skin on display when she pranced about the house. And, of course, an excellent bisexual.

Dylan's hand meandered south, stopping at Raffo's breast. She cupped it gently, her thumb lightly brushing against Raffo's nipple. The way her hand roamed across Raffo's body so delicately was so quintessentially Dylan—and quite different from what she and Mia did in bed—and therefore, it was perfect. Because this wasn't Mia by a long stretch. Mia was gone. Mia would never touch her again, would never see her naked again. Mia was the past, and this was now. Raffo had no use for looking into the future, past this night. This night was all she had and it was all she needed, as long as Dylan's fingers whispered across her skin like that.

Raffo groaned deeply when Dylan wrapped her lips around her nipple, when her tongue softly skated over it. While her tongue licked Raffo's nipple into a rock-hard peak, her hand drifted from Raffo's other breast to where it had been before. Dylan's touch might be delicate, but it wasn't less effective for it —on the contrary. A fingertip slipped through her wetness and Dylan moaned against Raffo's breast. She let go of Raffo's nipple and looked at her, the sexiest smile ever on her lips.

She looked into Raffo's eyes and pushed a finger deep inside.

Raffo was not used to so much tenderness, to such delicacy, when doing this. She certainly wasn't used to Dylan's face so close to hers. The truth was that she wasn't really used to any of this anymore. This slow acquisition of a new person's body. The lying awake wondering whether they'd really been flirting or just talking a bit more openly than two acquaintances would. The befriending of someone unlikely. And most of all, for Raffo, the pure joy she felt when she worked on her painting of a topless Dylan. To feel her mojo course through her veins, pump in her blood, as though it was an inextricable part of her. It was all because of Dylan. This unlikely, extraordinary woman who was stroking inside her.

There was not a hint of smile left on Dylan's face. Not even a tiny grin. Her face was all solemn gravity as she slipped her finger out of Raffo and replaced it with two. Despite the desire to close her eyes, Raffo couldn't look away from Dylan's face if she tried. Dylan looked completely entranced, like earlier, when she'd discovered how wet Raffo had been for her. Like she was riding this wave of pleasure along with Raffo instead of merely bestowing it on her.

Raffo brought her hand to Dylan's face and, instantly, Dylan turned to suck Raffo's thumb into her mouth. All the while, her fingers worked their magic between Raffo's legs, and as the wave turned into an unstoppable flood, Raffo felt more than pleasure. Because only the gentlest, kindest touch could reach the grief that had settled so deep within her—and Dylan had that touch in spades.

Her thumb caught in Dylan's mouth, those knowing fingers working inside her, Raffo felt herself cresting. The waves hit hard—pleasure tangled with an unexpected surge of emotion. Not just grief for Mia, but for everything she'd finally been able to voice in those late-night talks with Dylan. When she caught her breath again, the tears on her cheeks felt more like release than sadness.

She felt satisfied and a little beside herself and a lot like she wanted to lie in Dylan's arms all night long.

Dylan had the sensitivity to not ask whether Raffo was okay. She just pulled her close, asking nothing and offering everything in the warmth of her embrace.

CHAPTER 18

Dylan woke with Raffo's arm around her waist and Raffo's cheek pressed against her shoulder. She took a breath. She tried to gauge the time by the light filtering between the curtains but the time of day didn't matter. No one, except Raffo, knew she was here. Today would be another day they would spend together, except now, they'd slept together.

Oh, fuck. The first thought that flitted through her head was that Connor could never know about this. She would tell him everything about why she was at Big Bear, but never that she'd slept with his best friend. Her breath turned into a sigh. Spectacular as it had been, it was also complicated. Raffo wasn't just anyone.

Dylan tried to shift in Raffo's embrace to look at her. Raffo stirred slightly, but her arm remained around Dylan's waist, and she showed no signs of waking.

Dylan studied Raffo's peaceful, sleeping face and the effect was immediately calming. Maybe it was complicated, but it didn't feel like a mistake. How could it possibly be when it had been so glorious? It certainly wasn't something that Dylan wanted to undo—if anything, she craved more. The memory of Raffo's tongue on her rushed back, of how Raffo had pushed

Dylan's arms above her head and, most thrilling of all, how electrifying it had been to have her fingers inside Raffo.

Unable to resist, she softly stroked Raffo's cheek, her fingers drifting along her neck to her small but scrumptious breasts.

Raffo's eyelids fluttered open for a second, then fell shut again. Being with Raffo made Dylan feel naughty and she gently rolled Raffo's nipple between her fingers. Raffo's lips stretched into a smile before she properly opened her eyes.

"God, you're insatiable," she whispered through half-lidded eyes.

"That's how you make me." Dylan chuckled at her own lame excuse.

"Aren't you supposed to have a drop in libido at your age?" Raffo asked.

"Wow. Good morning to you too." Dylan wasn't exactly miffed, but the brash reference to her age still shocked her.

"Sorry." Raffo quickly pressed her lips to Dylan's cheek. "My brain is in utter disarray."

"Understandably so." Dylan leaned into Raffo's kiss. "Did you get some sleep?"

"I did. You?"

Dylan nodded. She wasn't used to sharing her bed, yet falling asleep after Raffo was done with her hadn't been a problem.

"Do you feel bad?" Raffo asked.

"Loaded question." To distract herself, and perhaps also to make a point, Dylan cupped Raffo's breast in her hand. Instantly, her clit came to life—not a hint of a drop in libido. "I can't feel bad because last night was amazing and I'm so incredibly fond of you, but… there's the elephant in the room, of course."

"Can we agree not to tell Connor about this?" As usual, Raffo was much more direct about it.

"Most definitely." In any other circumstance, it was none of her son's business who Dylan slept with, but this was different. Raffo wasn't only his friend; she was also his star protégée.

Dylan was hungry and desperately needed a shower, but extricating herself from Raffo's embrace seemed impossible. And her hand on Raffo's breast felt like the only natural place for it.

"What happened last night?" Dylan asked. "Why did you come out of your room like that?" In her defense, she'd just been getting a bottle of water.

"I don't know." Raffo grinned. "I guess that's what happens when a hot cougar walks around barely dressed all the time." She followed with a rich chuckle.

"A hot cougar?" Dylan played along. "Don't you mean MILF?"

"Oh, no." Raffo groaned and shook her head. "No, don't say that."

Dylan pushed all thoughts of her son to the outskirts of her brain. She'd deal with her guilt later.

"How about some breakfast?" she asked.

"Before the cougar devours me again." Raffo pulled Dylan close and planted a trail of kisses on her neck, before, finally, letting her get out of bed.

———

"Here's the problem," Raffo said. She hadn't even glanced at her work in progress—Dylan guessed she had other things on her mind. "I want my hands all over you, but I also feel like I should never touch you again."

"That is, indeed, a problem." Dylan felt exactly the same. They'd kept their physical distance since getting out of bed, as though the action of showering—of washing off what they'd done in the darkness of the night—represented a clean slate. But it had still happened. And they were still sharing a house.

Raffo cleared her throat. "Should I, um, prepare to leave?" she asked.

"No," Dylan said before she could properly process the question, because, when she did think about it, maybe it was the only sane thing to do. To put distance between them and, at the very least, make sure it didn't happen again.

"What's the alternative?" Raffo asked, her dark gaze brooding.

"We stay." Dylan planted her elbows on the kitchen island. "Just because it happened once, doesn't mean it will happen again. We just had to blow off some steam. And we did. We can go back to, um, normal now."

"It's going to happen again," Raffo said so matter-of-factly, it might as well already have happened. "Let's not kid ourselves." Her dark eyes found Dylan's. "Unless, um, you regret it or… I'm sorry. I can only speak for myself, obviously. I have the hots for you, Dylan. I tried to ignore it and, also, you know, my heart is still in pieces and all that, so I honestly wasn't thinking about you like that, not consciously, but… I really like you. And I know I shouldn't, but you're kind of impossible not to like." She huffed out a sigh. "And last night was fucking amazing."

"It was." Dylan stretched out her hand toward Raffo.

Raffo looked at it for a split second, then wrapped her fingers around Dylan's wrist. "If I stay here, I'm going to want to sleep with you again, and I really don't think we should do that."

What Raffo said made perfect sense, yet Dylan couldn't imagine her leaving.

"I would like you to stay." It was selfish and reckless, but it was all Dylan wanted—for her and Raffo to remain in this joyous bubble they'd created in Big Bear. "Just a few more days."

"And then what?" Raffo didn't let go of Dylan's wrist— Dylan's clit was surely taking notice.

"I don't know. Then we'll reassess."

"It's a really dumb idea." Raffo's thumb stroked the inside of Dylan's wrist.

"Yet smart people do dumb things all the time."

"They sure do." Raffo abruptly dropped Dylan's arm. "But we're not teenagers unable to control our hormonal urges. I'll stay for a few more days, but only if we agree to not sleep together. That's my condition."

Speak for yourself, Dylan thought, regarding the hormonal urges, but her attraction to Raffo wasn't simply due to that— that would diminish it too much.

"Deal," Dylan said, while her clit raged between her legs— more frustrated than excited now.

She offered her hand and Raffo shook it chastely, then swiftly let go, as though holding onto to it for a split second too long may already have jeopardized the deal they'd just made.

"I'm going for a swim," Raffo said bluntly, before rushing to the stairs.

CHAPTER 19

Raffo might have to remain in the lake for the rest of her stay, that was the only way she could possibly keep her end of the deal. Leaving Big Bear was the only honorable way out—then it could still easily be explained as a one-night madness kind of thing—but Raffo didn't want to go back to LA just yet.

She could go somewhere else, but she couldn't tell Connor as long as Dylan hadn't told her son that she was also here—it would involve too many lies and half-truths. What a mess. And the simple fact was, also, that Raffo didn't want to leave Dylan. At a minimum, before she left, she wanted to finish her portrait. She'd planned to paint something for Dylan—one that didn't portray her and that Dylan could sell, if she wanted to. But that might have to wait.

Raffo swam farther from the house, then treaded water for a few minutes, looking at it all from a safe distance. How hard could it possibly be to not sleep with Connor's mother? The question was both ridiculous and excruciating. Most of all, Raffo didn't need this added aggravation to how lost she already felt after Mia. But that was just the thing. Dylan made her feel all sorts of things and sad and lost were not among them.

Earlier, trying to have a rational conversation with Dylan had been nearly impossible. Her tousled golden hair, those dreamy blue eyes, and the persistent memories of last night had clouded every thought. Here, by herself in the water, Raffo could think clearer. She asked herself what it was she really wanted? What was the one thing that mattered the most?

The answer surfaced effortlessly, because it never changed: Raffo wanted to paint. Her break-up with Mia had taken that from her, but two days with Dylan had reignited it with stunning force.

Connor would want her to prioritize her art—not at the expense of sleeping with his mother, but he didn't need to know about that part. What terrified Raffo the most was the possibility that leaving Big Bear—leaving Dylan—might silence her creative voice again. In her personal hierarchy, art ranked above the risk of falling into bed with Dylan again. A crude rationalization perhaps, but it felt true enough for now. She could own that decision, at least.

Raffo swam back to the house, dried off, and did what she wanted to most of all—even more than sleep with Dylan again. She went to work.

———

There were days when Raffo's artistic stars aligned and she managed to do in a few hours what, in lesser circumstances, could take days or even weeks. When she disappeared into a place inside herself that allowed her a hyperfocus that always produced swift and superior work. She wished all days were like that, but they decidedly were not. But today was one of those rare, special days.

She tried not to be flippant about it and attribute it to the orgasms that had freed up some blocked energy in her soul—or something woo-woo like that—but the thought persisted. Being with Dylan had been magnificent—unexpected yet inevitable—

106

tender and, somehow, strangely loving. Dylan was a loving person and that effortlessly translated into the bedroom. With Mia, the last few years, it had always been whips and hand-cuffs, whereas with Dylan it had been straightforwardly sweet —Mia would most certainly sneer at it as too vanilla, but Mia had nothing to do with this—and surprisingly arousing.

Either way, whether it was because of the wonderful sex with its subject or not, Raffo finished the painting of Dylan at five forty-five that day. She didn't just complete the work, she was over the moon with it. Because it was her first completed work post-break-up and also because it was fucking good— even if she did say so herself. The colors were spot on and if you didn't know, you might not recognize her, but Raffo saw everything of Dylan in it. The honey of her hair—rendered in a golden hue Raffo had mixed, as if by magic, only about an hour ago. The kindness in her eyes—their depth expressed in the bluest of blues she could make. The warmth in her smile. The delicious swell of her breasts.

The first thing she did, in her euphoria, was call for Dylan. She didn't go to the kitchen door and kindly ask if Dylan could spare a minute. Raffo yelled for her from her spot on the porch, probably loud enough for the neighbors to hear.

"Where's the fire?" Dylan asked as she half-jogged over.

Raffo's lips drew into an unstoppable smile. "Right here. It's done. I finished it."

Dylan's eyebrows arched up. "No way? Already?"

"Hell, yes. Do you want to see?" Raffo had to stop herself from jumping up and down.

"Is my name Dylan French?" Dylan rubbed her palms together.

"Come." Raffo stood behind Dylan and put her hands on her shoulders. She maneuvered Dylan around until she stood facing the canvas. "Ta-da."

"Oh my god," Dylan exclaimed. "Raffo. Fuck." Did her voice just break a little? Raffo couldn't see her face—and she also found it hard to remove her hands from Dylan's shoulders. "It's so beautiful. I'm—" Raffo did see how Dylan brought her hand to her mouth. "Speechless, but also… incredibly honored." She paused. "That you would see me like this and translate that into this gorgeous work of art."

She didn't sound so speechless to Raffo, but every single word was music to her ears.

Dylan's hand found Raffo's on her shoulder, warm and trembling slightly. "I want to turn around and thank you, but I can't look away from it."

"It's yours. You can look at it for the rest of your life." Raffo squeezed Dylan's shoulder. "And I should be the one thanking you. You made this possible for me. You have no idea what that means to me." Everything, Raffo thought. Absolutely everything.

"I'm also a little afraid to turn around." Dylan leaned backward a fraction, her behind pushing against Raffo's thighs.

"We're going to have to look at each other at some point." Raffo's voice had turned into a whisper.

Slowly, Dylan turned around. Their joined hands dropped, but remained clasped together.

"I'm going to say something that I shouldn't. I know this, but I'm going to say it anyway." Dylan's eyes were a little dewy. "I think that last night, for me—" She put a hand on her clavicle. "I think it was more than sex."

Raffo was not expecting that. What did that even mean? Where was the line? When was it just sex and when was it more?

"I know I shouldn't have said that." Dylan broke the short silence that followed. "But it's how I feel." Dylan pointed her thumb behind her. "And that? That's pure genius, Raffo. You're so fucking brilliant and I'm so lucky that you came here."

Dylan was probably a little overwhelmed by seeing that painting of her. Raffo could understand that. It was a brand-new sensation for her.

"I would also very much like to kiss you right now," Dylan said next.

What about the deal they'd shook on this morning? Not even a day had passed and Dylan wanted to kiss her again? And she had... feelings for Raffo?

"Dylan, um—" Raffo was the one who was actually speechless. It was all too much. Last night, followed by the rush of finishing the painting, and now this?

"I won't, of course. I'm sorry." Dylan took a step back. Their hands lost touch. "But I'm so impressed by you," she whispered.

None of this was rational. That painting behind a stuttering Dylan least of all. Raffo glanced at it and all she could feel was pure joy—especially because the one and only critic this particular work of art would ever have, had responded by wanting to kiss her. It wasn't as though Raffo didn't want to kiss Dylan again—she wanted to do so much more than that—but this was not the deal they'd made.

"Look." Raffo stepped closer again. She didn't want to leave Dylan hanging like that. "Let's take a breath. Let's talk this through. I know it's a lot." Paintings were emotions that couldn't be put into words. Maybe Dylan's brain, and a few other body parts, had interpreted it as much more than it was. To Raffo, it was a return to what she loved the most. But it was impossible for Raffo to know which sensations it elicited in Dylan, its subject—except that she wanted to kiss her.

"I'm sorry." Dylan swallowed hard. "I feel a bit silly but, Raffo, I also kind of don't. I am totally floored by this work. By you. This means something to me. It's hard to put into words what exactly, apart from what I just said, but... sure, let's talk."

"Please, don't feel silly. There's no need for that." Raffo's affection for Dylan was so big, she had to resist pulling her into her arms.

Then it hit her. Of course, last night had been more than sex. They weren't strangers who'd had a one-night stand. They were two people going through a very intense time together. Two people who hit it off and were attracted to each other and had profound conversations as well as breezy, flirty ones.

Then Raffo stopped resisting because if this moment called for one thing, it was a hug between the subject of that finished painting—its muse—and its painter.

"Hey." Raffo bridged the distance between them and opened her arms. "Come here."

Without hesitation, Dylan walked into her embrace. She folded her arms tightly around Raffo's waist and put her head on her shoulder.

"Thank you," Raffo whispered. "For everything. I'm so impressed with you as well."

"I want you," Dylan whispered back. "It's impossible not to want you after seeing that painting. I want you so much, Raffo." Dylan's breath was hot against the sensitive skin of Raffo's neck. So much for talking things through. But what would they say, anyway? Dylan didn't do anything, however. She just stood there, in Raffo's arms—waiting. She was leaving the next step up to Raffo. Dylan's skin was glued to hers. Her lips were a mere fraction removed from Raffo's. Moreover, much like last night, Raffo's body seemed to be taking over. Her arms had no inclination of letting go of Dylan and her feet did not want to walk away from this.

So she closed the tiny distance between their lips—easily and joyously. Of course she fucking did.

Dylan sighed into Raffo's mouth, then clawed at her T-shirt. The time for waiting was, clearly, over.

CHAPTER 20

There was no such thing as logic left for Dylan. Once she'd laid eyes on that miraculous, wondrous, beautiful painting, her brain had gone into tunnel vision and she could only think of one thing. Her fingers inside Raffo.

She wanted Raffo with a fierceness that was completely alien to her. She knew very well she shouldn't have said any of the things she'd said, per their agreement, but fuck their agreement. Dylan didn't care about their deal. She cared a lot about Raffo, though. Now she'd seen Raffo's work, her heart as well as her clit were about to explode. And yes, it made her feel silly, but it also felt completely inevitable. What did Raffo think? That she could just casually show her this work—this artistic depiction of Dylan's face *and* breasts—and get on with her day? That they would have dinner and some easy conversation about some mundane topic?

That painting most likely meant something entirely different to Raffo—she'd have to ask her later—but to Dylan it was a huge boost to her self-esteem. That someone so exaggeratedly talented as Raffo Shah would paint little old her? She, the woman who had lost all that money and who was hiding out from her life, and her son, because of it?

Dylan felt seen and heard and acknowledged as a fully accomplished human being for the first time since she'd arrived here. She wasn't just lucky that Raffo had come here and had wanted to paint her—and generally delight her with her company—but also that she, simply, was here, and had chosen to do *this* with her presence. Dylan wasn't foolish enough to mistake Raffo's desire to paint her as some artistic version of love at first sight. But there was something there—even if it was purely creative inspiration on Raffo's part, it still meant something.

Most of all, Dylan had wanted to kiss Raffo again because of the power that painting had over her. Because of the emotions it unleashed in her. Because of how it had shocked her, in the space of a few seconds, into thinking about herself as the opposite of a gigantic failure.

And then there was last night. All day long, Dylan hadn't been able to think of anything else, despite the deal they'd made. And then she saw the painting, which practically equaled the two of them naked in bed together, Raffo pinning Dylan's hands above her head. It was like Raffo asking her not to kiss her while her lips hovered a mere inch away. Dylan wasn't having any of that. She didn't want to ignore how she felt. She didn't even want to take the time to go upstairs.

While their tongues danced their delicious dance, she yanked up Raffo's T-shirt. That lounger over there would do nicely for what Dylan had in mind—for what she hadn't been able to stop thinking about all day.

Dylan's hands went for Raffo's bra clasp next. Oh, how she couldn't wait to wrap her lips around the tight bud of her nipple. To feel it go hard against her tongue. And then…

In no time, they were naked from the waist up. Dylan swiftly walked them to the lounger. Raffo sat, and Dylan straddled her. Raffo cupped Dylan's breast while she peppered kisses along her neck. Raffo would probably scoff at the notion, but seeing that painting had left Dylan starstruck.

There was no other word for it. Raffo hardly had an abundance of women to choose from in this house but still, they could also not be doing this. Raffo could also not have ogled her more ostentatiously as the week progressed. Raffo could also not have painted Dylan's bare breasts—her nipples painted in the most improbable colors that were, somehow, just right. Dylan was starstruck and flattered and aroused beyond anything—beyond her common sense, that much was for certain.

There was something dangerous about feeling like this. The last time Dylan had lost her common sense, she'd also lost half a million bucks. But she was convinced she only stood to gain by doing this. By pushing Raffo down in this lounger and making quick work of unzipping her shorts, lowering her panties, and having her lie deliciously naked in front of her.

Raffo was not a tiny woman—to Dylan's endless delight— and it took some maneuvering for Dylan, after she'd slipped out of her own shorts and underwear, to slot into the lounger with her. But they didn't need much room for what they were doing—as long as Raffo could spread her legs.

Dylan lay on top of Raffo and, in between kissing her, she simply couldn't stop smiling. Happiness rushed through her, mixed with unbridled, unstoppable lust. Dylan's clit pulsed hard between her legs. She let her knees slip either side of Raffo's upper thigh and the mere touch of her clit against Raffo's leg sent a sparkle of heat along her spine.

When they broke from their kiss, Dylan looked into Raffo's eyes. "Can I fuck you," she asked, in between the shallowest of breaths.

Raffo swallowed hard, then nodded. "Yeah," she said on a throaty moan.

Dylan slipped off Raffo as best she could. The armrest poked into her behind and her left arm was awkwardly stretched under Raffo's neck, but none of it mattered. Any discomfort was easily overridden by the heat in her flesh, by the desire that made her fingers tremble as she skated them along the skin of Raffo's belly.

Dylan angled herself toward Raffo's breast and licked her nipple into the hardest pebble, while her hand, slowly, drifted between Raffo's legs.

To find her wetness was another jolt to her revved-up system. Dylan circled Raffo's clit and it felt like her own clit was being touched at the same time, that's how out of control it pulsed between her legs. When Dylan slid a finger inside Raffo, her breath stalled in her throat. Dylan had done this with other women before—two to be exact—but she didn't remember it feeling this way. This hot and intimate. This excruciatingly arousing—as though she might come just by having her fingers inside Raffo.

"Aah," Raffo moaned. "Oh, Dylan."

Dylan's clit reacted as though instead of saying her name, Raffo had just swept her tongue over it.

Raffo's hips moved toward Dylan's hand, meeting it, demanding more of her fingers—and Dylan gladly gave them. She pushed two fingers inside Raffo and was floored again by the warm grip Raffo had on her. She could feel it in places that weren't her fingers. Her clit, first of all but, also—and she wouldn't be sharing this information with anyone any time soon—a little around her heart.

It wasn't because she was extraordinarily aroused, to the point of orgasm, that Dylan couldn't tell the difference between doing this now and having done it last night. Already, it felt like a world apart. Because when Dylan gazed at Raffo's scrunched up face, her eyes closed and her mouth wide open, she didn't just see the exquisite woman, she also saw the magnificent artist who produced magical paintings with colors so improbable, she must be inventing new ones. That touch of green in Dylan's nipple that, realistically, shouldn't even belong there, was kind of like the green of the fir trees on the mountains at the very height of summer, but it also decidedly wasn't. It was its own green. It was Raffo's green and it made all the other colors she used shine and come together in a way that Dylan had never seen before.

Dylan's body was in thrall to everything that was happening —and had occurred the past week. To her fingers inside Raffo. To the look of bliss on Raffo's face. To the groans rising from her throat. To Raffo's body surrendering to her touch so willingly and easily—despite their dumb deal. But also to Raffo's finished painting and to how Raffo had come to her in the middle of the night. To everything Raffo had revealed about herself and, perhaps, most of all, to how it felt for Dylan to simply be with Raffo. Not just in this fiercely intimate moment, nor to see her paint, but just to be in the same space as her. To look at her as she moved across the deck, or inadvertently swayed to a song on the speaker. To simply see her as she was, which was like the best fever dream you could ever have.

So, of course Dylan's body surrendered at the same time as Raffo's. As Raffo clenched hard around her fingers, spreading even more delight through Dylan, heightening her own plea- sure. Dylan came hard, her untouched clit throbbing, and her moans of ecstasy mixing with Raffo's as they bathed the deck in the most rapturous sound ever.

———

"I would like to propose a new deal," Dylan said. "The old one isn't really working for me."

They'd jumped into the lake, skin bare to the cool water, and rested their arms on the weathered wood of the jetty extending from Dylan's property.

"The old one isn't even old yet." Raffo's gaze was soft, her features a mask of satisfaction.

"It was a bad deal. Completely unrealistic. What were we even thinking?" Beneath the surface, Dylan caught Raffo's ankle between her legs, drawing her closer. Even inches of space felt like too much distance now. "We both have our reasons for being here," Dylan said. "Let's stay and agree that resisting each other is not an option. It's simply not. But let's also agree to leave Connor out of this. Connor is not here and he has nothing to do with this. This isn't about him. This is about us, here and now. In Big Bear, in this house, where I want to stay. With you."

Raffo lay her head on her crossed arms and gazed at Dylan. "I'd like to stay. I'd like to paint something else. I feel if I can paint one more, and feel that thing inside myself that I so crave, I'll be ready to go back to LA. I don't feel ready yet." Raffo nodded as best she could in the position her head was in. "Your new deal is pretty easy to agree to because it basically means we do what we want without worrying about the consequences."

"Why wouldn't we?" A flutter of anticipation danced through Dylan's core.

"Because of Con, but you're right. This isn't about him. As long as we agree, and this is a deal I will not come back on, to never tell him about us."

"Deal," Dylan said. "Connor doesn't have to know and he never will." They'd agreed on a deal before and failed miserably to keep it, but this was different. The stakes were much higher.

"I can already guess what you want to do to seal this new deal." Raffo smiled, her tilted head and half-lidded eyes pure seduction.

"Me?" Dylan scooted closer, their legs now completely intertwined under the water. "Let's not point fingers. Let's use them for far better things." A frisson of lust ran up Dylan's spine.

"I'd like to create a painting of your house next," Raffo said, again taking Dylan by surprise. "So you have something to remember it by if you decide to sell."

"That would be so amazing." The prospect of having to sell the holiday home she had owned for twenty-five years didn't hit Dylan as hard in the gut any longer—she had other things on her mind. "It would also remind me of the time you and I spent here."

"And there's that." Raffo briefly sunk her teeth into her bottom lip. "There is something special about this place. I can feel it now."

"Are you sure that's not just the orgasms talking?" Dylan rested her chin on Raffo's elbow.

"Maybe just a little, but that canvas didn't paint itself."

"It sure as hell didn't." Dylan no longer had to stop herself, so she leaned in and kissed Raffo full on the lips, naked in Big Bear Lake.

CHAPTER 21

Another week had gone by. When Raffo first arrived in Big Bear, she had expected this to be one of the most painful times of her life, pining after Mia and stutteringly trying to paint again. Instead, it turned out to be, without a doubt, one of the best, most magnificent weeks of her entire life.

The weather was sunny. Her mojo was flowing. And Dylan was just as kind and caring and hot as she'd been from the start, but they also slept together every night. After Raffo packed up her paintbrushes for the day, they sometimes danced on the deck together, the music turned up loud, their bodies always moving toward each other. And yesterday, when Raffo had joined Dylan for her afternoon 'nap', they'd listened to Ida Burton's naughty story together—Ida had not disappointed.

Thoughts of Mia had faded as Dylan filled every corner of her world. In the kitchen. At the table across from Raffo. On the deck. In her head. And all over Raffo's body. It was like a dream, and sometimes, when she woke in the middle of the night to find Dylan sleeping beside her, Raffo had to pinch herself. Because this was real. Though it was just a secret affair strictly relegated to their summer in Big Bear, a veritable summer fling, every single second of it was still real.

Raffo walked onto the deck where Dylan was lounging, her head angled toward the setting sun.

Without asking, Raffo refilled Dylan's wine glass from the bottle in the ice bucket next to her. Settling into the adjacent chair, Raffo couldn't help but smile. Even when she tried to turn down the corners of her mouth, they didn't obey. The joy was beyond her control.

Dylan stretched out her hand, as she always did, and Raffo took it in hers. She swiped her thumb over the softest part of Dylan's palm.

"How was painting?" Dylan asked, as she slowly turned her head to look at Raffo.

"Excellent." Raffo couldn't shake the niggling feeling that the triumphant return of her mojo might be too connected to this place—and to Dylan. But she wouldn't know until she returned home. And she didn't want to think about that yet. Dylan's trip to Europe was supposed to last two months. She could stay in Big Bear without raising suspicion for another month. So could Raffo, although she imagined Connor would want to hear some news from her soon. "I kind of miss working on my previous painting, though," she joked.

"You don't have to paint my breasts to see them." Dylan smiled at Raffo. "They're all yours whenever you want."

"What are you going to do with it?" Raffo asked. Dylan had put the painting in her bedroom, right across from the bed—it proved a powerful aphrodisiac.

"I don't know. I haven't thought about it." Dylan squeezed Raffo's hand. "I want to take it home so I can enjoy it, but I can't risk Connor seeing it."

"Yeah." Raffo just nodded. There were things she simply didn't have a reply to, like any mention of Connor in the context of their affair, which would have to find a way to magically not have happened in a few weeks' time.

"I seem to be feeling my age today. I'm exhausted," Dylan said.

"I'll cook for you tonight," Raffo said without hesitation. "I should really respect my elders and their limited energy more." After all, Dylan was almost twice Raffo's age.

"But you hate cooking."

"Not when I cook for you. Don't worry. I have a few dishes up my sleeve and I promise not to poison you."

"Thank you."

"Thank me later." Raffo lifted their joined hands and kissed the inside of Dylan's wrist.

Dylan only groaned in response.

———

It was a pity she hated it so much because Raffo wasn't that bad a cook. When she made biryani for Dylan, it didn't feel like a punishment, although it wasn't exactly enjoyable either.

Raffo took her time and thought about her mother while she prepared the meal. She could hear her mother's voice when she added the spices—"more isn't *always* better, Raffi"—and maybe that was just another magical thing about Big Bear but by the end of it, Raffo was able to serve Dylan a decent plate of food.

"You keep on surprising me," Dylan said. "Is there anything you can't do?"

"Too many things to mention," Raffo replied. "I pretended Mom was helping me, guiding me through the dish. I think that's why it tastes okay."

"Do you get it from her? Your art?" Dylan popped another bite into her mouth and sent Raffo a gentle smile.

"Partly. My father can—or could, at least—draw really well. But my mom, she was the queen of color. She wasn't a painter, but you should have seen how she looked. How she dressed. So bold. So gorgeous. She taught me to be unafraid of color. To embrace it. It wasn't just in how she dressed or decorated our house. Every single meal she made was a feast of taste *and* color." It was entirely possible that Raffo remembered her mother as a touch too perfect, but that's what happens when the better of two parents dies way too young.

"Do you have a picture of her?" Dylan asked.

"Of course." Raffo looked around for her phone and realized, not for the first time, that she'd simply forgotten to keep it on her. She had no idea when she'd used it last. That was also what being in Big Bear did to her. She was more off the grid than she'd ever been, which was quite the achievement for a Millennial. Dylan probably had something to do with it as well. "Let me just find my phone. I'll right back."

Raffo located her phone in the kitchen. It had been on silent and her heart leapt in her throat when she noticed she had three missed calls from Connor.

"Connor tried to call me." Raffo rushed onto the deck in a panic.

"Did he leave a message?" Dylan's posture went rigid in her chair—her shoulders square and her lips a tight line.

"He sent a text." In her panic, Raffo hadn't read the text yet. "Fuck, I hope he's not on his way here or something like that." Heart hammering in her chest, Raffo opened the message.

Call me asap. I have huge news. xo

Raffo showed it to Dylan. They both took a deep breath. It was all well and good to claim Connor had nothing to do with what was happening between them, until he called, and reminded them of his importance in both their lives.

"Do you want to call him?" Dylan asked.

"I should." Raffo was curious what the huge news could be. She reached for her wine glass and downed a big gulp. She paced on the deck as she made the call.

"Oh my god, Raff. Are you sitting down?" Connor didn't bother with any niceties.

"No, but tell me." Raffo kept her back to Dylan so it was easier to pretend she wasn't there.

"You know Over The Rainbow, the queer merch company?"

"Yeah." It was hard to escape when you were queer. Their products were everywhere these days.

"They want to license your rainbow heart painting." One of Raffo's most famous—Connor liked to call it iconic—works was of a heart painted in the colors of the rainbow. It was simple—it had only taken a few days to create—but extremely effective.

"What does that mean?" Raffo asked.

"It means you're going to be one rich lesbian painter. They want to put it on everything. Mugs. Pillows. Whatever you can think of. They're not kidding around. They're offering a substantial advance and a generous percentage on sales."

Raffo didn't know what to say. She'd never had an offer like this. She didn't even know Connor was pursuing deals like this.

"When I say substantial, I mean half a million bucks, Raff. This is the big league. They are truly not fucking around. They want your work and they're willing to pay the price." Connor left a dramatic pause. "A price I expertly negotiated, I might add."

"You've been talking to them for a while?"

"Yes, but I didn't want to disturb your peace in Big Bear until I had an offer you couldn't refuse. That's why I'm your amazing gallerist-slash-agent-slash-best-friend-in-the-whole-wide-fucking-world."

"Half a million? Are you sure?" Raffo's hand was trembling, making her phone shake against her ear.

"I have it in writing. I'll email it over as soon as we end this call so you can have a look at it. My lawyer is scrutinizing the offer as we speak."

"My god, Con. What the hell is happening? First, a show in Chicago, and now this?"

"It's your time, Raffo. It's all coming together." Connor sounded a little out of breath. He must be beside himself. "Can we set up a call for tomorrow to discuss this further?"

"Um, yeah. Sure."

"Let's try FaceTime. I miss you. LA isn't the same without you," Connor said. "Aren't you lonely all by yourself by that big lake?"

Oh, boy. "I'm good. I've been working a lot, actually."

"Can't wait to see the results," Connor said.

"Thanks, Con. For everything. You're awesome."

"Do you have any idea when you might be coming back? Or if a quick return trip is an option? I might need your signature soon."

"Let's talk tomorrow." It was dreadful to have Connor call her with such amazing news and then having to lie to him.

"Sure. Check your email in one minute, okay? Love you, babe."

They rang off, and Raffo took a beat before turning around to face Dylan. The previous time Connor had called, Raffo hadn't yet been sleeping with his mother. She just had to hide that Dylan was in Big Bear. What she had to conceal now was a million times more excruciating. But Raffo didn't have time to consider her secret affair, because she'd just gotten the offer of a lifetime.

She explained to Dylan what Connor had just told her.

"Half a million?" Dylan whistled through her teeth. "That's a lot of money."

"Plus a percentage of sales," Raffo repeated. Connor was right. If this deal went through, she would be a rich lesbian painter.

"Are you okay?" Dylan asked. "You look a little… taken aback."

"I'm both stunned and elated, but, I—I hate that I wasn't able to fully share my joy with Connor about this. He made this happen for me. He has done so much for me and my career and this is how I repay him? By deceiving him?"

"You're not deceiving him," Dylan said.

"It sure feels like it."

Dylan rose from her chair and crossed to Raffo with that

fluid grace she always moved with. "I know you want to cele-brate with Connor, but you can celebrate with me instead." She curled her arms around Raffo's waist, her touch both comforting and dangerous. "I'm so happy for you. Please, try to enjoy this special moment. You deserve it so much."

"He wants to FaceTime tomorrow." Raffo didn't get how Dylan could be so casual about this.

"We'll make it work. Don't worry about it."

"I *am* worried. I'm the one who has to talk to him so I'm the one lying to him. I'm the one pretending you're not here and… well, all the rest."

"I'll make it up to you." Dylan nuzzled Raffo's neck. She wasn't taking this seriously at all. Raffo extricated herself from Dylan's embrace—it no longer felt right.

"This is going to hurt Con. We can choose to ignore that all we want, but that doesn't make it less true."

"I'm well aware, but I've had to flip a switch in my head. For as long as we're here enjoying this glorious but all-too-brief time we have together, that's what I've decided to do." She sent Raffo one of her more seductive smiles. "Weren't you going to show me a picture of your mom?" She took a step closer, but left a respectable distance. "And while you're at it, show me that half-a-million-bucks painting as well, please."

CHAPTER 22

Dylan gazed at a picture of Raffo's mother on her phone and it was like seeing a femme version of Raffo.

"You look so much like her," Dylan said.

"Yeah." Raffo still appeared a little distracted after her phone call with Connor, which was perfectly understandable, but Dylan had meant what she'd said—she had no choice. She had flipped the switch in her head.

The woman in the picture who had Raffo's dark eyes and her raven-black hair and the same solemn, I'm-not-here-to-kid-around expression was dressed in a golden-yellow embroidered sari with sleeves hemmed in sky-blue silk, the fabric luminous against her skin. She wore an emerald silk scarf, dramatic hot-pink earrings that nearly brushed her shoulders, and a state-ment necklace studded with gemstones that caught the light in every color of the rainbow.

It was like looking at one of Raffo's paintings. It shouldn't work, yet it did—spectacularly. Also as with one of Raffo's paintings, Dylan couldn't look away.

"You don't dress like her," Dylan said after she managed to tear her gaze from that very illuminating picture.

"Nah. That's not my style. I don't wear dresses or skirts."

Dylan remembered a question that had popped into her head not long after Raffo's arrival, but she'd been afraid to ask then. Things were very different now.

"Do you identify as butch? Is that even still a thing?"

Raffo shrugged and Dylan could have so easily predicted her laconic response. It was so quintessentially—so irresistibly —Raffo.

"I don't dress for the male gaze, because I couldn't care less about it. I simply dress how I like." A hint of defiance played at her lips. "It drove my mom crazy that I didn't want to wear dresses, even when I was little. But I just didn't. It didn't feel like me. She got over it soon enough, unlike my dad." Raffo rolled her eyes.

Dylan smiled, picturing a tiny Raffo, arms crossed, refusing to put on a dress. "I see your mother's influence in how you use color in your paintings," she said, deliberately steering away from any mention of Raffo's father.

"I don't have to dress like her to honor her. Her use of color is inside me." Raffo still looked kind of deflated.

"Are you okay?" Dylan's change of conversation hadn't seemed to help a whole lot.

"I'm just wondering, again, if we should cut our stay short. If I should go home."

Dylan shook her head feverishly because as soon as one of them went back to LA, it was all over.

"I love Connor more than anyone and I sure as hell don't want to hurt him. And I won't. I will have to fess up about hiding out here, but it will be fine. I'll explain it to him, and he will understand."

"Have you thought about what happens when we go back?" Raffo asked. "To us?"

"When we leave here," Dylan admitted, her heart shrinking in her chest. "There will no longer be an 'us'."

"Exactly." Raffo's voice broke. "We're going to have to pretend to someone we are super close to, and who knows us both really well, that none of this ever happened. I don't know how I'm going to do that."

On top of that, Dylan thought, they would no longer be able to see each other. Except, maybe, when Connor went to New York to—no, she had to stop this ridiculous train of thought.

"It will be hard but maybe not as hard as we imagine." *Christ.* Dylan couldn't seem to stop lying, even to herself. "Things will be different once we put some distance between us, and then time will do its thing, and we'll be back living our ordinary lives, our idyllic bubble will have burst, and…" Dylan ran out of steam. Even though she had her former life waiting for her, she didn't want to imagine going back.

"I'll sleep on it, but…" Raffo's pause made Dylan's stomach twist itself in knots. "Instead of hopping on a call with Connor tomorrow and lying to my best friend's face, I would like to text him that I'm coming home instead."

"But you wanted to stay," Dylan tried. "You needed to paint more before going back."

"That was before Connor called and…" Raffo's scoff cut through Dylan like a blade. "I'm beginning to think that this combination of the two of us together is making us lose our minds. We're fooling ourselves into thinking there are no conse-quences to what we're doing simply because we're doing it here, in Big Bear, away from LA, which is some truly high-level irrational thinking." She shook her head. "This is not me, Dylan. I don't recognize the person talking on the phone with Connor earlier. I trust that guy with my life and I don't want to break his trust in me." She shrugged dramatically. "Although I already have. And so have you."

"You're being too hard on yourself." Although it was compli-cated, Dylan meant it. She knew there were times when you had to be lenient with yourself and your principles—almost six decades of being alive, more than half of those as a mother, had taught her as much. But this was the kind of wisdom you couldn't simply impart on someone younger, someone whose principles were still cut in stone, someone who hadn't lived enough life yet to see that gray areas were where most of real life played out.

"Maybe," was all Raffo replied. "But I can't live with this ambivalence."

"Sleep on it, please." Dylan stretched out her hand. "With me."

Raffo peered at Dylan's hand through narrowed eyes. She swallowed hard. It took a few very long seconds before she, finally, took Dylan's hand in hers.

———

"I propose a compromise," Raffo said. She'd been waiting for Dylan to wake up and every minute she'd watched her sleep had made it more difficult to say this. She couldn't afford to wait any longer.

"Good morning to you too." Sleep had left creases on Dylan's face, softening her features in a way that made Raffo's chest tighten.

"Three days," Raffo said, ignoring the seductive smile on Dylan's face and how her blue eyes already sparkled so brightly just after waking up. "That's my compromise."

"Then you're leaving?" Dylan scrunched her lips into a pout.

"Ideally, you would leave first so you can tell Connor that you didn't go to Europe and we were here together all this time, but that's probably too much to ask." Raffo had tried to think through all scenarios, but none of them included telling Connor the full truth, so she would do what she had to do to minimize the hurt for everyone involved.

Dylan rolled onto her back and expelled a deep sigh. "I'll do it. I won't have you go back to LA and lie to Connor about me being here. That's not fair. None of this has been fair on you. I just… wish we could have longer," Dylan said to the ceiling.

"Me too, but—" The words died in her throat. There were no buts. Her painting of Dylan's lake house would be finished tomorrow. One more day together. One final night. Then everything would end. Real life was beckoning. While frightening, it was also exhilarating. Because Raffo was not the same person that had arrived here a few weeks ago.

Mia had faded more each day, crowded out by everything else. Once Raffo got back, she'd have a million things to do, like find a new home, prepare for Chicago, reconnect with her friends, discover if her mojo would follow her to her old studio —or if she needed to find a new one. All the while trying not to tell Connor she'd slept with his mother.

It was a lot and quite a few things seemed impossible yet, as always in life, she'd just have to do it. Hardest of all would be to pretend Dylan barely existed in her life, that Dylan was anything more to her than Connor's mother whom Raffo had spent some time with in Big Bear, but nothing more than that.

"This gives us three days to get our story straight," Raffo said, watching Dylan's profile. "When you tell him we were here together, he'll assume we became friends—it's the only explanation that makes sense for why I stayed."

"We'll just tell him that we got along but we need a break from each other after spending so much time together."

"You make it sound so easy." Raffo assumed her relationship with Connor was very different than the one he had with his mother. She and Connor shared information that you didn't tell a parent, no matter how close you were. She also predicted that Connor would scrutinize her in a very different manner than his mom. With Dylan, he'd need to get over the fact that she lied about her whereabouts for so long first. Raffo, on the other hand, would probably need to answer a fair few questions about Dylan's state of mind and exactly how worried Connor should be about her.

"Some things we will have to play by ear. We can't rehearse

a few lines and then repeat them to Con verbatim. That's not going to work."

Raffo cleared her throat. "Have you ever asked yourself whether it would be easier to just tell him the truth?"

"No." Dylan's voice was firm, but she kept staring at the ceiling. "It's none of his business."

"It is, though."

"I get that it's more difficult for you." Dylan's voice softened and she turned on her side. "You're friends. It's not the same."

"Ordinarily, me sleeping with someone new would be huge news." Raffo tucked a strand of golden hair behind Dylan's ear. "I was already with Mia when I met Connor. He's only ever known me with her."

"I get that you're worried, but it's always better to assume things will work out."

"You're so philosophical about this. It baffles me some-times." Raffo curled an arm around Dylan's waist, now that she still could.

"In the grand scheme of things, of our lives, this is just a tiny blip. When I look back on this summer, I'd rather remember the amazing time you and I had together than the money I lost or that I couldn't tell my son about it."

"Oh, god," Raffo groaned.

"What?" Dylan painted on one of her sexy half-smiles.

"When you say things like that, I like you even more." Raffo scooted closer. "And I don't know what I'm going to do without you."

"You're going to Raffo-Shah the hell out of life." Dylan pushed her nose into Raffo's hair. "You have so much to look forward to."

"I'm a verb now, am I?"

"You're everything," Dylan whispered, the words barely audible but striking Raffo's heart like thunder.

CHAPTER 23

Three days was nothing. Three last days with Raffo might as well have been three minutes for how quickly they vanished.

After dinner on their final evening together, Dylan wanted to stretch out the night as long as possible, because she didn't want morning to come. She had a whole life in Los Angeles. She had friends—and a son she had missed the hell out of. She had a house with neighbors who believed she'd been living it up in Europe all this time.

Maybe it was the time pressure they were under or maybe it was the simple fact that Dylan had fallen deeply, hopelessly, and recklessly in love with Raffo. She'd only fully admitted this to herself the day before, when Raffo had revealed the painting of the lake house, and Dylan had felt it so bone-deep, so clearly, it simply could no longer be ignored. She had to ask.

"What if we did tell Connor?" Suddenly, even for Dylan, it was a viable option to be explored.

"What?" Raffo turned away from where she'd been silently gazing into the fire. "Where does that come from all of a sudden?"

"Raffo—I—" But Dylan couldn't put that kind of pressure on Raffo. This was never supposed to be *amorous*. It was a summer fling—all the ingredients had been present. She shook her head. "Forget it. It's crazy." Though she'd admitted to having feelings weeks ago, Dylan couldn't confess she'd fallen in love. Raffo's heart was still raw from Mia, even if her ex's name had barely crossed her lips this past week. Moreover, Raffo was thirty-two years old and things were happening for her, while Dylan was considering her final professional hurrah before retirement. And Connor would never accept it. What would they even do? Go on dates in LA? Have Sunday brunch with her son? None of it seemed remotely plausible.

"I'm going to miss you," Raffo said, her voice rough. "So fucking much." The smallest smile touched her lips. "It's okay to be sad it's over. It *is* sad. But it's only sad because we had such a great time."

"Yeah." Dylan took in Raffo's face, the gravity of it—and how different it looked to when they were in bed together.

"Have you figured out what you're going to do?" Raffo asked. "Get a job or sell this place?"

Dylan shook her head. Right now, as they were sitting by this glorious lake, on their last night together, Dylan couldn't fathom selling her Big Bear house, and all the memories they'd made in it. First, she would tell Connor about losing her savings. Then, she'd try to pick up her life in LA, after which she would try to make a decision.

"Can I ask you something?" Dylan didn't know how Raffo would react, but she still thought it a fair question for their last night.

"Sure." Raffo nodded.

"What if as soon as you're back, Mia comes to see you and claims she made the biggest mistake of her life when she left you."

Raffo scoffed. "Fuck that." That, too, was such a Raffo response—economical with words even now. Still, Dylan gave her time to elaborate. Raffo looked into the fire again. "Maybe, one day, I will be able to accept that she fell out of love with me.

Rationally, I know that is something that happens to couples all the time. That it can just be over like that. I can forgive her for that but never for how she handled it. For how she treated me." Raffo shook her head. "It's not going to happen, anyway, because she doesn't love me anymore."

But I do, Dylan thought, the words burning in her chest. *I'm so stupidly, crazily in love with you.*

––––––

When Raffo woke, Dylan was no longer in bed. She groaned as reality washed over her. Dylan was leaving today. Fuck, fuck, fuck. Raffo had suggested it, but now that it was about to happen, she wished she'd never proposed this particular compromise. Because their last night together hadn't just been sensual and explosive and passionate—it had cracked something open between them, something raw and honest and terrifying.

Raffo would never get the image out of her head of a naked Dylan straddling her underneath the sheet, like some super-sexy ghost who couldn't get enough of her, with breasts so improbably perfect, Raffo might just have to paint them all over again. Maybe that's what she would do as soon as Dylan left. Paint her. A full-body work this time—completely naked.

She could already see it in her mind: Dylan stretched out on the lounger, sunlight playing across her skin, those knowing eyes fixed on some distant point across the lake. The painting would capture everything—her strength, her vulnerability, her impossible grace. But Raffo would have to keep it hidden away, like so many other memories of their time together. Another secret to carry home.

"Where are you?" she shouted, because, for one final minute, she wanted Dylan back in bed with her.

"I'm here." Raffo couldn't make out where Dylan's voice was coming from, but she appeared in the room a moment later.

"I've been awake for a while. Going home jitters. So much to pack."

"Come here, please." Raffo opened her arms.

Dylan was already fully dressed in crisp linen pants and a blue blouse that made her eyes look like pieces of sky—maybe that was for the best.

Raffo pulled her into a fierce hug. Because she didn't know what to say she sighed deeply into Dylan's soft, sun-streaked hair. They lay like that for long seconds, moments Raffo never wanted to end.

"It's so hard." Raffo breathed in Dylan's familiar scent—expensive moisturizer, coffee, and something uniquely her—trying to memorize it. In a few hours, this would all be just another memory, like the way Dylan looked in the morning light, or how she laughed when Raffo said something unexpectedly funny. All these little details that had become so precious. "Why is it so hard?"

"You probably can't imagine life without access to my breasts," Dylan joked, but there was a clear sadness to her tone.

"That must be it." Raffo held onto Dylan a little tighter. "Why are you Connor's mother? Why can't you be someone else?" It wasn't a rational question. Nothing about this was rational. It was all emotion.

"Why?" Dylan's voice was muffled because her face was pressed against Raffo's neck. "Would you ask me on a date in LA if I weren't his mother? Am I not too old for you?"

Raffo didn't reply because it was futile, although she didn't consider Dylan too old for her in the least.

"I will never forget our time in Big Bear. Thank you for everything. For all the meals and the excellent company and the mind-blowing orgasms." Raffo loosened her embrace a fraction.

"Thank you for the amazing works of art." Dylan pushed herself up and gazed at Raffo, her eyes all moist. "And for being my third woman." Dylan swallowed something out of her throat. She swept at her cheek. "Sorry. I'm just, um—you made me feel good about myself again, Raffo. That means so much to me." Tears streamed down her face. Dylan didn't bother catching them any longer. "I'm going to miss you so much."

"Me too." The tears that pricked behind Raffo's eyes soon rolled along her cheeks, onto the sheets of this bed where everything had changed.

They sat still, looking at each other, only the sound of sniffling between them. Then there was nothing left to say, though a thousand words pressed against Raffo's lips. This was it. It was all over. The vacation. The time-out from life. Their red-hot and strangely restorative affair. Their secret fling in Big Bear and whatever feelings it may have produced. As soon as Dylan's car rolled off the driveway, it was all over and done with.

CHAPTER 24

After barely holding it together in bed, Dylan had to get out of there. If she'd stayed any longer, she would have told Raffo how she really felt about her. She would have been in danger of blowing up her life, which was already so torn to pieces.

She glanced in the rearview mirror, watching Big Bear shrink behind her. Each mile seemed like another brick added to the wall she'd have to build between herself and Raffo. The lake house disappeared around a bend, and Dylan's chest tightened so sharply she had to remind herself to breathe. Everything about the past few weeks—the painting sessions, the late-night conversations, the way Raffo looked at her like she was the most fascinating person in the world—all of it would have to be locked away somewhere deep inside her.

She banged her fist against the steering wheel. Why, of all the billions of people in the world, did she have to fall in love with Raffo Shah? With her son's best friend?

It was hard to focus on the road, especially after the night they'd had. Dylan didn't know how it was possible, but it had been a million times hotter than all the nights before combined.

"Are you into anal play?" Raffo had asked, long after midnight—the only appropriate time for a question like that.

Dylan hadn't known what to reply. It was a question she didn't know the answer to because no one had ever asked her before.

Raffo had devoted a lot of attention to Dylan's behind by then, her fingers gently skimming the sensitive skin there, but Dylan'd had no way of knowing things were headed in that direction.

"It's okay if you're not," Raffo had said, in that matter-of-fact way that really didn't suit the situation, but made it all the more thrilling. "But if you want the climax of your life, an orgasm to always remember me by, you should give it a try."

What was Dylan supposed to say to that? She had become a woman who was into anal play there and then. And the real kicker? Not a word of what Raffo had said had been a lie. She'd asked—demanded, really—Dylan to touch herself while she got out the lube and played with her there and, fuck, Dylan could never, ever forget. The sensation was etched sharply into her memory because of its utter ecstasy combined with Raffo's audacity and the general addictiveness of her personality.

But Dylan had to ban these memories swiftly from her brain. She gripped the steering wheel tighter, remembering how Raffo had whispered encouragement in her ear, how she'd known exactly when to push and when to be gentle. It wasn't just the physical sensation that had been extraordinary—it was the trust between them, the way Raffo had made her feel completely safe while simultaneously driving her wild. Dylan had never experienced anything like it, that perfect balance of tenderness and raw desire. How was she supposed to forget any of this? But she had no choice. Los Angeles wasn't far. She'd be reaching the city limits soon. She took a few deep breaths and made the call she'd been dreading for weeks.

She called her son.

———

It was the middle of the afternoon when Dylan arrived in LA and met Connor at his gallery.

"Oh, Mom." He wrapped her in his arms, and Dylan felt herself go a little limp against his chest.

"I missed you so much," Connor said. "I'm all for spiritual journeys but it was too long, even though you came back early."

"We have to talk, darling," Dylan said. "I have to tell you something."

"Did something happen on your trip?" Connor held her at arm's length. "You look good, Mom. Healthy and strong and, I don't know—I can't quite put my finger on it, but I have a feeling you're about to tell me all about that."

Connor didn't have a clue—how could he possibly imagine what had really happened in Big Bear?

"Shall we go into your office?" Dylan needed all the privacy she could get for this conversation.

"Sure." Connor walked them into his office and the first thing Dylan saw was, unmistakably, a Raffo Shah painting. It was one of her earlier works—all bold colors and sharp angles, so different from the softer style she'd developed in Big Bear. Dylan's throat tightened as she remembered watching Raffo paint, how her whole body would become part of the process, how she'd bite her lower lip in concentration. The memory felt dangerous here in Connor's office. But Dylan had to keep it together.

Connor poured them both a glass of water and they sat in the lounge chairs by the window. "Tell me everything. I'm absolutely dying to hear about your adventures."

Here we go, Dylan thought. This confession felt almost easy compared to the secret she'd never be able to share. In the pause before she spoke, Dylan imagined telling Connor about Raffo and her. Would it really be so atrocious? Wasn't Connor always saying that love is love? But Dylan pulled herself together again.

"Darling, um…" She tried to look at Connor's face but her

gaze skittered away. "There's no easy way to say this and I should have told you weeks ago, but I… I didn't go to Europe. I made a bad investment a few months ago and I lost a lot of money. I spent the summer in Big Bear instead."

"What?" Connor knitted his eyebrows together. "What do you mean? You're not making any sense, Mom. Are you okay?" He slanted his head. "Raffo's in Big Bear, anyway. You can't have been there. I would have heard by now. She tells me everything." The penny seemed to drop—slowly. A shadow crossed his face. The confusion in his eyes slowly transformed into something darker as the pieces started fitting together. His jaw tightened, and Dylan could practically see the wheels turning in his head as he connected the dots about his mother and his best friend sharing the same space all summer, keeping secrets from him.

"Raffo was there. I asked her not to tell you. Please, Con, don't be mad at her. Raffo didn't want to lie, but I begged her to. It's not her fault."

"But, um—why wouldn't you tell me?" He rubbed his chin. "How much money did you lose?" He inhaled sharply. "What on earth is going on here?"

"A year or so ago, I met this guy. He was big into crypto and it piqued my interest. I got involved, did my research—at least I thought I did. I bought a couple of thousand dollars' worth and it kept on going up and up, so I kept buying more and more. Then, after I'd gone all in, the crypto exchange I used was hacked, losing billions in customer funds. Then the SEC cracked down with strict new regulations, and the coin I'd invested in crashed to nearly zero overnight."

"That doesn't sound like you at all, Mom," Connor said, his voice icily calm.

"I'd just quit my job and was making plans to start a new agency after my trip to Europe. I got carried away because I figured the more seed money I had, the bigger the chances of my new ad agency succeeding. I should have pulled out much earlier. I should have had my ear to the ground more. I was blind to the reality of it and oh-so stupid. God, I've never felt so stupid and utterly dumb in all my life. Which is why I didn't tell you. I couldn't. I needed some time to process my humongous failure, but I also could no longer afford to go to Europe. I canceled everything, got refunds, and I hid out in the lake house instead."

Connor didn't say anything for a while, then he shook his head. "I can't believe you didn't tell me."

"I was ashamed. I hope you can understand that."

"But you lied to me and then… you made Raffo lie to me. *My* Raffo. My best friend." He scoffed. "I can't believe she went along with it."

"She didn't want to, but… that's all on me. I explained to her why I needed more time and then days turned into weeks and then, a few days ago, you called with the news about the licensing deal and then Raffo really couldn't take it anymore. She made me come back because she couldn't lie to you any longer." Dylan buried her head in her hands—it all sounded so much worse now that she was telling her son. "I'm sorry I made Raffo hide this from you."

"Jesus, Mom. Raffo's not… she's not a liar. She's—fuck, I sent her to Big Bear because she was in pieces and then she finds you there, because you lied to me about being in Europe and if that wasn't bad enough, you then make her lie to me too." He expelled a sharp breath, running his hands through his hair in frustration. "How is she?"

"Raffo's, um—" Dylan bit back the tears. She couldn't start crying about Raffo in front of Connor. "She's much better. She's painting again. I think she'll be all right."

"Thank fuck." Connor threw his head back dramatically.

"I'm so sorry, darling. I know it's a lot right now, but I hope you can accept my apologies at some point. I never meant to hurt you. I surely never meant to drag Raffo into this. None of this should have happened, but it did."

"How much money did you lose?" Connor leaned forward with his elbows on his knees.

Dylan cleared her throat, as though that would make admitting the ludicrous amount she invested easier to confess. "Half a million." No matter how much time had passed, and how much Raffo had propped up her self-esteem, the shame about her mistake still burned savagely inside her when she recited the amount—it probably always would.

"Oh, fuck. Mom!"

"I know. It's bad. I feel bad. I will never feel good about that. I—I might sell the house in Big Bear. It's a mess, Connor, and I didn't want to saddle you with all of that before I could start forgiving myself."

Connor looked a lot paler than he did before. Any joy at seeing his mother again after weeks of absence seemed to have dissipated. He took a sip of water.

"I'm rarely lost for words, but I don't know what to say to this. I am sorry that you felt like you had to go through this alone, Mom. You should have told me. If only to share the burden."

I wasn't alone, Dylan thought. "Raffo, um, helped me come to terms with it. To be honest," she paused, choosing her words carefully, "it was a blessing that she arrived when she did."

"Really?"

"She's… very special."

"Oh, I know. And she's having a moment. I'm so excited. I can't wait for her to come back. Tomorrow, right?"

Dylan nodded while swallowing the dryness out of her throat.

"I'm glad that your—and Raffo's—future is so bright, darling. I'm so happy for the two of you. You make me really proud, Con."

"I know you will automatically say no, but, Mom, if you need money… I can help. I want you to know that."

Dylan would rather sell her Raffo Shah paintings than take money from her son. "That's very kind of you, but I'll be fine."

"You want to sell Big Bear?" Connor's face didn't look so ashen anymore. "You love that house."

"I'll see. I can also just go back to work. I'll figure it out." Dylan leaned forward and took her son's hands in hers. "Now enough about me, tell me what you've been up to this summer." Luckily, Connor was the kind of guy you didn't have to ask twice to talk about himself. And Dylan loved hearing his stories about the gallery and Murray and New York. For an unguarded few moments, she simply enjoyed being with her son, listening to the sound of his voice, and pretending that she wasn't in love with his best friend.

CHAPTER 25

"You bitch," Connor said while he hugged Raffo tightly. "I'm so happy to see you, even though you lied to me all this time."

"I couldn't tell you, Con. I'm sorry."

"I know, my mom made you do it. Good grief." He let go of Raffo and gave her a once-over. "You look about a gazillion times better than when you left, so that's something."

"I feel better," Raffo said, although she wasn't sure how painting would go when she went back to her studio. "Your mom took great care of me." The words tumbled out before she could stop them.

"You're besties now after bonding over keeping a secret from me?" Connor joked.

If only he knew. But being here, in Connor's house, around his energy, made everything, instantly, feel different. The hankering for Dylan that Raffo had suffered from since she'd left had disappeared at the sight of her best friend. Being with him in person, having a conversation, made Raffo able to see reason again. She hadn't expected it to be so easy, but there you go.

"You're very lucky to have a mother like that, despite... well, you know."

"Despite her being a two-hour's drive away from LA all summer? Tsk." Connor shook his head. "Despite her lies and deceit." He brought his hands to his chest. "But I love my mom. And we can't all be flawless, like *moi*." It was good to see Connor was already in a joking mood about it.

"I need you to know that I felt awful every time we talked on the phone and I couldn't tell you she was there. I hated lying to you."

"Ah. I'll forgive you soon enough." He shrugged. "I get it. You were staying at my mom's house." He cocked his head. "You must really like her then, if you were willing to lie to your best friend for her, and stayed with her all those weeks."

"She's, um, very easy to be around." Raffo's cheeks burned but, luckily, she had the kind of complexion that could easily absorb a blush. "Are you angry at her?"

"Not so much angry, more like utterly shocked. I've always thought of my mom as this really smart woman and then she goes and loses all this money. It doesn't make any sense to me." He tapped this chin. "I've had a day to think about it and, I mean, she looks fine, and she's not even sixty yet, but you hear about these cases more and more. People with early-onset dementia."

Raffo wasn't sure if Connor was still joking or not. "I think she just got carried away."

"She's never displayed any signs before, as far as I know. But what do I really know? And then she goes and hides out in Big Bear for months? I mean, come on. Why didn't she just tell me? We're family. We're meant to share the hard stuff."

"She felt extremely stupid and ashamed and she didn't want to worry you." Raffo couldn't help but defend Dylan.

"She said you made her feel better." Connor looked Raffo straight in the eye—as though he knew something, which was impossible—and her stomach coiled itself in a knot.

"We talked a lot. And she made me feel better, too." *Argh.* "I was painting again after two days there."

Connor clapped his hands together. "Hallelujah." His face split into the widest smile. "When can I see?"

"It's not commercial work. I gave it to your mom for letting me stay at her house." This part wasn't so easy, because it involved omitting more truth—but Connor could never see the first painting Raffo made after she got her mojo back. "It was a picture of the lake house, so."

"You gave my mom a painting?" Connor emitted something between a chuckle and a snort. "That should help with her money issues."

"How have things been here?" Raffo had come straight to Connor's house, where she would be staying. Her first order of business, now that she was back, would be to find a place of her own. "Have you seen you-know-who?"

"Only once or twice and just in passing. You know I'm firmly in your camp, Raff."

"She's still with my impossibly long-legged, blond replacement?"

"No one can replace you, but yes, I think so. I mean, I don't really know. We're not in touch." Connor gave her a look. "Instead of talking about the evil ex, let's talk about Chicago and Over The Rainbow."

"Fuck yeah." Raffo pointed at Connor. "You're the man, Con."

"Your one and only—man, I mean." He walked into the kitchen. "I have a bottle on ice to celebrate."

Raffo fetched the glasses and then clinked rims with her best friend who had made all this happen for her. She sipped from her champagne and let the happiness course through her. It was a straightforward kind of happiness that didn't involve any ambivalence—or lying to people she loved—and that she could enjoy for a full one hundred percent. So she did and, while she was at it, pushed any lingering thoughts of Dylan all the way to the outskirts of her brain.

"By the way," Connor said. "We're not done celebrating.

We're having a party on Saturday. You're the guest of honor, *bitch*."

Raffo could only hope that Connor hadn't planned on inviting his mother—but why would he?

————

Raffo's champagne glass had been refilled too often, her pleasant buzz sliding dangerously toward drunk. She could easily tell because, as the evening progressed, and more people arrived at the party, she wished one of them *was* Dylan. But this was not the kind of party you invited your mother to, no matter how close you were.

Murray was in town, and she watched him and Connor dance together. Murray was seven years older than Connor, nothing compared to the age gap between her and Dylan. Not that it mattered. Fuck. Raffo had been back for five days now and she'd been happily caught up in the whirlwind of settling back in and picking up her life again. She'd already inspected a potential new home but when it turned out to be on the border of WeHo, Raffo had decided she didn't want to tempt fate. What if she ran into Dylan at the local coffee shop? No thank you, please.

She refocused on Murray and Connor and on how seeing them together made her happy. Connor's house was packed with all their friends—minus Mia, who was no longer considered a friend.

Raffo joined Connor and Murray on the makeshift dance floor and let herself be swallowed up by the love of her friends. She could enjoy this again now. Connor, who liked to throw a party for every possible occasion, had tried to wrangle Raffo into having one for her birthday a few weeks before sending her to Big Bear, but Raffo didn't want a party then. There was nothing to celebrate because Mia had left her, and she could no longer paint, and she couldn't even bring herself to go back to the house where they'd lived together for six years. The house they'd bought, renovated, and decorated together. The house that was such a symbol of their love, of their beautiful relationship, that Mia, nonetheless, had thrown away like a piece of stale, old bread.

Returning to her and Mia's house would have to be the next step. But for now, Raffo was staying at Connor's place in Silver Lake. It didn't come with a lake attached and a gorgeous woman who cooked all her meals—and made her come like crazy every night—but it had her best friend in it and, oh, it had been so good to be reunited with Connor.

Tonight, Raffo wanted to celebrate. She was back and ready for whatever life had in store for her next—most probably a vicious hangover in the morning.

CHAPTER 26

"Oh, fuck, Tiff," Dylan said to her best friend, because she had to tell someone. She was afraid of falling to pieces if she didn't. "Promise me that this will stay between us. Neither Connor, nor Joe can ever find out about this." Tiffany was Dylan's ex-sister-in-law but still very current confidante. She was the only person in the world that Dylan had confided in about her bad investment and, in case of an emergency, her stay in Big Bear instead of Europe. Even though Tiffany was Connor's aunt, Dylan trusted that her secret was safe with her. Tiffany had kept many secrets for her over the decades they'd known each other, and vice versa.

"I wish I'd known you were going to tell me secrets. I would have made the tea stronger." Tiffany was a recovering alcoholic who was twenty-five years sober.

"Connor sent Raffo to Big Bear because her girlfriend broke up with her and she couldn't paint anymore and she just needed a break from everything," Dylan blurted out.

"And Connor didn't know you were there," Tiff said.

"No, so Raffo arrives." Dylan skipped the part where Raffo walked in on her sleeping topless. "Expecting to find the house empty, except it's not. I'm in hiding. And I have to convince her not to tell Con, who she's incredibly close to, but… that's not what I want to tell you." Dylan wished she had something stronger than tea, although she also knew—from Tiffany—that booze was rarely the answer to anything. She took a deep breath, realizing there was no way she could say this without sounding ridiculous and like a horrible almost-sixty-year-old cliché. "I fell in love with her," Dylan whispered. "I fell in love with Raffo." Her voice became more powerful as she repeated it. "She is one of the most amazing people I've ever spent time with."

"I'm sorry, but… what?" Tiffany's brow was a nest of wrinkles. "You fell in love with Raffo Shah? Connor's friend and protégée?"

How Raffo would balk at being called Connor's protégée, but that wasn't the point here.

"I know how it sounds. I know it's absurd. But it's also the truth." Dylan, who had missed her son so much, could barely bring herself to call him for fear she would crack and tell him. Or, even worse, that he would mention Raffo and Dylan would burst into tears. "I'm so in love with her and we're meant to have distance between us, and LA might be big, but we're in the same city, and she's living with Connor at the moment, and it's driving me completely insane."

"Back up a little, please. What happened? You say you're in love with her, but… does she know? Does she have feelings for you? Did you… I don't know. Tell me."

"We were both in Big Bear nursing our wounds and we spent a lot of time together. We talked a lot. Shared a lot. And then one night, it just happened. We slept together. And then it proved impossible to stop, even though we tried. The only way to stop was to leave Big Bear and come home, which we did. That was a week ago and I've been losing my mind ever since."

"You haven't been in touch since you left Big Bear?" Tiffany wasn't one to judge.

Dylan shook her head.

"Did you tell her how you feel about her?"

"Yes and no. I might have alluded to it being more than sex for me, but we never expanded on that. And I didn't want to make a big love declaration before leaving, before jumping back into our real lives. That hardly seemed fair. And also because it doesn't matter. It's not like we can ever be together."

"Because of Connor." Tiffany nodded her understanding.

"Yes, most of all, but also because she's only thirty-two and she just came out of a long-term relationship that ended badly and… there are so many reasons, but mainly Connor, of course. Yes." As long as Dylan could focus on her son, and the effect her ridiculous feelings for his best friend would have on him, she could keep it somewhat together.

"I'm sorry, Dyl. I'm sorry you feel that way about someone you can't be with." Dylan had known Tiffany would never try to talk her into giving into her feelings—because she didn't believe in love-at-all-cost like that and because she was Connor's aunt.

"I'll get over it." Dylan gazed into her tea. "I just wish I was over it already." Dylan couldn't believe she'd been the one claiming it wouldn't be as hard as they thought it was going to be—it was so much harder.

"Do you wish Raffo had never shown up at Big Bear?"

"No way. I wouldn't have missed that for the world."

"What's so special about her, anyway?" Tiffany asked.

What's not? "She's been through so much in her life yet she carries herself with such grace and…" There were things Dylan couldn't share, even with her best friend. "She's so crazily talented. I watched her paint. It was like watching pure magic unfold, no tricks needed." The first piece Raffo had painted for Dylan stood in her bedroom for now, although Dylan knew she'd have to put it somewhere else so as not to be constantly reminded of Raffo. It was just like their clandestine affair. She wanted to keep it and cherish it so badly, but she couldn't because of the possible consequences. "But mostly, she's just such a joy to be around. She's so calm and down-to-earth and serene and…" Dylan let her eyes fall shut. Instantly, on the back of her eyelids, an image of Raffo in one of the Adirondack chairs by the lake materialized. Her still face. The way her dark gaze would light up when Dylan approached. Dylan quickly opened her eyes again. "I don't know how to get over someone like that."

Tiff regarded her intently. "You didn't feel worthy of her?" She had a knack for cutting to the chase.

"No, because I felt like such a fuck-up when I arrived in Big Bear. Such a loser. And I was a mother lying to her son. But Raffo, she… she liked me, just for me." *And maybe for my breasts and my legs.* "But, in the end, I have to be realistic about that as well. She was so hurt. Her break-up really devastated her. I'm smart enough to know that I was also a distraction for her— from her heartache. But, um, the sex… My god, Tiff."

"That good, huh?" Tiffany sipped from her tea stoically. She reminded Dylan of Raffo—or maybe it had been the other way around. They both had a calmness about them that Dylan enjoyed. Tiffany was the opposite of a dramatic person—maybe because, like Raffo, she'd been through a thing or two in her life as well.

"Out of this world." Dylan used up so much precious energy trying not to think of Raffo in bed, of how she looked when she surrendered but, most of all, of how she looked when she did the opposite of surrender. It sent a shiver down her spine every single time.

"I wish I could give you some sage advice, but I don't think I have any," Tiff admitted. "The only thing you can do is live your life and let time go by. Many hearts have been healed like that."

"I have a lot to do in that respect," Dylan said on a sigh. "To sort out my life."

"On the bright side," Tiffany said. "You're on the cusp of sixty. You know this will pass. You're not a teenager unable to control your hormones. You have experience and the kind of wisdom that can only come with age. Use it to your advantage."

Dylan didn't feel wise or that life experience could help her get over Raffo more quickly. She just missed her every second of every day.

"Thanks, Tiff."

"And you have me," Tiffany said. "Whenever you feel like you might do something… unwise. Call me. Come and see me. We'll talk it through."

If only it were that easy, Dylan thought, even though she had no choice but to do just that.

CHAPTER 27

In many respects, almost three weeks after Big Bear, life seemed to be falling into place. Raffo had signed the licensing deal with Over The Rainbow. In a few days' time, her bank account would reach an all-time high. She had an option on a Craftsman in Silver Lake, just five minutes from Connor's place. She'd had the most amazing Zoom call with Dolores from the Dolores Flemming Gallery in Chicago who had sung her praises until Raffo's cheeks burned so hotly, she could barely take it.

In other respects, things were stalling. She hadn't been able to bring herself to face Mia, too afraid of what seeing her might do to her. She'd used the Over The Rainbow money as an excuse, because it would be more than plenty for a deposit on a house of her own. Raffo knew she and Mia needed to sell their house eventually—she wasn't just going to let Mia keep it as a reward for falling in love with someone else—but she preferred to practice avoidance for now. Before she spoke to Mia, Raffo would like to paint something she could be happy with—like the two paintings she'd made in Big Bear.

Raffo'd had an inkling from the start that the spectacular—and ultra-swift—return of her mojo in Big Bear was tied to that particular place—to the lake house and its gorgeous occupant.

Her studio had always been her sanctuary, even more so now she'd left the home she'd shared with Mia. Raffo had always thrived there. She'd fallen for the space as soon as she'd laid eyes on it. For the light most of all, because it was always what was most important. But this was not the same light as Dylan's porch in Big Bear. And Dylan wasn't prancing around in her skimpy bikini. There were no delicious cooking smells coming from the kitchen. And the only picture Raffo wanted to paint—Dylan, naked in bed, that sultry half-smile on her face—was the one she most certainly wasn't allowed to paint. Only if she wanted to give Connor a heart attack.

Raffo had begun drawing a puffy cloud in the vague shape of a snoozing cat, but she thought it was too childish, too not-her, too not what she so desperately wanted to paint. Her heart wasn't in it and it was as though her mojo knew this.

"I thought I'd find you here." Out of nowhere, and just like that—as though time had rewound itself a couple of months—Mia appeared in the doorway of her studio. Raffo's paintbrush clattered against the easel, leaving a stark blue streak across her abandoned cloud.

"What the h—" The words caught in Raffo's throat.

Mia stood framed in the doorway, backlit by the hall lights, looking both familiar and like a complete stranger.

"I come in peace." Mia raised her hands, one of which held a bottle of champagne. "I hear massive congratulations are in order." The forced cheerfulness in her voice made Raffo's skin crawl.

Mia lowered her hands. "I'm sorry for showing up like this. Can we talk, please?" The question hung in the air between them, heavy with all the conversations they should have had months ago.

"What do you want?" Raffo found it impossible to inject any friendliness into her voice.

"Just to… talk and, um, tell you something that I really need to say and haven't yet had the chance."

Raffo took a breath. She was never going to be ready for this but she had to talk to Mia at some point. After so many years together, they had a life—and a lot of admin—to untangle. Although Mia didn't look as though she had admin on her mind. She looked pale and skinnier than before with not a hint left of the smugness with which she'd introduced Ophelia into their lives.

"Can we sit?" Mia gestured at the lounge area in the corner where she'd spent a lot of time the past decade. The worn leather armchair still bore the indent from where she used to curl up with her laptop. Mia had always loved coming to the studio and she'd been in constant competition with Connor as to which of them was Raffo's biggest supporter.

"Sure." Raffo was more than happy to put her brushes to the side. And Mia was smart enough not to ask how her work was going.

"I'm sorry for how things went down," Mia said as soon as her behind touched the chair. "I'm so sorry. I need you to know that." She put the bottle of champagne on the table between them. It couldn't have looked more out of place. "I've been an inconsiderate bitch. I'm well aware of that."

Raffo didn't say anything. She just listened while her heart alternately flung itself against her ribcage and seemed to want to shrink away into the farthest corner of her body.

"She's not like you, Raff," Mia said, wiping her eyes.

"What? W—who?" Raffo stammered.

"Ophelia, she… she's really smart, like, with an IQ up to here and all that." Mia actually held her hand above her head. "But she's not serious. She's… I don't know how to put it. The best I can come up with is that she's not like you. She's the opposite of you."

"Mia, um, I don't want to hear this. If you want to complain about your new girlfriend, please have the courtesy to do that to someone other than me."

"She's not my girlfriend anymore. I broke up with her."

The words hit Raffo like a physical blow. Wasn't this what she'd been dreaming of, secretly, when she allowed herself a little less anger at Mia?

"I—I don't know what to say to that." And she didn't. The studio suddenly felt too small, too full of their shared history, of the future they'd planned together between these walls.

"I'm not here to… beg for your forgiveness. To beg you to take me back. I'm not that foolish and I know you, but… I miss you. I know I fucked everything up. I dropped this massive bomb on our lives. I hurt you so much, I know that, and you didn't deserve that." Mia locked her gaze on Raffo.

A tremor started in Raffo's fingers and rippled through her entire body, as if every cell was trying to reject Mia's words.

"You are so… gorgeously you," Mia said—had the audacity to say, after she'd ripped Raffo's heart to shreds. "And I'm so very sorry. I just wanted you to know that." Mia rose. "That's what I wanted to say to you." She took a few steps toward the door. "Maybe we can talk some more later? I would like that."

Raffo couldn't move and she certainly couldn't speak. She just watched as Mia walked out of her studio, as though she'd had any right to come here in the first place. What the fuck? She glanced at the bottle of champagne and fought the impulse to smash it into smithereens. She tried to calm her trembling body and control her breathing so that, at the very least, her hands would stop shaking. As soon as she was able, she reached for her phone and called Connor.

"Mia just came to my studio," Raffo said.

"No way. What did she say?" Connor sounded as though he was in traffic.

Raffo told Connor the bits her shocked brain could remember.

"I'm just pulling up to my mom's house," Connor said. "Do you want to come here?"

"What? To your mom's?" That would be the day. "No."

"She's having an issue with her iPad again. I was going to

stay for dinner, but I can skip that if you need me to come home and be with you."

"No, it's fine. Have dinner with your mom."

"Why won't you come over? Aren't you friends now after all that time together by the lake? She knows all about Mia, doesn't she?"

Oh, Jesus. "I—I don't really want to see anyone right now. I'll just go to your house and I'll meet you there later, okay?"

"Sure. I'll tell her you said hi. Love you and, Raff, don't let Mia get into your head."

With Mia's apology and Dylan's memory warring in her head, Raffo packed up her things—ignoring that wretched bottle of champagne—and made her way to Connor's house.

CHAPTER 28

"I just spoke to Raffo," Connor said, barely through the door, his keys still dangling from his fingers. "She's in a state. Mia turned up at her studio unannounced."

Dylan's heart nearly exploded out of her chest. "Is she okay?"

Connor shook his head dramatically. "No, I really don't think so." He kissed Dylan on the cheek and gave her a brief hug. "Apparently Mia broke up with her new girlfriend and, from what I gather, she's already planting seeds to get back into Raffo's good books."

"What do you mean?" This was none of Dylan's business— and yet.

"Oh, I don't know." Connor sighed. "All this lesbian drama. Us gays are supposed to be the dramatic ones, you know?" He sagged into his favorite chair by the kitchen window. "I asked if she wanted to have dinner with us, but she declined."

Dylan grabbed onto the kitchen countertop.

"There's something I just don't get, Mom." Connor toyed with his keys before putting them in his pocket. "You claim she helped you, and Raffo says you helped her with the whole Mia business while you were in Big Bear. You spent weeks together, just the two of you, up there by that lake, building campfires and singing 'Kumbaya' and whatnot, and then you come back, and what? You're not friends? Did something happen? Did you have a fight near the end or something? Is that why you came back early?"

"No, darling, just—" *I fell in love with her.* "It was a bit much, I guess. Quite intense." Dylan tried to sound casual but she had no idea if she was succeeding. "We both have so much to sort out now that we're back."

"So you didn't fall out?" Connor looked her in the eye.

"No." Dylan tried to hold his gaze, but it was impossible. She grabbed her iPad and thrust it into his hands. "My email won't sync again. Can you work your magic, please?"

"Sure, Mom." Connor just put the iPad in his lap. He rubbed his chin and sighed. "I worry about Raffo so much. I know she'll be all right, but I would hate for Mia to get her claws back into her."

Me too, Dylan thought.

"I was over the moon when Raffo told me she was painting again. Because it means she's ready to transform the pain. Because that's what she does. It's what makes her work so special and what makes people respond to it in the way that they do. What attracts them to her paintings so irresistibly. On the canvas, she turns her pain into this incredibly colorful expression of joy that makes it impossible to look away. That's her real talent. She's so fucking special and I don't want Mia to fuck her up all over again."

Dylan couldn't agree more. Connor was pretty fucking special too for saying that, and for seeing that in Raffo when he signed her to his gallery.

"Do you think I should talk to Mia or stay out of it?" Connor asked.

"Oh, darling, I don't know." Dylan could do so much better than that. "Raffo's strong. Don't underestimate her," she tried again, and it was easy—a relief, even—to say these things about

Raffo. "Of course, she's going to be in shock when Mia shows up out of the blue like that, but she'll regroup. She'll find her genius again. It's in her. I've seen it in action."

"You watched her paint?" Connor's eyebrows arched all the way up.

Dylan nodded while a lump grew in her throat. The evidence was on display in her bedroom, on the floor above right where Connor was sitting.

"Do you want a glass of wine?" Dylan asked, eager to change the subject.

"Nah. I'm driving. Just water, please." Connor lit up Dylan's iPad and went to work.

———

"Mom!" Dylan was in the pantry when she heard Connor cry out. "Mom?!"

"Where's the fire?" Dylan joked as she exited the pantry.

Connor sat staring at her iPad with his mouth wide open.

"What's wrong?" Dylan asked. Maybe she needed a new iPad—she'd probably asked Connor too many times to fix a silly issue for her.

"Why is there a picture of Raffo totally naked on your iPad?"

"What?" Dylan's heart dropped all the way to the floor. "What are you talking about?"

Connor covered his eyes, as though a naked picture of Raffo was the worst thing he'd ever seen, and turned the screen toward Dylan.

And then there she was. On their last day in Big Bear, in that weird headspace of knowing what they had to do and clinging onto the last shreds of rebellion in their hearts, Raffo and Dylan had posed naked for each other. Raffo had instigated it, claiming she might need a nude picture of Dylan when her mojo disappeared again—and how could Dylan say no to that?

167

But Dylan had most certainly not transferred that photo to her iPad. How the hell did it get on there and, more importantly, what was she supposed to say to Connor? More lies or the truth? Dylan couldn't lie anymore and she was certain, in every fiber of her being, and despite the inevitable fallout, that Raffo wouldn't want her to lie either. She'd want for that picture to never have appeared on Dylan's iPad screen, but that could no longer be undone.

Dylan took a breath, ignoring the hot shame burning her cheeks, and said, "I'm sorry. You were not supposed to see that."

"Duh. What the hell, Mom?" Connor screwed his eyes shut. "But I can't unsee it."

"Look, we—" Dylan started, but she didn't know how to say this, how to explain it to her son in a way that he could understand, let alone accept. "It must have synced from my phone. We took some pictures in Big Bear. It was—"

"Nude pictures?" Connor threw the iPad on the table and started pacing. "Why?"

Dylan could spin a tale of Raffo needing them for inspiration, but it would all just be more lies. She'd lied enough to the person she loved most in the world—her son.

"Raffo and I, we, um, we had a thing at the lake house, but it's all over now, so we don't need to make a big song and dance about it, darling." *Yeah right*. Connor was nothing if not a drama queen.

His eyes went wide. "What's a 'thing'?" He shook his head. "It better not be what I think a thing is."

"An affair. A summer fling," Dylan admitted and it felt horribly awkward but strangely relieving at the same time.

"Sex?" He said it as though it was the most disgusting word he'd ever uttered in his life. "You had sex with Raffo?" He looked as disgusted as he sounded. "That's just not possible, Mom. I mean—" He shook his head vigorously, as though the harder he shook it, the more he could undo it all. "You're, like…

you're my mom," he croaked. "You can't have an affair with my best friend. No. That didn't happen. Please, tell me that didn't actually happen."

"Look, darling, what happened doesn't matter. It's over. It's not a thing anymore. All that's left of it is that picture." And that painting in her bedroom and all the mad yearning in Dylan's heart.

"Of course it matters. You slept with my best friend. For how long? Was it just once?"

"Con, please, calm down. Take a breath. You're upset."

"Of course I'm upset. Wouldn't you be upset if you found out I slept with… I don't know. Whoever your best male friend is." He dropped his head in his hands.

"Yes, of course, but still. Please, sit."

"With Pete," Connor said, lifting his head. "Or with Carl." He refused to take a seat, while continuing to name all of Dylan's male friends and acquaintances. "Or Kevin. Ugh," he said.

Dylan let him run out of steam. She'd have to call Raffo as soon as Connor left. If he was going to be railing like this to her, after what she'd already been through with Mia today, she needed a heads-up.

Connor finally sagged against the kitchen island, his elbows gliding along its smooth surface. "All this time, you've just been lying to me more. Both of you." That was the real kicker. What hurt him the most. Two people he was meant to trust with his life had, again, kept something crucial from him.

"Darling, sometimes a lie is kinder than the truth. You didn't want to know this."

"But I do know," he said on a sigh.

"It was just… comfort," Dylan lied. "We were both hurt and depressed and… we were there. It was more a proximity thing than anything else." Of all the lies she'd told, this one felt the worst—and the most untrue.

"I just can't wrap my head around it, Mom. I just can't."

169

"That's okay. You don't have to." Dylan could barely wrap her own head around it, and she'd been a part of it.

"Did you… seduce her? Take advantage of the vulnerable state Raffo was in?"

"No!" Dylan took great offense at that and she made sure Connor could hear it in her voice. "Of course not."

"I just don't get how this happened." Connor inhaled sharply and took a long time expelling his breath.

"Sometimes, in life, things happen that you don't get, or don't want to have happened, or…" This was hardly the time for a life lesson, but Dylan was only trying, with the tiny amount of energy she had left after… everything.

"But it's really over?" Connor fixed his gaze on Dylan. "You haven't been carrying on behind my back all this time?" It was a fair enough question under the circumstances.

Dylan shook her head. "I haven't seen Raffo, nor spoken to her, since I left Big Bear."

"That's why she didn't want to come to dinner. That's why you haven't acted like the friends you claimed to have become at the lake house. But fuck, Mom, I never would have guessed this."

"I know. It's a lot. I'm sorry." It felt odd to apologize for something she had enjoyed so much, but Connor deserved the apology. Unwanted, he stood in the middle of this whole mess. "For everything." Dylan was still apologizing for keeping her financial embarrassment from him as well, making her feel like the worst mother in the world.

"Oh, Mom." Connor just stood there, speechlessly processing the second bombshell Dylan had dropped on him. "Is there anything else, now that we're getting into it?"

"No." Except that Dylan couldn't get Raffo out of her head, but she—wisely—didn't share that information. "I promise."

"What am I going to say to Raffo when I get home?" His eyes were pleading, as though he genuinely had no idea how to talk to his best friend any longer.

"Just give her a break if you can." Dylan's voice softened despite herself. "She's been through so much."

"Argh." Connor pushed the heels of his hands against his eyes. "The most unseemly images are flashing through my brain."

"I know this is not something you ever wanted to hear and that it's shocking." Dylan kept her voice steady, measured. She smoothed her hand over the kitchen towel, a nervous gesture she'd had since Connor was small. "But in the end, we were simply two consenting adults who liked each other."

"A lot, apparently." Connor's jaw tightened.

"Raffo's pretty amazing," Dylan allowed herself to say—the full truth, for once.

"That she is." Connor swallowed slowly, his Adam's apple bobbing up and down. "I get that you would be attracted to Raffo but, no offense, Mom, that it would be mutual?" He shook his head as though Raffo wanting to be with Dylan was the biggest head-scratcher he'd ever faced in his life.

It was hard not to be a little offended, but Connor was upset, so Dylan could hardly hold it against him.

"What I mean is that I just don't see you that way. Since Dad, all you've ever been with are these mediocre middle-aged men and now… Raffo? Just like that?"

"You know I'm bi," Dylan said, weakly, not protesting the characterization of her previous relationships.

"Intellectually, I do know that, but I've never seen you with a woman… and now suddenly my brain has to parse you and Raffo all over each other at the lake house. Maybe if it was anyone else, but not Raffo. She's my best friend, Mom. No, she's more than that. I won't say she's like a sister to me, coz, ew, gross, but we work very closely together. We tell each other everything… until now. I had no idea. She's been back, living with me for three weeks, and I had no fucking clue."

"I know. I'm sorry. We had to make the decision very early

on that we would never willingly tell you. That we had to protect you from that."

"Early on? Do you mean you were sleeping together all the time you were there? Raffo was in Big Bear for five weeks."

"Not all the time," Dylan said.

"And if I hadn't seen that picture? You would have lied to me for the rest of my life?" He sounded more deflated than dramatic.

"It's hard to say, darling." Dylan resisted the urge to hug him—this was not a time for physical affection.

He heaved a sigh. "I don't feel like going home and having this conversation all over again with Raffo."

"You're very welcome to stay here."

"I don't want that either. Besides, Raffo's waiting for me. She has to process this Mia-business that went down today." He nodded, as though he suddenly understood something. "She was hurting and you're very caring and motherly. That does make sense to me. That it must have been comforting for Raffo in that respect." He pulled a face again. Poor Connor. He wasn't supposed to be thinking of scenes like that involving his own mother. "I think I'm going to go now."

"Don't be a stranger, you hear me?" Dylan did put a hand on her son's shoulder now. "I'll call you tomorrow to check in."

"I love you, Mom, and I want you to be happy, but…" He took her hand in his. "Should I be worried about you? Clearly, you haven't been yourself these past few months. Are you okay? Like, truly? No more lies. No more protecting me. I'm a big boy. I can take it."

"Oh, Con." Something inside Dylan crumbled. "I'm okay. I'm fine. I just made some not-so-good decisions, but you don't have to worry about me."

"The worst thing," Connor said, his voice shaky, "is that I'm not sure I believe you. That I *can* believe you."

Dylan deserved that, perhaps, but it still broke her heart into a million pieces.

CHAPTER 29

Raffo was flicking through TV channels in Connor's living room. The images blurred together, a meaningless stream of colors and faces that couldn't hold her attention. Mia's impromptu visit to her studio had left her numb more than anything and she was glad to have the house to herself for a while, to just wallow in it all. Mia with her idle, stupid words. That dreadful cat-shaped cloud she was trying to paint. Connor inviting her to dinner at his mother's. The thought of sitting across from Dylan at a dinner table made her stomach twist in ways she wasn't ready to examine.

But most of all it was what Mia had said. That she broke up with Ophelia, who wasn't serious enough. What did that even mean? Raffo's train of unstoppable thoughts was interrupted by the ringing of her phone. Her palms started sweating because she had a feeling it might be Mia and she wasn't in the mood for another confrontation. When she looked at the screen, Dylan's name appeared. Her pulse jumped, a complicated mix of relief and anticipation flooding her system. Not Mia—but somehow this felt even more dangerous. Her finger hovered over the screen for a heartbeat before she answered.

"Hey, Dylan. What's up?" The forced casualness in her voice made her wince.

"Raffo, I'm so sorry. Connor knows. He's on his way home and he's in a state, as you can imagine."

Everything that could tighten in a human body, tensed up inside Raffo. "Connor knows? How?"

"Oh, god. Something really stupid. One of the pictures we took synced from my phone to my iPad and he saw it and I just couldn't come up with another story. I couldn't lie to him anymore, Raffo. I'm so sorry."

"He saw one of the naked pictures?" Raffo closed her eyes. *Oh, no.*

"Yes, I'm sorry. I'm so very sorry."

"Oh, fuck. How did he react?" Raffo took a breath, sinking deeper into Connor's couch, as though its familiar embrace could shield her from what was coming. She had never wanted Connor to find out but, deep down, perhaps she'd always known it was inevitable, that it was impossible to keep that kind of secret from someone you were so close to—and neither she nor Dylan could be any closer to Con.

"Upset. Like he didn't get it. Grossed out. In shock. All of it."

"How are you?" Even though the circumstances weren't ideal, it was kind of nice to hear Dylan's voice.

"Mortified," Dylan said. "Or maybe mortified about having to be mortified is a better way to describe it."

"I'm sorry, what?"

"Nothing. Um, Connor told me about what happened today. That Mia stopped by your studio. How are *you*?"

"She broke up with her girlfriend and apparently I needed that information." The words came out bitter and sharp-edged with anger.

"Yeah." On the other end of the call, Dylan swallowed. "I'm sorry, Raffo. I asked Connor to give you a break because of today, but… he's hurt because I lied to him. Again."

"*We* lied to him again."

"I feel terrible. I really do, but—" Dylan didn't finish her sentence.

"But what?" Raffo asked.

"It's good to talk to you, even if only for a few minutes, and to give you this shitty heads-up. I—"

Raffo waited for Dylan to continue.

"Will you let me know how it goes with Con?"

"I have to talk to him first," Raffo said. "See what we agree on."

"Sure." A resigned sigh came through the phone. "I'm sorry again and, um, well, I don't really know how to end this call, but I'll just leave you to it." Without further ado, Dylan hung up.

Raffo sat staring at her phone. She hoped Connor was stuck in traffic. Life had been so much simpler in Big Bear, when she didn't have to take anyone else into account. Although the fact that she hadn't was exactly what had made this happen. Poor Connor. He didn't deserve this.

Raffo did the only thing she could do: with her heart beating nervously in her throat, she waited for her best friend to come home.

———

The front door burst open with familiar drama, followed by the clatter of keys hitting the entry table and designer shoes clunking on hardwood. Connor arrived home in the way he always had, all noise and look-at-me-I'm-here energy. Raffo uncurled from her spot on the couch, relieved that the news of her sleeping with his mother hadn't dampened his personality.

"I had a long chat with Murray on the way home," Connor said as soon as he clocked Raffo. "I don't know how he did it, but he somehow convinced me that you and my mom lezzing it up together isn't the worst thing in the world, and maybe it's not, you know, but fuck, Raff, how could you keep this from me for so long?"

"Because she's your mom," Raffo stated the obvious.

Connor shook his head. "I feel like I'm in a really bad soap opera."

Raffo knew exactly how he felt, except that she hadn't been lied to by her best friend.

"You're Raffo Shah." Connor sank into a chair, his shoulders slumping as though the weight of this revelation was finally hitting him. He gestured vaguely at the living room walls where several of her paintings hung. "You can get with anyone you want. Hell, even your ex wants you back." He ran a hand through his perfectly styled hair, messing it up in a way he'd never normally allow.

Raffo swallowed hard at the reference to Mia.

"Why, of all the women in the world, did you have to get with my mom?"

She also didn't know how to reply to that. She could hardly share the reasons of her attraction to Dylan with Connor. It was simply impossible.

"*My* mom." Connor shook his head dramatically.

"I'm sorry, Con. I can't really explain it."

"Mom said it was more proximity than anything else."

Raffo's muscles tightened further. That's not how Dylan had put it to her, but she could understand why Dylan would say something like that to her son.

"Yeah. I guess that it was."

"You don't, like, have any feelings for her, do you?" He looked at Raffo with such desperation in his eyes, as though it would be the end of him if Raffo felt something for his mother.

Raffo knew, rationally, that a simple no was the best—and only—way to go here, yet she found herself saying, "Your mother is an extraordinary woman. She was there for me and she… gave me back my mojo, Con. That's a huge deal for me."

"What does that mean?" There was a hint of venom in his

tone. "You started sleeping with her so you could paint again? She's your muse now?"

"Not exactly, but… she had this soothing, healing effect on me. She's so kind and giving and…" *Hot.* "I just really like her."

"So it wasn't just sex?"

"No," Raffo said, because she'd be damned if she told Connor another lie, no matter how much the truth might upset him. "I kind of miss her, but I'm trying to get over that. We haven't been in touch. We're keeping our distance. Out of, um, respect for you." That couldn't sound sillier if she tried.

Raffo braced for a vicious reply, but Connor remained silent for a few moments. "Look, Raff, apart from the fact that you sleeping with my mom grosses me out big time, you and I, we're more than friends. We're building something big and important, something I believe in with all of my heart. I believe in you and your talent so much, there's nothing I wouldn't do for you. But this…" He huffed out some air. "We can't risk our relationship because you have a crush on my mom."

"What are you talking about? Our relationship is not at risk." *Was it?*

"I don't want to be the person to deny you whatever it is you need, but please, don't start up with my mom again. I can't stomach that. You're *my* friend. I need you too."

"Con, come on, our friendship is not in danger."

"You say that now."

"Your mom and I, that's over. Okay? That's the decision we made." For you, she didn't add. "You don't have to worry about that."

"I'd hate for you to be my stepmom." He painted on a forced smile.

"That would be the day." Raffo chuckled, because what else was she going to do? "You'd never listen to me, anyway." Raffo made a mental note to text Murray later to ask him about his conversation with Connor.

"Damn right I wouldn't." He blew some air through his

teeth. "Now tell me about Mia? Because I'm seeing through her gameplay already, Raffo, and I'm not going to let that bitch get her claws back into you just like that."

"I've had some time to mull that over and I don't think that's what her visit was about."

Connor gave her his quizzical look, one eyebrow arched up and his lips pursed judgmentally.

"I think that, maybe, everything that's happened is catching up with her. She went from dumping me to jumping into this thing with Ophelia and now that it's over, she's probably grieving both relationships. Even though she fell out of love with me, we were together ten years. We've been through a lot together. We became grown-ups together, really. That's not something you can shake off that easily." That's how Raffo had decided to spin Mia's visit in her head.

"We'll have to see about that." Connor pulled his lips into a sweet smile. "Were you painting when she arrived?"

"Trying to." Raffo sighed. She always told Connor precisely how her work was going. He was her artistic sounding board in that way—although he didn't always have the answers both of them craved. "It's not coming together just yet."

"I'm not sending you back to Big Bear." Was that a hint of glee in his voice?

"Did your mom say whether she would sell the house or not?"

"I think she hasn't decided yet." Connor's tone was neutral again, as though his mother wasn't the subject.

Raffo, somehow, would hate if Dylan resorted to selling the lake house. Still, it was none of her business.

"Oh god." Connor went rigid in his chair. "If my mom has naked pictures of you on her phone, does that mean you have nudes of her on yours?"

A flush spread from Raffo's neck to her cheeks. "For the sake of our friendship," she said, trying to keep her voice level, "let's not discuss that."

"I'll take that as a yes," Connor groaned.

CHAPTER 30

As soon as she parked her car in the driveway in Big Bear, in the spot where Raffo's truck had been for five delicious weeks, Dylan made the decision—or, better, the decision was made for her.

She couldn't sell her house in Big Bear. She couldn't bring herself to do it. It had too many beautiful memories attached to it. Not just from her time with Raffo, although those were freshest in her mind, but from when Connor was little and he still loved coming here—before he became the very definition of a city slicker and, apparently, allergic to country air. She remembered him at nine, helping her plant the row of pines along the property line, his small hands covered in dirt, his face serious with concentration. Those trees now towered over the house, marking the passing years like silent guardians.

This house was much more a part of Dylan than her main residence in West Hollywood. She could sell that house and rent a small apartment until she got back on her feet. Or she could get another corporate job. She could take the path of least resistance—and least fun. But this was life, and it definitely wasn't turning out to be Dylan's best year.

First, she'd lost half a million bucks and then, she'd also

gone and lost Raffo. Although she could hardly compare her time with Raffo to money in the bank. There was no comparison. She'd happily lose all her remaining money if it bought her a solution to the paradox in her heart. To how much she wanted Raffo and, at the same time, didn't want to hurt her son. But Connor came first. It was the most important principle of being a mother. From the minute Connor had been born, Dylan had happily and easily—and forever—put herself second.

Raffo had probably moved on by now. Maybe Connor had been right, and Mia was finding a way to get back together with her. Or she'd simply met someone else. Or she just relished being on her own. Dylan didn't know because they didn't discuss Raffo any longer now that Connor knew. As though by not talking about it with Dylan, Connor could erase their affair from his consciousness.

Dylan was wise enough not to push him on the subject even though, some mornings, she woke, feverish and wanting, desperate for the tiniest morsel of news about Raffo. Because almost five weeks after leaving Big Bear, Dylan still couldn't forget Raffo. Now that she was back at the place where it had all transpired, she understood why.

Their connection had been brief, but incredibly powerful. It wasn't the amount of time they'd spent together, but the intensity of it. And the sex. Dylan couldn't even bring herself to think about the prospect of going on a date with someone else— let alone a mediocre middle-aged man. Not after how Raffo had made her feel. Some nights, she felt it in her bones as though it had happened only yesterday and, of course, Dylan did her part to keep those blissful memories alive. She hadn't masturbated so frequently, and with such gusto, her mind ablaze with images of Raffo, her wrists tingling as she imagined Raffo's fingers curled around them, since she'd been a teenager and first discovered what a climax felt like.

Dylan sank into Raffo's favorite lounger, wondering if the impossibility of their romance only intensified her desire—that bone-deep yearning that kept her company through endless days and sleepless nights. Time was not doing its job, on the contrary.

Dylan walked inside the house and her gaze fell on a small bronze statue of a merman that Connor had always coveted. She put it in her bag so she could give it to him the next time she saw him. It was the least she could do for her son.

———————

The day after, when she put her bag into the car, the weight of it reminded her of the statue for Connor. She called her son and invited him to her house so he could pick it up.

"Actually, Mom, can I ask you a huge favor?" he said in his sweetest voice.

"Sure, darling."

"I'm in a major time crunch and my assistant is swamped. I forgot my suit—it's hanging on my bedroom door, and I need it tonight. Could you possibly stop by my house and bring it to the gallery, please? My day is so insane."

"Sure. No problem. I'll be there in three hours tops."

"Thanks so much, Mom. You're a life saver. Love you." He said something to someone else in a muffled voice. "I have to go. See you later."

Before Dylan had a chance to ask whether Raffo would be at the house, or was even still living with him, Connor had hung up.

As she pulled up to Connor's house, the answer soon became obvious because there was Raffo's silver truck parked in front of the garage.

Dylan didn't use her key. Her heart hammered in her throat as she rang the bell.

Raffo opened the door wearing nothing but a robe, water dripping from her dark hair onto her shoulders. Dylan's mouth went dry.

"Dylan?" She pulled the robe tighter around her body. "Um, I wasn't expecting you."

"Connor asked me to pick up his suit for tonight and bring it to the gallery. I'll be in and out in two minutes." Dylan was rambling, her mind racing. There was so much she wanted to say to Raffo but wasn't allowed to. And fuck, how she wanted to push her against the nearest wall and just kiss and kiss her. *Argh.* She had to get a grip.

"Come in." Raffo opened the door. "I had an incident with a paintbrush at my new house," Raffo said as she led Dylan into the living room. "I know how ironic that sounds."

"You found a house?" Dylan unearthed the merman statue from her bag and put it on the dining table. Raffo eyed it quizzically but didn't say anything.

"Yeah. A five-minute drive from here. So Con and I can be even more joined at the hip." That did a good job of reminding Dylan of how close Raffo and her son were. It helped a fraction with squashing the increasing desire to kiss Raffo, but not a whole lot, if she was honest.

"That's great." Only immediate physical distance could save Dylan from her desire. "I'm sorry, but Con is waiting for me. I'd best get that suit."

"Sure." Raffo's smile held something Dylan couldn't read— or didn't dare to.

Dylan nearly tripped on the stairs, her legs betraying her state of mind. In Connor's room, she took a few deep breaths to steady herself—and the insane lust rushing through her veins. With a heavy heart, Dylan made her way downstairs because it had instantly become clear to her that the only way she'd ever get over Raffo was if she didn't see her again. If two minutes in her company could unravel Dylan so swiftly, she shouldn't take any chances. On the upside, Dylan would just be doing more of what she'd been doing for five long, Raffo-less weeks already.

"How's the painting coming along?" Dylan asked as she

was already crossing to the hallway. It was only polite to inquire.

"My house or my art?" Raffo leaned with her shoulder against the wall and she looked so damn sexy, Dylan had to avert her gaze.

Dylan chuckled like the schoolgirl she felt she was on the inside. "Art," she managed to say.

"Not so good since I left Big Bear, to be honest." Raffo was still her old, straightforward—and delicious—self.

"I'm sorry to hear that." Dylan wanted to ask a million questions, but she couldn't let herself. She had to get out of there, she had to get away from Raffo's energy before it sucked her all the way in. "I'd better go. Good to see you," she mumbled, as she made her escape—because that's what it felt like—from Connor's house.

On the way to the gallery, she repeated the words out loud like a mantra. "Connor comes first. Connor comes first. Connor comes goddamned first."

CHAPTER 31

After Dylan's impromptu visit, Raffo poured herself a large glass of water and slowly sipped it while hoping the bell would ring again. But it didn't. Dylan had barely been able look at her. Then, she couldn't leave quick enough, as though Connor was waiting somewhere cold and naked for his suit.

Raffo dragged herself up the stairs to get dressed, the brief but intense encounter leaving her shaken. Just as she made it to the top of the stairs, she heard a noise below. It wasn't the bell. It was someone letting themselves in. It couldn't be Connor because, apparently, he was so busy he'd had to dispatch his mother to pick up his dry-cleaning.

She thundered downstairs, deliberately heavy-footed to warn off any potential intruder. But the person standing in the middle of the living room was hardly an intruder. It was Dylan.

"Did you forget something?" Raffo asked. Her robe had fallen open—she knew because Dylan's gaze had dropped to her chest, lingering there instead of meeting her eyes.

"I did," Dylan said, her breath ragged, as though she had jogged back here instead of driving. She took a step closer, grabbed the side of Raffo's robe, and pulled her close. "I forgot this," Dylan said, then kissed Raffo full on the lips.

Raffo's knees went weak instantly. Because the very thing she'd been too afraid to dream of—to hope for—was exactly what was happening. Dylan's soft lips against hers. Dylan's hand letting go of Raffo's robe and slipping inside it. So, of course, Raffo kissed Dylan back, despite the fact that they were in Connor's house and despite Raffo believing, to her very core, that she'd rather give up painting forever than come between Connor and his mother.

Apparently, Raffo's core was not to be trusted when it came to Dylan. Nor was her common sense. Dylan's touch was too powerful. She'd gone without it for too long because despite what Raffo wanted to believe, and what she'd been telling herself—tried to convince herself of—Dylan's hands were exactly where they belonged right now. On Raffo's skin. Driving her crazy at lightning speed. Deactivating whatever flimsy amount of rational thought Raffo had left. But she was only human and, like most humans, she was ruled by her emotions more than anything.

"For the life of me," Dylan breathed into Raffo's ear. "I can't forget you. I think about you all the time."

Raffo pushed her hands into Dylan's hair and pulled her closer so she could kiss her again. So her tongue could dart in and out of Dylan's delicious mouth and Raffo, just for one minute—or maybe five—could take everything she'd denied herself for Connor's sake. It was just a kiss. Just a moment of temporary insanity. They'd come to their senses soon enough, after a few more of Dylan's divine kisses.

They stumbled backward until Raffo stood with her back against the door Dylan had just walked through for the second time in half an hour.

Dylan's hand sneaked up Raffo's belly and, softly, landed on her breast.

For five endless weeks, Raffo had tried so hard to push thoughts like this away as soon as they surfaced. She knew giving in wasn't an option, that she shouldn't try to keep the memories from Big Bear alive. But now it was actually happening, Raffo had no defense. Dylan had driven herself back here. She had instigated this, and it didn't look as though she was going to put a stop to it any time soon. Raffo had to be the wiser one, although she had no clue how. Not yet. She would in a minute. Just one more minute of Dylan's soft hands on her breast and her tongue in her mouth.

Dylan's hand grew bolder, her touch more insistent as she broke their kiss.

Fuck, she was so gorgeous, so utterly beautiful, so everything Raffo had denied herself.

"I want to make you come," Dylan said, her words so breathtakingly sexy, they almost made Raffo come there and then simply because it was Dylan who said them. "God, I want to," Dylan groaned. "Is that okay?"

Dylan was still fully dressed whereas Raffo's robe was barely still covering her. Raffo nodded because it was all she wanted. Just for another few minutes. Saying no was not an option in the state she was in. In this dream that she hadn't allowed herself to have that had, somehow, become reality.

"I'm going to lick you," Dylan whispered, her eyes blazing pure lust. She kissed Raffo again, her lips hot on Raffo's mouth, while her hand trailed down. Then, she broke the kiss and kneeled between Raffo's legs.

Through half-closed eyes, Raffo glimpsed the strange little statue Dylan had put on the table when she'd arrived earlier, reminding her why Dylan had come here in the first place—for Connor—but then Dylan's hot tongue swept along Raffo's clit and all thoughts were instantly erased from her brain.

Raffo forgot about the reasons this shouldn't be happening and tuned into her biggest desire. She wanted Dylan. Her body surely wanted Dylan. Raffo had been afraid to touch herself since Dylan had left Big Bear. Afraid of what she might feel, of what it might unleash in her. Afraid of what it might turn her into—a person living in her best friend's house while lusting after his mother. A person she didn't want to be. But oh, how she was that person now. And she was doing a whole lot more than just lusting. Dylan's tongue licked her to ever greater heights, awakening every nerve in her body, her clit surging to life.

The orgasm that seized Raffo brought her to her knees, and not just metaphorically. Her body as exhausted as her mind—both worn out from weeks of trying to forget what they desperately wanted to remember—Raffo collapsed beside Dylan. She reached for Dylan blindly, pulling her close.

"After I saw you," Dylan muttered under her breath, "I couldn't stay away."

Raffo maneuvered into a sitting position and tugged Dylan close. It was a warm day and she was only wearing a light blouse, but she still felt way too dressed next to Raffo.

Raffo didn't know what to say. Nothing had changed and everything had changed—again. So instead of talking, she started to unbutton Dylan's blouse. Dylan stopped her by putting a hand on hers.

"I can't have you touch me," Dylan said. "I won't know how to recover from that again."

That was rich. "And how am I supposed to recover from that orgasm you just gave me?" Raffo tried to inject some gravitas into her voice, but failed miserably.

"You will," Dylan said flatly. As though she suddenly came to her senses, her body went rigid and she put some distance between them. "I'd better go."

"Shouldn't we talk about this?" Raffo asked. "At least a little bit?"

To Raffo's surprise, Dylan's eyes moistened. "What's there to say? We can't be together."

"We have to tell Con. We can't lie to him again." The rush of Raffo's climax was quickly replaced with a crushing sadness.

"I'm sorry for coming back. I shouldn't have done that, Raffo. I shouldn't have put you in that position."

Raffo shook her head. "I'm not sorry, but… it shouldn't happen again. We can't do that to Connor or ourselves."

Dylan closed her eyes when she spoke, as though what she was about to say couldn't be said while looking at Raffo. "I miss you so much. I don't know how it's possible. I don't know why I can't seem to get over you."

"Maybe you just need a little more time," Raffo offered. She and Dylan both.

"Time?" Dylan opened her eyes. "I'll be sixty in a few months. When am I going to feel like this again? I may never feel like this in my life again."

It was high time for Raffo to be the wiser one, although she was, by almost three decades, the younger one.

"You have to think of Connor. It's the only way." Raffo made to get up.

"Yeah." Dylan pressed her thumbs against her eyes and then pushed herself up. "It would be a whole lot easier if I wasn't so damned in love with you."

Raffo did a double take. "What?"

"Oh, come on, Raffo. Isn't it obvious? I'm in love with you. I think you are so fucking amazing. I wish I could watch you paint again. I wish I could make you a meal. I wish I could take you out. I wish I could just sit with you and chat. I wish I could—"

"Not much painting to watch," Raffo said stupidly, because all the things Dylan had just said, Raffo wanted as well.

"I so want for you to get your mojo back. I really do." Dylan stepped closer and Raffo could smell herself on her skin. Dylan stroked Raffo's cheek.

"I think for that to happen you're going to have to show me your breasts again," Raffo said, even more stupidly.

Dylan smiled and her smile soon turned into a giggle and it removed a whole lot of tension from the heavy air between them.

"I'd love to come by your studio and make that happen,

but..." Dylan grabbed Raffo's hand and squeezed it. "For my own sanity, I need to stay far away from you."

Raffo wrapped her arms around Dylan and prepared for another last goodbye. Then they both froze as a key turned in the front door lock.

"Oh, fuck." Raffo pulled her robe tightly around her. "Connor isn't supposed to be home for hours."

"Hello?" A familiar male voice came from the hallway. "Anyone home?"

"Oh, thank fuck." Raffo exhaled sharply. "It's Murray." She moved toward the lounge door.

Dylan put a hand on Raffo's forearm. "He shouldn't see us together." Dylan frantically rubbed her fingers along her chin.

"It's okay. I'll talk to him." Raffo opened the door.

"I wanted to surprise my boo," Murray said. "Con has no idea I'm coming." His eyes widened. "Oh, hello, Dylan."

"Hi, Murray. How lovely to see you." As though a massive stick had lodged itself up her backside, Dylan strutted toward Murray and stiffly kissed him on the cheek. "I was just dropping something off for Connor."

Murray tilted his head, and his gaze skittered from Dylan to Raffo and back.

"Sure," he said, because he wasn't stupid, but he was kind.

"How long are you in town for?" Dylan asked. "You and Con should come to dinner."

"I'd love to." Murray painted on an innocent smile. "I'm here until Sunday night, if his Connor-ship will have me."

"He'll be delighted." Dylan turned around and looked at Raffo. "I have to go. Have fun." She suddenly looked as though she couldn't be out the door fast enough.

Murray put his hands on his hips and stared straight into Raffo's eyes, clearly conveying that he most certainly wasn't born yesterday. Raffo only wearing a robe probably wasn't helping.

"It's not what you think," Raffo said, although it was. "I mean, not really."

"Would you like to tell me what it is?" Murray opened his arms to Raffo and she rushed into them. Then she cried on his shoulder until she could find the words to tell him the reason for her tears.

CHAPTER 32

"Are you in love with her too?" Murray asked once Raffo finished explaining the afternoon's events.

"I don't know. I haven't let myself explore those feelings— and what's the point? We can't date. We can't... We can't do anything." Raffo was still in that damned robe and she felt a lot more naked than earlier when Dylan had pushed it off her shoulders. "I will tell Connor about this. I promise you, no more lies. I can't deal with any more lies."

"Listen," Murray said. "Connor's your chosen family—I get that. But he has me, he's in a great relationship, even if I do say so myself. You deserve that too. You deserve to be happy."

"Sure, but not with his mom."

"But what if she's the one who makes you happy? And vice versa? I saw the look on Dylan's face just now, Raff. I've never seen her like that."

"I can't. I won't come between them." Raffo shook her head. "They have such a warm, respectful relationship. I refuse to be the one who fucks that up."

"What if I tell you that Connor is a big boy who can step into his big-boy pants and accept that his mother is in love with his best friend?"

Raffo scoffed. "He shouldn't have to do that." Not that Raffo believed for one second that Connor ever would.

"Con's happiness doesn't outweigh yours or his mother's. That's my view. I've told him this, by the way." Murray's laid-back nature hadn't rubbed off on his partner, even after three years together.

"What did he say to that?" Raffo asked.

"You know Con—drama queen, highly strung, gay alpha. Perfect for running an art gallery, not so great at empathizing with loved ones."

"Next you'll tell me he's a top," Raffo joked.

"I won't go that far." Murray shot her a smile. "Once a power bottom, always a power bottom."

Raffo chuckled and oh did she need a laugh. "Now that I'm single, Connor is the most important person in my life. I've been living in his house for months. There's nothing he wouldn't do for me. The least I can do is not fall in love with his mother."

"Yes, Connor is a sweetheart, but your friendship is not a one-way street, Raff. You are also his most important client. By a very long stretch. He's so lucky to have you at his gallery and to represent you. Besides, I know you, and there isn't anything you wouldn't do for him either. Case in point, you are clearly smitten with Dylan, yet you tell me you hadn't seen her in five weeks until today. How's that for sacrifice for the sake of friendship?"

"You have a very different take on this, Murray. Although refreshing, it's not very realistic."

"Says who? Maybe I see it more clearly because I'm not tangled up in it. Yes, Connor's my boyfriend—I don't want him hurt. But this won't hurt him. Not the way you both think it will. You know what real pain is, Raff. I know it, too. And it's not having to accept that two people that you love also love each other. That's just an abundance of love, really. And sure, it's awkward and maybe not ideal or how Connor prefers it, but it's hardly the end of the world. Nobody's dying here. Nobody has a life-threatening illness. Nobody's going bankrupt. It's just family."

Raffo so yearned to believe Murray's utopian words. But she couldn't. It was simply impossible. "Let's see how he reacts when I tell him about this afternoon." Not a conversation Raffo was looking forward to.

"Would you like me to be there for that?" Murray sent her an encouraging smile.

"I would like that very much." Raffo would take all the moral support she could get. "He'll be home late, so it will have to wait until tomorrow."

"And he'll find me in his bed, so he will be otherwise engaged."

Raffo made a mental note to put in earplugs tonight. "At least he'll be ecstatic that you're here."

———

Even through her earplugs, Raffo had caught Connor's arrival well past midnight—his delighted shriek at finding Murray in his bed piercing the house's silence.

Too restless to stay beneath the covers, Raffo rose early. Connor and Murray, evidently free of this affliction, stayed in bed well past ten. She might as well be productive and move some more boxes to her new house.

Once there, she was instantly drawn to the canvas she'd set up by the living room window. She'd put it there in case inspiration struck. Her studio hadn't brought her much in the way of that lately—especially not since Mia's visit.

Raffo stood in front of the canvas, closed her eyes, and allowed herself to see the image she had forbidden herself to see. Just as she had allowed Dylan to kiss her—and to make her come—yesterday. It was infuriating that it was that simple and so excruciatingly difficult at the same time.

Raffo wanted to paint Dylan. Of course she did. What else was she going to paint? Her subconscious must be filled to the brim with all things Dylan—her easy kindness, that devastating beauty, those piercing blue eyes, the way she'd said she wanted to make Raffo come—but Raffo hadn't allowed them to rise to the surface. Because she didn't want to hurt Connor.

But yesterday had happened and she couldn't turn back the clock on that—nor did she want to. Connor was already going to be upset, so fuck it. Raffo just wanted to paint. And just like in Big Bear, she wanted to paint the one and only image in her head. She wanted to paint to her muse. She craved the process of going through those ecstatic motions and the pure satisfaction of creating something new.

She might never allow herself another moment like yesterday with Dylan, but she could allow herself this. When it came to painting, to what was her deepest artistic expression, she could take Murray's unrealistic words to heart.

So Raffo began and, just as in Big Bear, it was so easy, as though images of Dylan were all she was meant to paint from now on. It made Raffo replay what Dylan had said—that she was in love with her.

Raffo didn't know if she was capable of that herself so shortly after Mia, after all that dreadful heartache, but then again, she'd barely let herself think about all those insanely hot summer nights in Big Bear with Dylan. She'd pretended they hadn't really happened, that they were some foolish fever dream.

Her paintbrush told a different story. Because the image that slowly emerged was a full-body one of Dylan in all her gorgeous naked glory. No wonder Raffo had felt so blocked before. It no longer had anything to do with Mia ruining her mojo. Raffo had made the beginner's mistake of trying to paint something that wasn't in her heart. All she had to do was let herself.

When she stepped back and looked at her canvas, there was no denying what was in her heart.

―――――

Connor's eyes lit up at the sight of Raffo, his hands clasping together.

"You're all smudged up." Hope radiated from his face. "Is that good news?"

"Yes," Raffo said. "I've been painting and it was great, but…" She sought Murray's gaze for courage. He gave a slight nod. "It's not as straightforward as I would like it to be or, um, you would like it be." Raffo pulled back a chair from the table where Connor and Murray were sitting. "Can we talk?"

"Of course. What's up?" Connor rested his gaze on her.

"Something happened yesterday that allowed my painting juices to flow today." Raffo thought it wise to start with that.

"That's great, Raff. What happened?" Connor wasn't one for strategic silences that let his conversation partners find their words.

"I was here when your mom came by to pick up your suit."

"Oh. Okay. So?" He shuffled in his seat. Despite trying to sound casual, Connor was getting antsy already. Raffo knew him so well.

"I'm only telling you because I don't want any more lies between us, okay?" Raffo hated going on the defensive like this. "Not because it will happen again or anything like that." This was never going to be an eloquent monologue.

"What won't happen again?" Connor drummed his fingers on the tabletop, indicating his rising annoyance.

"We kissed and…" Raffo stopped—details would only hurt him more. "We talked and, well—"

"Wait!" Connor held up his hand. "You kissed my mom in my house?"

"Babe." Murray put a hand on Connor's shoulder but he shrugged it off. "Let Raffo finish, please."

"Finish what? Telling me that she and my mom had sex in my couch? No fucking thank you."

Murray, steady as always, returned his hand to Connor's shoulder. "Don't be a baby about this. It's not helpful."

"A baby?" Connor scoffed. "I'd like to see your reaction if your best friend told you she'd been sleeping with your mom."

"Sandy's straight," Murray said matter-of-factly.

"Okay. Fine." Connor took a breath. "What are you trying to say?" He glared at Raffo, his face stripped of its usual kindness —that gentle warmth he'd inherited from Dylan.

"At my house earlier, I felt it again—that deep joy of painting. For the first time since Big Bear. Because I was painting Dylan."

"You can paint as many pictures of my mom as you like. As long as that's all you do with her."

"That's not the point, Con," Murray said. He looked at Raffo. "I'm so happy you've got your mojo back, Raff."

"What do you want from me?" Connor's voice rose. "My blessing to date my mom because she's your muse now?" He huffed some air through his pursed lips. "I know you've been through a lot, Raff. And I'm super sympathetic. I'll do anything to help, you know that. But you were a fantastic painter before your break-up, and you will be again. You don't need my mom for that. You just need a little bit more time."

"You're right," Raffo said, because it was true. Nevertheless, her stomach tightened.

"No he's not," Murray interjected. "For crying out loud, babe. They're in love. That's what Raffo's trying to say."

"They're not in love." Connor made a face as though someone had just told him his gallery had burned down. "I'm thirty-three years old and you know how many times I've known my mother to be in love with another woman in all that time?" He made a 0 with this thumb and index finger. "Zero times. And now, all of a sudden, she's in love with my best friend?" He took a breath and rubbed his fingertips against his forehead. "I'm actually really worried about my mom. She's not herself. First, she loses all that money, which is so unlike her and now…" He waved his hands about. "This."

"I don't think you have to worry about your mom," Murray said.

"There could be something wrong with her. Something serious." Connor sounded genuinely concerned.

"Whether you like it or not," Raffo said. "I spent a lot of time with your mom and I second Murray. There's nothing medically wrong with her. She made a mistake with the money and, in my opinion, she also made a mistake when she decided not to tell you and hide out in Big Bear. People make mistakes, but that doesn't mean there's something wrong with them."

"But, Raff… what about you? I mean, come on. I'm no shrink, but you were so heartbroken when you left for Big Bear. That's why I sent you. And my mom, she's my mom. I know what she's like. She's all like, sit down, darling, I'll make you some dinner, talk to me, here's some wine, we can fix this together. I get it, okay? You're right, I don't like it, but what happened in Big Bear, from your perspective, I get it. You were hurt and my mom was there, even though she was supposed to be in fucking Europe. But has it not been enough, now? Seriously?"

"Con," Murray said softly. "It's just love. Think about it. Do you really want to be the one standing in the way of that?"

"Fuck, yeah. When it's my mom and my best friend, I will damn well stand in the way of it."

Raffo didn't know how to fight for this—she didn't even know if she wanted to. She was being torn right in half.

Raffo cleared her throat. "As I said earlier—" She sought Connor's eyes, but he looked away. "It won't happen again. I just wanted you to know." She pushed back from the table and stood. Walking back to her house, she knew it was time to move out of Connor's place for good.

CHAPTER 33

Dylan was researching the company where she had an upcoming job interview when the doorbell rang. With all her heart, she hoped it would be Raffo. She practically sprinted to the door.

"Hey Mama." Murray stood in the doorway, holding a bunch of flowers.

"What's that for?" Dylan asked, kissing his cheek as she ushered him inside.

"The other day was a little awkward, so I figured I'd break the ice with some fresh daisies and lilies."

They settled at the backyard table with fresh coffee, the LA sun warming their shoulders.

"I haven't heard from him, but Connor must be thrilled about your surprise visit." Dylan forced warmth into her smile. When she'd tried to call her son yesterday as well as this morning, he hadn't picked up, nor replied to the messages she'd sent inviting him and Murray to dinner.

"Raffo told him what happened and he's not being a good sport about it," Murray said.

"Understandably so." Dylan sipped from her coffee. "How's Raffo?"

"She's been staying at her new place—camping out there until she gets furniture or reclaims her stuff from Mia's. But she's painting again, so that's good."

Dylan stopped herself from asking for Raffo's new address. The last thing she should do is show up there.

"How are *you*?" Murray put a hand on Dylan's arm and the gesture was so kind and warm, it nearly moved Dylan to tears.

"I hate all of this," Dylan said. "Connor's coldness. These feelings for Raffo I can't control. My weakness in going back to her, undoing weeks of trying to get over her. And now this job interview next week for a position I don't even want."

"I'm sorry." Murray gave her arm a gentle squeeze. "I'm working on Connor and I'll make sure he comes to see you before I leave. I promise you that." He followed up with a sweet smile. "That's the only promise I can make, however."

"I don't want to be estranged from my son," Dylan said. "But, damn it, I'm so crazy about Raffo." She shrugged. "In the end, the choice is easy. I will always choose my relationship with Connor over everything else. I'm just not really there yet, you know? It still hurts so damn much that I can't be with Raffo. I keep thinking that Raffo and I aren't even really a thing. We just had a summer fling in the sort of idyllic location that lends itself to that perfectly. It might very well be the sort of thing that doesn't work in real life. We might be completely incompatible. I'm way too old for her. And she might not feel the same way about me. But the fact I'll never know is just killing me because…" Dylan shook her head. "I'm crazy about her. When I saw her at Con's house yesterday it was so crystal clear. Of course I went back. It's like my car drove itself back there. I haven't felt this way about anyone in such a long time, but Connor will always be my priority." *Yeah right.* Some useless mantra that had been. She'd repeated it the whole drive yesterday, then turned right back around to kiss Raffo anyway.

She found Murray's gaze. His face was all understanding and empathy. At least, Dylan could be happy for her son that he was with such a wonderful guy. "What do you think about this mess?" she asked.

"I think that when two people fall in love like that, nothing should stand in their way, because life is too damn short. But you're not my mom, so."

"I don't blame Connor," Dylan said. "I understand completely. No child should have to accept this from their parent. It's right there in the parenting manual: don't fall in love with your kid's friends. Easy-peasy."

"And yet," Murray said.

"I'll get over her eventually. There's no choice."

"I wish you didn't have to. Love is too precious to turn away from like that. I wish I could make Connor see that, but you know what he's like."

"He's just being a normal son with completely ordinary feelings about this."

"But that's the thing. Connor is not ordinary and he doesn't give a damn about being normal. There's a reason why he and Raffo found each other, that they make each other better and are having so much success. They're special. I know that I would say that because I'm his boyfriend, but I'm a little disappointed in his norm-core reaction to this."

"Really?"

"Fuck yeah. You know my story. And you know my dad's story. If my mom fell in love with my best friend, I'd be the first to congratulate them. I'd get ordained just so I could officiate their wedding."

Murray's dad had died of a heart attack last year. One moment he was there, the next he was gone, leaving his family completely shattered.

And before meeting Connor, Murray had nearly died of Covid. Despite being young and healthy, he'd spent a week on a ventilator, his life hanging by a thread. So of course Murray had a different view on something as beautifully gorgeous and heartbreaking as love. Still, Dylan would never wish hardship on her son, even if pain might grant him Murray's perspective on love. If anything, Dylan was glad that Connor had lived such a charmed life.

"Your mom's wedding?" Dylan joked, because she could do with a chuckle. "Things are moving quickly."

"Hypothetical wedding." A shadow crossed Murray's face.

"How's your mom doing?" Dylan asked.

"Okay under the circumstances. She'll be all right. But it takes time to get over a sudden loss like that. To pick up your life again."

"Give her my love, please."

"I will." His features softened. "She's so fond of Con." His eyes lit up as though he suddenly remembered something. "He gave her a Raffo Shah painting not long after my dad died, because Raffo's work has such a joyful, cheerful quality to it, you know? She has put it front and center in the living room. My mom was really touched by that."

"Yeah." Despite what she couldn't have, Dylan experienced joy and cheer—and many other emotions—every time she looked at the artwork Raffo had painted of her.

"Hey," Murray said. "You're not just Connor's mom. He's also your son. He can go out of his way for your happiness as well. It doesn't have to be a one-way street."

"Connor makes me very happy. He's the best son a mother could wish for." Dylan meant it from the bottom of her heart. "This is not something a parent should ask of their child."

"I couldn't disagree more." Murray pursed his lips.

Dylan appreciated the sentiment behind Murray's words, but it didn't change anything about the situation.

CHAPTER 34

Because Raffo didn't want Mia to know her new address—lest she turn up out of the blue again—she had only shared it with a few close friends. The afternoon light slanted through bare windows, casting long shadows across drop cloths and the few cardboard boxes she'd bothered to unpack. She was putting the final touches on Dylan's portrait, savoring that rare satisfaction of perfect execution, when the bell rang.

"Hey stranger." Connor stood in the doorway.

"Oh, Con." Even now, Raffo was happy to see Con. Things weren't quite right between them, but they weren't exactly fighting either. She'd been avoiding him lately, telling herself it was to give him time with Murray while his boyfriend was in town. "Come in."

"Love what you've done with the place." Connor's voice was full of irony because Raffo hadn't bothered yet with procuring much furniture. "Looks like you may need Connor Hart's magic touch with your interior design."

"Maybe, yeah." The words came out softer than she intended, weighted with everything she wasn't saying. Raffo had plenty of flair for decorating a home, but she simply didn't have the energy to decide which couch she wanted and what color her bedroom should be. It reminded her of the confrontation she needed to have with Mia, the gorgeously decorated house they needed to sell, and the furniture they would have to divide—all the things she was afraid of.

Connor paced through the sparsely furnished house. His eye must have been drawn by the colors of Raffo's just-finished painting, because he walked straight toward it.

"Fuck me." The words punched through the careful distance they'd been maintaining. "That's my mom?" He leaned in to examine the canvas up close, then took a step back.

Raffo could hardly deny it, but it felt weird to confirm the subject of her painting to Connor.

"It's a little different than what I'm used to from you. Not as whimsical. More… I don't want to say serious, but there is a certain gravitas to it that is incredibly compelling."

Raffo couldn't help but chuckle at Connor's pretentious art critic voice.

Connor turned to her. "I'm not even kidding, Raff. Fuck. It's astounding." He gave her the same once-over he'd just given the painting. "It's like you've taken things up another notch after your… hiatus."

"I'm quite pleased with it," Raffo said.

Connor grinned. "Being an expert at Raffo-speak, I know what that really means and I'm thrilled." The familiar teasing felt like a lifeline thrown across the divide between them.

Connor was right. Raffo was more than just pleased with that painting of Dylan. The process of painting it had offered her a much-needed escape from the reality of her messy life while also giving her immense creative fulfillment. The canvas held everything she couldn't say aloud: desire, fear, the strange peace she'd found in Dylan's arms.

She didn't know how many more portraits of Dylan she'd have to make to get over her, but Raffo did know that, for her, it would probably be the only way to get Dylan out of her system. She was lucky that art was her job as well as the therapy that had always worked best for her—except after Mia. Maybe finally giving in to the urge to paint Dylan—to paint what she really wanted—was exactly what she needed to put her desire as well as her botched relationship behind her.

"I can totally see this as the center piece at your Chicago show," Connor said.

"Are you serious?"

"Yes." Connor drew in a sharp breath. "Intellectually, I know that's my mom. Naked. But I'm choosing to see past that. What matters is its impact—the obvious beauty and this new... quality it has. I'm really floored by it, to be honest. As long as we don't mention the M-word."

Denial was one way to go about it, Raffo guessed, even though it caused quite the conflict inside her. She had needed to paint Dylan like this. It had poured from her heart and soul out of pure necessity. That's probably why Connor noticed a different, perhaps more profound layer to it. But that she was now unable to discuss this with him, her best friend and gallerist— the most loyal admirer of her work—was complicated to say the least. Connor could pretend that wasn't Dylan in that painting all he wanted, but the fact that it was Dylan was the whole point for Raffo. And then there was another matter.

"I'm not sure this should be a commercial work," Raffo said.

"Oh." The single syllable carried volumes of unspoken tension.

"We have to ask *her* permission." Christ. Raffo couldn't bring herself to say 'your mom'—how ridiculous was that?

"That won't be a problem." His voice had taken on that brittle quality it got when he was trying to maintain control.

"How do you know? She hasn't even seen the painting. She doesn't know it exists." This was still Raffo's work, an intimate portrait of what burned inside her heart, and Connor couldn't just come in and take over.

"Out of guilt. She owes me," Connor had the audacity to say.

"She's your mom, Con. Have a little respect."

"Respect? Like she respected me when she kissed you in my living room?"

Raffo shook her head. "It's my decision, and that painting's not going anywhere until I've shown it to Dylan."

Connor was visibly taken aback by the sharpness in Raffo's tone.

"Of course," Connor said, his tone equally biting. "As long as I don't have to be there for that *special* moment."

"We are trying, Con. We are only doing our best, for you, even though, frankly, what happened between me and Dylan had fuck all to do with you." Raffo surprised herself. She hadn't been herself since Dylan had come back to kiss her—to make her climax against Connor's wall like that. Then again, she hadn't been herself for months. Not since Mia had dumped her. Not in Big Bear—not for the most part, anyway. And certainly not since she'd returned to Los Angeles. Even when she was painting—really painting and not fruitlessly noodling around with a work she couldn't put her heart into—something was different with her, hence the finished work on that easel over there. Being with Dylan had changed her.

"What do you want me to say?" Connor exploded. "I'm sorry for being my mother's son? I'm sorry for standing in the way of whatever it is you want to do with each other?"

"I have feelings for her." Raffo glanced at the painting—it couldn't be more obvious to her now. "Genuine feelings. And I don't know how to deal with them. I have no clue."

"For crying out loud." Connor was obviously not ready to be understanding about this. "We've all been there. We've all had feelings for someone we shouldn't have feelings for. It's not as uncommon or special as you'd like to believe. We've all had to make an effort to get over things like that. If you can't do that for me, your best friend, I'm not sure this is even still a friendship."

"Oh, please." Raffo rolled her eyes. What was Connor even

talking about? Who was he referring to that he'd had to get over in his own life? "Don't be so dramatic. It drives me up the wall."

"And I can't stomach the idea of you in bed with my mom, so there you go."

When he reduced it to two selfish people consumed by desire, blind to everyone else, it sounded indefensible. But what she and Dylan shared had evolved far beyond that after their first night together.

It's not just sex, Raffo wanted to scream. If it was, she wouldn't still be pining for Dylan so many weeks later. She wouldn't have painted that image of Dylan. But she didn't want to incense Connor further by using the word sex in relation to his mother. Clearly—and she completely understood this—he couldn't see past that.

"Maybe we should press pause," she said instead. "Take a little breather from each other."

"A breather? What does that even mean?" He huffed out some air. "We work together, Raffo. Your show in Chicago isn't that far away. We have to select works. We have that thing with—"

"Con," Raffo said. "Look at that painting you were just admiring. That's what I want. It's all I want. If I can't paint like that, I'd rather not paint at all."

"What are you talking about? You can paint whatever you want. I just literally told you so."

"I can't be judged for it. Not by you."

"I'm not judging you. I'm separating the two for the sake of our friendship." At least he still considered them friends—for now.

"The fuck you are, Con."

"But she's my mom." He shook his head. "I just… can't."

"I know." Raffo was so done with this conversation. She walked into the hallway, hoping Connor would follow so she could show him out.

"I'm calling you tomorrow." Connor stood very close to her. "Please don't make me the bad guy in this. I love you both." He planted a quick kiss on her cheek and walked out the door.

Connor was right. Of course he wasn't the bad guy and none of this was even remotely his fault. If only that could be the end of it, but the problem was that it couldn't.

Raffo shuffled back to her painting. She took a picture of it and sent it to Dylan, who had the right to see it, no matter the circumstances. Raffo just typed 'You' in the message. After she'd sent it, and the message showed as 'Read' on her screen, she couldn't tear her gaze away from her phone. At first, for a few agonizing moments, there were the three dreaded dots as Dylan typed a message back. Then, for the rest of the night, until Raffo could no longer keep her eyes open, there was nothing.

CHAPTER 35

Dylan stared blankly at Raffo's message, at a loss for an appropriate response. She typed and deleted, typed and deleted, until she drove herself crazy, and put her phone away.

She couldn't look at that painting of herself any longer, either. It was much more explicit and much more recognizably her than the one Raffo had made in Big Bear. She could only hope Connor hadn't seen it. He and Murray were finally coming to dinner, so she would soon find out.

When they arrived, Murray's hug was noticeably warmer than Connor's. Dylan could immediately tell Connor was in a mood. She felt sorry for him, because she was probably responsible for it.

"He and Raffo had a fight," Murray said, not wasting any time. Maybe because he had a plane to catch later tonight and he didn't want to leave Connor in this state.

"For the millionth time, it was not a fight," Connor said.

"I'm sorry, darling." Dylan couldn't help herself. She put an arm around her son.

"In case you're wondering, it was about you," Connor said, contradicting himself.

Dylan didn't know how many more times she could apologize. She had just about run out of I'm-sorries when it came to this—also because it was very difficult to actually regret her time with Raffo. If only she regretted it more, that would make everything so much easier.

"She painted you and…" Connor didn't sound very angry, more despondent and a little sad. "Ugh, the work was so good. So exceptional. So Raffo on absolute steroids but it was you, Mom." He scoffed. "All of you. Naked."

"It's art," Murray said. "I went to see Raffo earlier to say goodbye and she showed me. It's beautiful, Dylan. You need to see it." Murray sounded so casual about all this.

"I have seen it. Raffo texted me a picture."

Connor's eyes went wide. "You've seen it?"

Dylan nodded.

Connor bit his lip, as though trying to stop himself from saying something vile.

"My flight's in three hours and I would like to say something before my taxi gets here." Murray had that air about him that made you want to listen when he spoke—or maybe Dylan was just really curious about what he wanted to share. "Con, babe, I love you and I understand why you feel the way you feel about this."

"But?" Connor's voice couldn't sound more sarcastic.

Murray pinned his gaze on Dylan. "You don't give up on something potentially great just because it's difficult," he said.

Both Connor and Dylan protested at the same time.

"Stop." Murray held up his hands. "Please, let me finish." He looked at them as though he was the principal who'd called two wayward teens into his office for one last chance before expulsion. "You can't see any of this clearly because you're in it. You're too involved. Dylan, you're smitten with Raffo and that, too, I totally get. And Con, Dylan's your mom so of course you're freaking out about it. It's normal. But—"

Connor started to say something, and Dylan was infinitely

impressed with Murray's power to stop her son from talking simply by holding up a finger.

"The fact that I don't live here gives me more of a bird's eye view on all this than either of you. From this vantage point I'm telling you that love, just as life, is precious. Just like that." He snapped his fingers. "Someone you love can die. I don't mean to be grim, but it's true." He paused. "Ask Raffo."

"That's a little unfair," Connor said. "And quite emotionally manipulative."

"It's not," Murray said. "If only you could see that."

Dylan stood there, witnessing this bizarrely intense conversation between her son and his boyfriend, of which she was the subject. She and Raffo. Raffo would be mortified by all of this—or would she? The truth was that Dylan didn't know. She hadn't even replied to her text. She hadn't even complimented her on that magnificent painting she'd made. This work of art that conveyed, without words, exactly how Raffo felt about Dylan. And wasn't that what art was for? To say the things that couldn't be put into words?

"Mom gets why I can't accept her having an affair with my best friend," Connor said. "Don't you, Mom?"

"I do," Dylan confirmed. It was hardly a matter of not getting it.

"That's not the point." Murray put his hand over Connor's. "You know that rainbow heart that Raffo's being paid a massive amount of money for," he said. "I think you have forgotten what that stands for, babe."

"No, I haven't. It's not because they're two women—"

Murray cut Connor off. "It stands for *all* the love, Con. That includes the love between your mom and Raffo."

"*Love?* They slept together a couple of times in Big Bear." Connor spat out the words. He pointed a finger at Dylan. "Where you weren't even supposed to be, by the way. In case we all forgot that my dear mother, aside from sleeping with my best friend, also lied to me about a bad investment and where she was spending her summer. And what? Now it's all on me? Now I'm the one standing in the way of their 'love'?" He curled his fingers into air quotes. "Give me a fucking break."

"Okay," Dylan said. "That's enough." She started to walk out of the kitchen, but turned around. "You two, make nice before Murray leaves. Make sure there are no hard feelings before saying goodbye. I'm done with this conversation." Contrary to what she'd just said, Dylan walked back into the kitchen and planted a quick kiss on the side of Murray's head. "Thank you for what you said. I really appreciate it. Have a good trip back to New York." She headed over to her son and mussed his hair about, knowing full well how much he hated that. Still, Dylan couldn't help herself—it was the story of her life lately. "I love you, Con," she said, before going up to her bedroom, where she stopped in front of Raffo's first painting of her.

You don't give up on something potentially great just because it's difficult.

Murray's words swirled in her head. There might be some truth to what he said, but Dylan not giving up on Raffo could equal losing her son, so that battle was already over before it had even begun. There were some risks Dylan would never take.

Still, Dylan fished her phone out of her pocket and—finally —texted Raffo back.

> It's insanely beautiful, and I'm not just saying that because it's a picture of me.

CHAPTER 36

Raffo's palms sweated. She couldn't bring herself to use the key to her own house, which was ridiculous, but what hadn't been utterly ludicrous about her life the past couple of months? Since it had all started falling apart? She rang the bell and, as though she'd been waiting on the other side, Mia opened the door instantly.

She had the courtesy to not try to hug, or worse, kiss her. Mia kept a respectable distance as she led the way into their house. Raffo's knees went a little soft as her gaze drifted along the quirky wallpaper in the hallway and the second-hand table she'd painted in two complementary colors, the dividing line just off-center so it made everyone wonder if there was something wrong with their eyesight. As much as she loved that table, she didn't know if she could just transport it to her new home. It had too many memories of good times in this house— and with Mia—attached to it.

"Congrats on the new house," Mia said, her collarbones sharp beneath her shirt. She'd always been slim, but now her face held shadows Raffo had never seen before.

"Thanks, um, are you okay? Physically? You don't look so hot."

"I'm fine." Mia poured them each a glass of water and just pushed Raffo's toward her across the kitchen island. "My appetite has plummeted since…" She didn't finish her sentence, as though it should be obvious to Raffo.

"Is this a good time to talk about all this?" Raffo asked.

"Is this a good time to ask if you will ever forgive me?" Mia countered with a swiftness her fragile looks didn't suggest she had in her.

"No." Raffo said. "That's not why I'm here. We need to deal with this house. With our stuff." What was Mia playing at now?

"I'd love to buy you out," Mia said with a weary sigh, "but I don't think I can afford it."

"For real? You'd want to stay here?" They'd decorated the house together, but Raffo's style dominated every room. "Does it not remind you too much of, um, us?"

"Maybe that's exactly why I want to stay."

"Mia, come on. Don't be like that. It's not fair."

"It is unfair, Raff. I know that. And I apologize, but I can't help how I feel."

"You caused how you feel. You are the reason I don't live here anymore." Raffo shook her head. "I don't understand why you're suddenly so convinced that you didn't stop loving me and destroyed our relationship because of it."

"I did not stop loving you." Mia sounded as though she genuinely believed what she was saying.

Raffo could only scoff. "I'm not having this conversation. I'm serious. That's not why I'm here." Raffo needed some chairs to sit on in her new house and some clothes from her closet, but most of all, already, she felt as though she needed to get out of there. She'd buy new chairs. She didn't know why she'd been postponing the simple purchase of a couple of chairs. Was it because she'd been subconsciously waiting for this moment? For some sort of cathartic event between her and her ex? If this was it, it was highly inefficient and anti-climactic.

"I do still love you," Mia said. "I made a lot of mistakes and

I didn't treat you right and I'm so sorry, Raff. You have no idea." Tears dripped onto the marble of the kitchen island.

Raffo's heart shrank. She wished she didn't care. She wished she could face Mia's tears with nothing but indifference. Raffo took a breath and closed her eyes. What she saw on the back of her eyelids was her latest painting of Dylan. Dylan who had given her so much comfort in Big Bear, who had listened to Raffo's sad tales of Mia and how much she'd hurt her, who'd let her cry on her shoulder—and so much more.

"I hope you understand where I'm coming from when I say that I can never trust anything you say or do again," Raffo said, her voice barely a whisper—because this was a hard thing to say to a crying woman she'd once loved with all her heart. *Once.* Not anymore. Because there was no room for two people in Raffo's heart to love, to be involved with *amorously*. And Raffo was in love with Dylan.

Unlike Mia, Raffo had the decency to not tell her that she'd fallen head over heels for someone else. She didn't want to rip Mia's heart to shreds like that. But she did do the only other possible thing she could.

"I can't do this with you right now," Raffo said. "Call me when you're ready to discuss a solution for the house."

Raffo left and instead of driving to her new house, she drove past her street, took a left, and headed to her best friend's place.

———

"I'd like to press play." Raffo tried her best grin when Connor opened the door to her. "I'm done with pausing."

Connor matched her grin. "Thank fuck." He all but yanked her inside. "I've missed my cash cow like crazy."

Raffo brushed off Connor's comment, knowing how much he genuinely loved her art.

"I went to see Mia," Raffo said, describing the brief ten

minutes she'd endured before fleeing what used to be their home.

"If you need anything from the house," Connor said, "I'll get it for you. No problem. I've got you covered." It wasn't the first time Connor had offered, but it had always felt like something Raffo should do herself.

"Thanks," she said, finally ready to take him up on his very kind offer. She looked at the glass of water he'd poured her after they'd sat. "We might need something stronger for what I want to tell you next," she said.

"Oh, boy." Connor strode to the bar cart and grabbed a bottle of tequila. "Will this do?"

"Perfectly."

Connor brought over the bottle and two shot glasses, not bothering with any accoutrements. He filled the glasses to the brim so they inevitably spilled some liquor as they brought the drinks to their lips.

"Hit me," Connor said. He locked his gaze on Raffo. "For the record, I know what you're going to say."

"No you don't." The shot of tequila made Raffo a little bolder already.

"Oh yes, I do. Hold on." He reached for his phone. "I'm going to make a note predicting what you're going to say and then I'm going to give you my phone so you can check after you've said it."

By the fuss he was making, Raffo was pretty sure Connor did know. He wasn't born yesterday. She didn't have a fool for a best friend. Connor was clever, kind, and just as strong-willed as Raffo at times. He quickly typed something into his phone— it seemed very short—then gave it to Raffo.

Connor refilled their glasses, knocked another shot back and gazed into Raffo's eyes. "I'm listening," he said.

"You know that when I'm painting, I have to feel it. If I don't feel it, I might as well forget it." Raffo thought of that cat-shaped cloud she'd tried to paint for days on end while stubbornly refusing to paint the only subject she'd really wanted to devote her time to. "If I don't feel it, I might as well not paint at all."

Connor nodded. He wasn't an artist, but Raffo knew that he understood completely. Connor had got it—and her—from the first time they'd met.

"Okay." Raffo gulped down another shot of tequila as she worked up to her conclusion. "Earlier, at Mia's, it hit me so clearly, Con. The reason why I didn't relent when she told me she still loved me, and that I'm well on my way to being over her, that I no longer want to be with her and no longer consider her the greatest woman I've ever met. It's all because… it's because of your mom." Raffo swallowed slowly. "Dylan helped me in ways I can't put into words. She was there for me so unexpectedly but so completely. She took care of me, Con. She really did. She gave me something that I didn't know I needed, and it moved me deeply. For the sake of our friendship, I was desperate to believe it was just a fleeting rebound thing, but I now know it was so much more than that. It *is* so much more than that. She made me feel like myself again. She gave me back my mojo. She's all I want to paint and that tells me all I need to know." Raffo's throat went dry. She glanced at her empty glass.

Connor took the hint and refilled it.

"Check my phone," he said.

The notes app was still open on Connor's phone.

Raffo <3 my mom, it read.

Raffo swiftly knocked back her third shot. Of course he knew. What else would she need tequila for to tell him?

Connor let his forehead fall against his spread out fingertips. "You're miserable. Mom's not herself. Murray's on my case all the time about love being love. It's hardly been an enjoyable situation for anyone, but what do you want me to do? Give you my blessing to date my mom? Do you know how profoundly weird that is?" He found her gaze. His eyes were a little watery, which could be due to the tequila. "There are things I simply can't think about, okay? I just can't. And you and me, we talk about everything. We're so open with each other and I'm so scared that this will change us forever. And the timing, Raff. It's all happening for you right now. You're going places. *We* are going places because I'm going with you on this journey." He interjected with a sigh. "But what I'm most afraid of is that two people I love so fucking much will end up hurting each other because I can't just believe this will magically work out, Raff. That you and my mom will be happy forever and everything will be hunky-dory. I'm terrified that things will never be the same between us."

"Things have already changed between us," Raffo said.

"That's true enough." Connor filled their glasses again.

Raffo happily drank. She didn't know how else to deal with asking her best friend if she could date his mother.

"This shouldn't be up to me," Connor said. "I want nothing more than for you and my mom to find love again, to have a Murray in your life, but fuck, why does it have to be with each other?"

"Look at it this way, Con. You're a great guy. There are so many reasons why you are my best friend. We have this chemistry, this undefinable thing between us. Maybe it's only logical that I would also have something like that with your mom. She made you." Raffo was beginning to slur her words—and talk nonsense. "She's just as wonderful as you, that's why I like her so much."

"What about my dad?" Connor was hardly still sober either. "He made me too."

"I'm not that into dads," Raffo said. "If I'd met your mother, you know, like properly met her and spent time with her, at any other time in my life, meaning before Mia dumped me, this would never have happened. It was something that only happened because of the headspace I was in, but also the physical place I was in, at your mom's house in Big Bear. It was all of those things but most of all it's because she's such an incredible woman."

"I know my mom is great, but—" He didn't continue, because all that needed to be said was in that 'but'. The 'but' that would always be there.

Raffo gathered all her courage. "I know it's too much to ask, but I'm asking you, anyway."

"Oh, god." Connor groaned. "Don't. You don't need my permission, Raff. That's just so wrong."

"Permission is the wrong word for it, but I do need something from you."

"How about another shot?" Connor asked. "Will that do?"

Raffo understood that Connor couldn't say it. He couldn't spell it out for her. It was unrealistic to expect him to.

"Yes," she said, because she had to take what she could get.

CHAPTER 37

Connor had made a reservation at their favorite Korean restaurant. Dylan was running late because her job interview had lasted much longer than expected. The three people who had interviewed her had all been at least ten years younger than her, one of them probably closer to twenty. She felt old and insecure, but also grateful that Connor had invited her to dinner. It was his way of supporting her after a stressful day.

Dylan rushed into the restaurant, gave Connor's name to the maître d', and followed her inside.

Dylan froze. Connor wasn't there—instead, Raffo sat at a table for two by the wall, and Dylan's heart couldn't decide between soaring or sinking. Min-ji, the restaurant's owner, was Raffo's friend, so of course Raffo might be here. But tonight? When Dylan was supposed to meet her son, with whom things hadn't completely returned to normal? She hadn't seen Connor since the night Murray had left. The only communication they'd had was this dinner invitation he'd extended this morning, when he'd called to wish her luck with her interview—he'd always been a wonderfully attentive son in that regard, no matter what was going on.

Dylan's head spun. Raffo looked gorgeous, and the thought

that she might be here on a date with someone else made Dylan's stomach clench.

The maître d' stopped at the table Raffo was sitting at.

"There you go, Mrs. French," she said. "Min-ji will take care of you personally, but we've been asked to give you ten minutes alone first."

"Wait a second." Dylan held up her hand. "I think there's been a mix-up. I'm meeting my son. The reservation is for Connor Hart."

"Connor made the reservation," the maître d' said. "But you're having dinner with Raffo, not Connor." She waggled her eyebrows and walked away.

Dylan stared at Raffo. "What's going on? Am I, or am I not, in an alternate universe? Do the doors to Min-ji's lead to a different dimension?"

Raffo rose from her chair. "I don't know. I was supposed to have dinner here with Connor tonight too." She scratched her cheek. Then a grin appeared on her lips. "When was the last time you spoke to Con?"

"He called me this morning to set up this dinner," Dylan said. They stood around awkwardly, towering over the tables around them. Dylan wanted to kiss Raffo—at least on the cheek —more than anything, but she had to figure out what was going on first.

Raffo chuckled. "I think this might be Connor's way of… saying we should date." Her face all lit up, she grinned at Dylan. "He set up this dinner—this date. For us."

"Are you sure?" Dylan found it hard to believe.

"Ninety-nine percent." Raffo did what Dylan didn't dare. She took a step closer. "Hi," she said, once she was firmly in Dylan's personal space. "It's fantastic to see you." She pressed her lips to Dylan's cheek.

Dylan pushed her cheek against Raffo's lips. Instantly, heat rushed from her neck to her face. It wasn't a hot flash—those were well and truly behind her. Dylan knew damn well what it was.

"Shall we sit?" Raffo gestured at the table.

Dylan was already feeling a bit wobbly in the knees and was glad for the support of a chair.

"What the actual fuck?" she said. "What happened?"

Min-ji approached their table. She and Raffo exchanged a long, close hug.

"Connor asked me to give you this. It will explain every-thing," Min-ji said. "I'll be right back with some drinks." She handed Raffo a white envelope.

Raffo tore the envelope open and pulled a card from it. On the back, there was a picture of Raffo's famous painted rainbow heart—Dylan would recognize it anywhere now.

"*Dear Mom, Dear Raff,*" Raffo read out loud. "*Dinner's on me. Have fun. Love you both, Con.*"

"Oh my god." Dylan didn't know what was going on, but tears pricked behind her eyes.

Raffo turned the card around in her hand and spotted her painting. "Fuck me."

"You didn't know about this?" Dylan dabbed at her eyes.

Raffo shook her head. "I talked to him a few days ago. I told him how I really felt about you."

"You did?" Butterflies danced in Dylan's belly. She extended a hand to Raffo.

Raffo nodded, then wrapped her hands around Dylan's. They felt warm and comforting, like the first sunlight after weeks of winter.

"There was this bullshit with Mia again and I so clearly real-ized that I wanted to be with you—well, that I wanted to try," Raffo said. "If you want to." Raffo fixed her dark gaze on Dylan.

"There's nothing I want more." They would need to get the food to go. Dylan was only hungry for one thing.

"It's still complicated but… Connor set this up so he must have found a way to be okay with it."

"I suspect that way goes by the name of Murray." Dylan picked up the card. "He referenced this painting while trying to get through to Connor about… us."

Min-ji arrived with two beers and a plate of food.

After she left, Dylan huddled over the table and whispered, "I so want to take you home."

"I get it, but we have to stay a while. For Min-ji." Raffo grinned as though this delighted her greatly.

"Because she's your friend and it would be rude?" Dylan asked.

"Yeah. Besides, we've waited this long." She slanted her head. "Granted, you've waited longer than I have, but that's your own fault."

Dylan couldn't get enough of this devilish side to Raffo.

"Let's talk then." She picked up the bottle of beer and held it up. "And toast. To my son."

Raffo clinked the neck of her beer bottle against it. "To Connor Hart."

"What did he say?" Dylan was dying to find out.

"Well…" Raffo held up her bottle. "We didn't so much talk about it as we… *drank* about it, if that makes sense." She put down her bottle, a grave expression crossing her face. "There are some things that best friends simply can't talk through and this is one of those things, but clearly Connor's willing to make an effort to live with it because he wants us to be happy, even if it costs him something—well, more than something. It's awkward and weird and all of that, but he knows me through and through and that's why he knows that I wouldn't have asked him if I didn't feel like I had any other choice."

Dylan's heart was about to burst out of her chest. Not just because her son was becoming more amenable to the idea of *them*, but because Raffo had just claimed that she didn't have any other choice but to be with Dylan—and go through the ordeal of asking Connor if he could find it in himself to be okay with that.

"Maybe nothing is really impossible," Dylan said, even though it sounded a bit silly. But she was intoxicated by the situation and, in that moment, it truly felt like everything was possible. The relief coursing through her was overwhelming because everything that had seemed so thoroughly impossible was suddenly within reach.

Raffo shook her head, because that's the kind of person she was—and that's the kind of life she'd lived. "I don't believe that, but I do believe in this, in… us. The potential of us."

A grin spread across Dylan's lips. "I guess this is our first official date."

"Maybe, even though we've done plenty of things that don't necessarily belong on first dates."

Dylan's mind flashed back to their last night together in Big Bear. Min-ji set down more food and left them alone.

"You're looking very different than what I'm used to from you," Raffo said after swallowing a bite of bulgogi. "Very corporate compared to those barely-there jeans shorts and see-through tank tops that you seduced me in."

Dylan ignored the playful jibe. "I had a job interview before I came here."

Raffo's eyes lit up. "I bet you crushed it. Did they hire on you on the spot?"

"No," Dylan said with a glance at Raffo. "They didn't have an instant crush on me like some people at this table."

"Don't blame me. Blame your naked breasts," Raffo said matter-of-factly.

Dylan nearly spat out the piece of shrimp she'd just popped into her mouth.

"Are you still not over that?" she asked.

"Scarred for life, but in the best way possible." Raffo plastered on the most delicious grin. "Seriously, though, how did the interview go?"

"Good." Despite feeling ancient and insecure, the interview

had gone well, although Dylan didn't really feel the spark for the job. "We'll see."

"You don't want to talk about it?" Raffo read her so well.

"It's not what I want to do, but I also don't want to sell Big Bear, so it's my only choice right now."

"You're not selling?" Raffo smiled widely. "Meaning we can go back any time?"

Dylan nodded slowly as memories of their time at the lake house engulfed her brain. It was more than enough to perk her up. Maybe, if she could date Raffo in her spare time, taking a job she didn't really want would be a piece of cake.

CHAPTER 38

Despite having known Connor for years, Raffo had never been to his mother's house. She didn't have much time to study the decor—or take in family snaps—because Dylan all but dragged her inside with an urgency that revealed exactly what was on her mind.

Raffo gladly let herself be pulled in, not just inside Dylan's house, but by everything. By simply being with Dylan. The delicious dinner they'd had, although they'd been too absorbed in each other, and Connor's surprise move, to fully appreciate Min-ji's culinary talents. But now that they could date openly, they had all the time in the world to return.

This was a date. It was nothing like a first date, however, because Raffo already knew so much about Dylan. She knew what she liked—she knew how she reacted when Raffo grabbed her wrists and pinned them above Dylan's head. When Raffo did that, something came over her face that gave away, so very clearly, what Dylan liked. Raffo had missed that look so much.

As an artist, most of the time, Raffo knew how to get out of her own head—because it was the only way to get where she truly wanted to be. She'd done it in Big Bear when her feet had led her to the landing in the middle of the night, Dylan not exactly waiting for her, but close enough. She'd done it the other night after visiting Mia, when she'd driven to Connor's house without thinking—because thinking was irrelevant at that point—and because she knew in her bones what she had to do. Most of all, she felt it when she was painting a picture of Dylan. And she sure as hell knew it now.

"I missed you so much," Dylan whispered in her ear. "God, the thought of never doing this again." Raffo felt Dylan's lips stretch into a smile against her cheek and it lit her entire being on fire. She'd missed Dylan's smiles the most because they'd been the hardest to forget. Because they were so dazzling and intoxicating and so quintessentially Dylan.

Raffo leaned back to take in this particular smile, and it was just as glorious and arousing as she'd expected. But Dylan's captivating grin didn't blind her to the fine lines around her eyes or the creases on her forehead. Dylan wasn't just Connor's mom; she was also significantly older than Raffo, making her an unlikely candidate to fall in love with, at least by rational standards, yet that was exactly what Raffo had done.

It had happened months ago, in Big Bear—maybe even on that first day. Or maybe it had transpired more slowly, over the course of the weeks they'd spent together, Dylan simply being Dylan making it impossible for Raffo not to fall for her, despite all the logical arguments against it.

But Raffo was in love. Seeing Mia—hearing her hollow words—had only crystallized that truth. The first few weeks in Big Bear, Raffo's head had still been filled with Mia-Mia-Mia, until all those thoughts had been replaced with Dylan-Dylan-Dylan. And maybe there was something unhealthy about that, something a bit too escapist, but Raffo'd had plenty of time since returning to LA to question what she really wanted.

Falling for Dylan in Big Bear had been wonderfully distracting but coming back and having to face Connor most certainly hadn't been. This wasn't just lust. This was love. That, too, was as clear as daylight to Raffo. This, too, she felt in every last cell of her body when she got out of her own head. When she let herself.

Dylan led the way up the stairs, into her bedroom, where Raffo's first—scandalously topless—painting of her hung on the wall.

"Wow," Raffo exclaimed, not because she was impressed with her own work, but because of the impact it must have had on Dylan all this time. "You've basically been sleeping with yourself for weeks."

"I sure have." Dylan tugged at Raffo's shirt. "Thinking of you for every single second of it. You and me in Big Bear." Too impatient to undo the buttons, Dylan hoisted Raffo's shirt over her head. "I've been meaning to ask." She flashed one of her smiles. "Do you have any self-portraits? I'd love one of those."

"I don't do self-portraits," Raffo replied. Whenever the thought had occurred to her, or someone had suggested it, she'd dismissed it as ridiculous. Why would Raffo paint herself when there was an infinite number of much more interesting subjects to paint?

"That figures," Dylan said, "but you should really reconsider."

"I should, huh?" Raffo grinned at Dylan. "And who's going to make me?"

"Maybe you can start with a portrait of the two of us together to ease yourself into it."

Raffo chuckled but quickly lost interest in this topic. She knew exactly how to make Dylan stop talking nonsense. She kissed her gently on the lips and allowed herself to relish in the feeling—in this moment she'd been so afraid to dream of.

Raffo wasn't sure they'd be having this divine moment now if Dylan hadn't come back for her last week. If Dylan hadn't gotten out of her own head—bypassing the grievances of her own son—and driven back to Connor's house to kiss her.

But none of it mattered, because they were here now. It was

impossible to predict how Connor would react when he saw them together—*really* together—for the first time, but that was for later. Connor had given them the gift of tonight and the possibility of a future and, right now, that was everything.

They fumbled with their clothes in between kisses, in between the magical touch of Dylan's lips against her. Because there was something magical about it. This entire night had been magical. From the moment Raffo had spotted Dylan at Min-ji's, and the energy in the restaurant had transformed, there had been magic in the air.

Wasn't it magic that they stood here in Dylan's bedroom now? Wasn't it magic that they had ended up together in Big Bear? Two different people both looking for their own kind of peace of mind, for something they had lost—and while searching for that unquantifiable, seemingly impossible thing, they had found each other.

Every lonely night that had passed since, Raffo had relived that insane, hard-to-believe moment when Dylan had confessed that it had been more than just sex for her. Raffo hadn't been able to believe her then, not fully, because it was still impossible, and their feelings for each other too implausible, but there was nothing implausible about tonight. About how she felt. About how crazy she was about Dylan French.

Raffo wasn't as good as Dylan at expressing how she felt, but the words simply burst out of her now.

"You make me lose my mind," she whispered in Dylan's ear. "Utterly and completely."

In response, Dylan maneuvered them onto the bed until she lay on top of Raffo.

"I'm so in love with you." Dylan looked straight into Raffo's eyes. She swallowed slowly, as though she was overcome by her own words. "I'm not letting you go again."

Raffo folded her arms around Dylan's neck a little tighter. She pulled her close, until their noses touched.

"I'm not going anywhere," she said.

"Good," Dylan whispered, then kissed her again. First on the mouth, but her lips soon drifted to the sensitive skin of Raffo's neck, driving Raffo even more crazy.

Raffo ran her hands over Dylan's soft skin, wanting to feel all of her. She held onto her, because she'd lost her once before and she now totally understood what Dylan had said about not knowing how to recover from Raffo's touch again. It made perfect sense to her now as Dylan's lips trailed a moist path to Raffo's breast and she wrapped them warmly around her nipple.

Dylan's hand meandered between Raffo's legs, teasing her above the flimsy fabric of her panties. Dylan gazed into her eyes and Raffo couldn't look away if she tried.

If someone had told her at the beginning of summer, at the height of her heartbreak, and before Connor had pushed her into her car to Big Bear Lake, that Raffo would feel like this about another woman, that she would fall head-over-heels in love again—with her best friend's mother, no less—she would have laughed hard in their face. She might have even called them a few names. She surely wouldn't have taken a word of it seriously because of the sheer improbability of it.

And look at her now. Her break-up from Mia that had so devastated her, that had left her heart—and her life and her art —in total shambles now just seemed like something she had gotten over—or was very close to being over. In fact, before she got out of her head completely, before Dylan hooked her finger-tips under the waistband of her panties, Raffo knew exactly what to do with the money from the sale of her and Mia's house. The sale she would no longer dillydally on. She'd done that long enough.

Because Raffo had learned two very valuable lessons at the tender age of thirteen. No matter that she'd been too young to understand back then, when there was only pain and loss and grief. She knew now.

Life was short, and love was never a given.

Then, Dylan's fingers slipped inside her panties and met with Raffo's wetness, and Raffo lost her mind completely.

CHAPTER 39

Dylan had waited weeks for this moment. At last, it was happening. Raffo's strong fingers curled around her wrist. Dylan wasn't sure why she was so hung up on this specific gesture, because Raffo had done many other things to her in Big Bear, yet this was the one her mind had been stuck on. Maybe because, subconsciously, it claimed a kind of ownership that was unthinkable outside of the bedroom. It drove Dylan wild when Raffo held her wrists above her head, even though her grip wasn't that tight and Dylan could easily shake herself loose, yet that was the very last thing she wanted to do.

Or maybe it was because it made her breasts jut out, vulnerably, but also irresistibly, to Raffo, who was as crazy about her breasts as she was about Dylan's personality.

The evidence was on display on the opposite wall to the bed they were in. Raffo had painted that topless image from a raw, primitive instinct. From a place inside her she couldn't hide from. Dylan had spent many hours staring at that painting, and she'd given it a lot of thought. That was the only and inevitable conclusion she had drawn.

And now, she could actually ask Raffo. They could lie in Dylan's bed together and study the painting and spend hours discussing its myriad meanings—Dylan looked forward to how adorably uncomfortable that would make Raffo.

For now, she lay panting in Raffo's grasp. Dylan tried to steady her breathing, but it was futile. Her body was all revved up from watching Raffo climax earlier, her voice deliciously low and her face all tortured satisfaction.

Raffo caught Dylan's hard nipple between her lips, then swept her soft, warm tongue over it. It was, contained in one second, the very thing that made Raffo so enchanting. She was soft and hard all at once, her hardness an undertone that never overshadowed the softness at her surface.

One night in bed in Big Bear, Raffo had told her a few things that she and Mia had done in bed—from what Dylan could gather, mostly on Mia's insistence. Although, from the start, Raffo had struck her as someone not easily swayed by what someone else wanted from her. But maybe that was the power Mia'd had over her at the dying end of their relationship. Maybe giving in to Mia's whims—for whips as well as open relationships—had been Raffo's last-ditch attempt at trying to salvage things. And she had learned the hard way that it didn't work.

Just as Raffo's grip on Dylan's wrists wasn't one-sidedly tight, and the clasp of her lips on her nipple wasn't just agonizingly sharp, Raffo was so many delicious things gathered in one person. Principled enough not to date her best friend's mother but also strong enough, when she simply couldn't take it anymore, to change her mind and stand up to Connor. To do that for Dylan—for them. No wonder Dylan hadn't been able to get over her.

Dylan no longer had any intention of getting over Raffo. Sure, she was aroused to the point of no return, because Raffo's hand was traveling across her belly, leaving a field of goose bumps in its wake, but it wasn't just infatuation tingling in every one of her nerve endings. When Dylan had seen that card from her son, when she'd gotten the permission she had hoped for, in a flash, Dylan had known.

Raffo was the one.

She could fill a dozen sheets of paper with an endless list of reasons, but the reasons didn't matter, in the end. The only thing that mattered was how she felt. How her body had told her, as she sat opposite Raffo, that despite everything, despite the glaring obstacle that her own son represented, this was the only way it was meant to be. Despite their age difference and Raffo only being Dylan's 'third woman', they were meant to be together.

Dylan wasn't so deluded that she believed she and Raffo would magically be together forever—she didn't have a crystal ball, and life had taught her better than to make such silly, absolute predictions. Yet Dylan knew, in every fiber of her being, that she should be with Raffo now. That Raffo was the one for her now. That she could no longer date—what had Con called them?—mediocre middle-aged men and expect to feel the same way she did when she was with Raffo.

Oh, how Raffo was the one for her. Being with her was like experiencing all over again, as though for the very first time, how utterly breathtaking sex could be.

Right now, Raffo clasped Dylan's wrists above her head with one hand, while her other reached the apex of her thighs.

Dylan's clit thumped wildly.

Age melted away as her body responded with the vigor of someone three decades younger. Although she would need lube. There were some things that would always betray her age. But Dylan didn't want to be younger, and clearly, Raffo didn't need her to be younger, either.

Raffo gazed down at her with her bottomless, pitch-black eyes. She tugged at her lower lip with her teeth, as though an idea had just occurred to her. Or maybe she was trying to figure out where the lube was—mercifully, it was right there on the nightstand. After their encounter at Connor's house, Dylan had needed copious amounts of it to quiet her needy body. Instead, Raffo sucked her index finger between her lips, and the sight made Dylan's clit beat in triple time.

Raffo brought her wet fingertip between Dylan's legs and, ever so gently—with that soft, tender touch she had—circled it around Dylan's pulsing clit.

A deep groan escaped Dylan. She'd dreamed of this moment —had actively envisioned it on the backs of her eyelids—countless times. The more profound her desire, and the wilder her fantasies had become, the less chance they'd seemed to have of coming true. But this was very real. Raffo's body was warm against hers. Her dark gaze was intoxicating and her face only a fraction removed from Dylan's. Her grip around Dylan's wrists was far more arousing than the one in her imagination. And that fingertip edging along her clit was about to drive her to utter delirium.

The half a million dollars Dylan had lost seemed like a small price to pay for this—for her dreams coming true. She would never have gone to Big Bear if she hadn't lost the money. She would never have spent all that time with Raffo. She would never have fallen in love with her. Dylan would give every last penny she possessed for a night like this with Raffo. And she had every intention of turning one night into many.

"Come for me," Raffo said—instructed, really.

Dylan nearly lost her mind entirely.

Raffo's finger grew a little more insistent but this wasn't about the pressure of a finger on Dylan's clit, it wasn't even about how her hands were held above her head. It was all about how Raffo looked at her with that glint in her eye that told Dylan everything she needed to know. It was about the two of them in this bed together finally being able to give in to what they'd both wanted. It was only about Dylan's dreams coming true, because that's what being with Raffo felt like.

So, of course, Dylan came. She cried out as the orgasm

washed over her, as the pleasure took her, as her body surrendered easily and desperately to Raffo's touch. To all of Raffo.

————

Dylan believed she must still be dreaming when she opened her eyes because Raffo was lying next to her.

She blinked several times, then trailed a finger along Raffo's arm to confirm this wasn't a dream. She was very real. All of this was real. And they were no longer in Big Bear. They were back in real life. Connor knew about them. Dylan would call him later to thank him for his grand gesture because, without it, she might never have given herself permission to do this. Perhaps she and Raffo would have sneaked a desperately illicit kiss at an event some time, but Dylan would never have invited Raffo into her home—into this very bed—without Connor's approval. The ambivalence of being in love with her son's best friend hadn't suddenly disappeared after last night. It was still odd and tricky but, now, it was also possible and something they could all work with instead of something to avoid and most certainly to never speak of again.

"Half a million for your thoughts," Raffo said, a naughty grin on her lips.

"Half a mil?" Dylan could now even joke about the painful amount of money she'd lost—about the reason she'd had that job interview the day before. She hadn't given the interview one more thought since she'd clasped eyes on Raffo. "That's generous."

"How much for a kiss?" Raffo narrowed her eyes. She looked deliciously sleepy and as though Dylan would have to hug her for at least the next hour.

"A kiss is free." Dylan scooted closer. She kissed Raffo softly on the lips. "And I was thinking of Connor."

"Hm." Raffo sighed. "After a night like that, he'd usually be the first person I'd call. But that's not the best idea this time around."

"I don't really know how to approach him either." It was an atypical feeling for Dylan, who was always very open with her son about everything and vice versa. "It's all well and good that he set up our date last night, but where do we go from there?"

"We can theorize all we want, but we won't know how he really feels until we talk to him."

Dylan nodded. "Let's talk to him separately for the first time, though. I wouldn't want him to feel ganged up on."

"Ganged up?" Raffo chuckled. "We're hardly a gang." She cupped Dylan's cheek. "Let's not overthink it. I mean it. Of course we will take his feelings into account, but… let's enjoy this." Raffo's smile was warm and also a little wild. "Last night was amazing and I want many repeat performances."

"Please keep in mind that my body needs more recovery time than a nimble thirty-two-year-old's," Dylan joked.

"You're already playing the age card with me? After our first night together?" Raffo swept her thumb over Dylan's cheek.

The loud ring of Dylan's phone interrupted them. What time was it? Dylan wasn't used to getting up for work any longer.

She found her phone on the nightstand. The call was from a number she didn't recognize. She picked up, anyway.

"Mrs. French, Gustavo Pereira from GMX here. I wanted to reach out first thing. We were incredibly impressed yesterday and I'm delighted to offer you the managing director position at our agency."

Dylan sat up a bit straighter. She should be beside herself, yet she wasn't. And after last night, she was intimately familiar with what that felt like.

"Thank you so much," she said, automatic politeness kicking in. "I truly appreciate that. I'm just in the middle of something. Can I get back to you later today?"

"Of course, I look forward to your call and I sincerely hope it will be a yes."

"Thanks, Gustavo. Talk soon." Dylan rang off and checked the time on her phone. It was 9:26.

"And?" Raffo's eyebrows were arched all the way up. She held up her hand. "Let me guess? They're cray-cray about you and they want you to start tomorrow?"

Dylan could smile now. "The job's mine if I want it."

"That's wonderful news." Raffo smiled widely. "Although you look as though someone just called to arrange your funeral instead."

"Argh." Dylan dramatically fell back onto the bed. "Not to sound petulant, but I don't want to be managing director at someone else's agency. The very reason I quit my previous job was to start my own." But Dylan had royally fucked that up for herself. She turned to Raffo, like she had done in Big Bear when this very subject had come up and Raffo, simply by widening her lips into a smile, could instantly make her feel better.

Raffo didn't smile and they were no longer in Big Bear. They were no longer hiding from real life.

"I know I'm being ridiculous," Dylan admitted. "I will take the job, obviously. I'm a fool to think I can have it all." She put a hand on Raffo's warm belly. "And I have you now."

"I want you to consider something." Raffo shuffled closer until Dylan's hand was flattened between their bodies. "Don't protest, okay? Just listen and then think about it." She actually brought a finger to Dylan's lips. "I've come into some money recently, in large part thanks to your son. And I have half of a house to sell. How about I invest in your new agency?"

Automatically, Dylan shook her head. She tried to open her mouth for the prompt 'no' she had at the ready, but Raffo didn't let her. Instead, she pressed her lips to Dylan's and then gave her a stern look—she had plenty of those, as well. "Don't imme-diately rebut my offer. Think about it for at least twenty-four hours."

"I don't have twenty-four hours," Dylan said. "I need to call Gustavo back today."

"If they really want you, they'll wait."

"Raffo, babe, I appreciate the offer, but I can't accept your money. That puts too much pressure on—"

"Do I look like someone who just gives money away willy-nilly?" Raffo interrupted her. "It would be an investment on which I expect a return. You spoke so passionately about the agency you want to start. I fully believe you can turn it into a success."

"What if I don't?"

"Then I will know what it feels like to make a bad investment." Raffo grinned. "I might have to hide away from the world in the house in Big Bear you would still own and would have to let me stay at." Raffo peered into her eyes. "All jokes aside, you have forty years of experience in advertising. I wouldn't offer you this money to invest in some obscure internet coin. I'm offering it to you as an investment in your new company, in you, and in your happiness, which means a lot to me."

"In that case." Dylan maneuvered herself on top of Raffo. "I'll think about it for the allocated twenty-four hours and by thinking, I mean doing this." Dylan peppered kisses all over Raffo's neck until her entire body shook with laughter beneath her.

CHAPTER 40

Butterflies somersaulted in Raffo's belly—and not the good kind. Just like the very first time she'd walked into the Connor Hart Gallery, her nerves were aflutter. But this time, years after that initial meeting, it wasn't because she was anxious about meeting the hot new gallerist in town. It was because she was sleeping with his mother.

There was only one way through it—by doing it. She opened the door, greeted Connor's assistant, and headed straight for his office.

"Hey." Connor studied her from his chair, taking a long appraising look before rising for their usual hello kiss. "Good dinner?" he asked as he hugged her.

"The best." God, this was weird. This was not the casual vibe Raffo enjoyed between them. She missed their easy friendship, but this awkwardness felt like a necessary toll for the happiness she'd found. The way Dylan looked at her, touched her, made every uncomfortable moment worth enduring. Still, sitting across from Connor now, she wished she could fast-forward through this particular growing pain.

"Let's skip the usual details," Connor said, settling back in his chair. Unlike her other gay male friends who avoided any mention of female intimacy, Connor had never been squeamish about such things.

"Words can't express my gratitude, so I won't even try," Raffo said, attempting to lighten the mood with their usual banter. She thought it was the best way forward. The sooner they could laugh about it, the better. "But still." This did need to be said. "Seriously, Con. Thank you. It means so much to me."

"I want you to be happy, Raff, and as my boyfriend has been telling me every day since he went home, my happiness isn't more important than my best friend's, let alone my own mother's."

"I'm aware that this is not effortless for you." Raffo took a seat at Connor's desk.

"Murray's very proud of me." His smile didn't quite reach his eyes, uncertainty lingering at its edges. "Especially of the little card with your very own rainbow heart on it. That was a lovely touch, even if I do say so myself."

"I hope you had the required copyright to have that printed onto a card. I hear licensing deals go for a lot of money these days." Raffo couldn't suppress a grin.

"I got it directly from the artist who happens to be my friend." His eyebrows danced with familiar mischief. "I'm also quite tight with her agent-slash-gallerist, who is awesome, by the way. Have you met him?"

"I have and you're right. He is a remarkable dude." Raffo hesitated, but only for a split second. "You should meet his mom, though."

Connor burst into a chuckle. "His mom most certainly is something else as well." He leaned over the desk. "She's not exactly aging gracefully—getting it on with younger people and everything. Women, no less."

"No fucking way! *Women!* You'd best get her head examined quickly."

They both laughed it off and maybe that was the thing with a friendship like theirs—it was strong enough to withstand this kind of initial tension. They wouldn't be going on family vacations any time soon, but their love for each other was big enough to adjust to this unique situation.

"We need to talk business, Raff," Connor said. "We have a job to do. Your Chicago show is approaching swiftly."

"I was thinking," Raffo relaxed into her chair. She could talk business, which equaled discussing her work, with Connor all day long. "I might have quite a few new pieces of work to show by then, after all." Ever since her night with Dylan, Raffo hadn't been able to shake the initially preposterous idea of a painting of her and Dylan together. It was what she wanted to paint most of all and if she'd learned one thing the past few months, it was not to ignore that particular persistent voice inside of her —no matter how absurd it might sound at first.

Connor reclined, amusement flickering across his face. "New work, huh? You mean in the 'I'm Crazy About Your Mom Collection'?"

Raffo couldn't help but chuckle. "Let's just say the muse has been generous."

"Do I even want to know?" Connor raised an eyebrow.

"Don't worry, I won't be painting your mom as Venus rising from the sea," Raffo teased. "But I've had some very inspiring ideas…"

Raffo was certain this would pique his interest, despite the subject of her new work.

"Go on." Connor nodded.

"I'm thinking of a series that captures moments of transition," Raffo explained, still feeling a touch insecure but her enthusiasm growing by the second. "Those in-between states where everything's changing but nothing's settled yet. Like dawn breaking, or the moment just before a storm hits."

Connor gave her an encouraging look. He lived for conversations like this. Nonetheless, she considered her next words carefully.

"Dylan's at this incredible point in her life. She's rediscovering herself, embracing new experiences. It's like watching someone emerge from a cocoon. I want to capture that energy, that sense of transformation." The words tumbled out easier than expected, fueled by the same passion that had kept her up half the night sketching. It wasn't just Dylan's transformation she wanted to capture—it was her own too, this shift from seeing Dylan as forbidden to seeing her as possibility incarnate.

The last traces of Connor's hesitation melted away. "That actually sounds really fucking amazing." He sent her a smile. "Even though this probably means more naked portraits of my mom."

"Almost certainly." Raffo grinned. "But I'll paint them so even you can look at them."

They shared a laugh, all of the earlier tension dissipating.

"To going places." Connor picked up a half-empty water bottle from his desk. "Together."

———

When Connor arrived, Dylan held him in an embrace that lasted longer than either of them was accustomed to. She must have done something right to have raised a son like that. A son who could accept that she was dating his best friend. Though 'dating' hardly described what she and Raffo had now. As far as she was concerned, they were in a relationship. That's what it felt like—like the most glorious, proper, satisfying relationship Dylan had been in since those early years with Connor's father.

"Raffo's inspiration is through the roof," Connor said as he walked into the house. "She's painting like they sometimes show in those completely unrealistic movies where an artist creates a work of genius in twenty-four hours." His lips curved into an enigmatic grin. "If I had known it was going to be like this when you got together, I wouldn't have objected so much." Dylan couldn't read whether he was posturing, joking, or something in between.

"Sit, darling. Let me get you a drink." Dylan needed Connor relaxed for the Raffo-related conversation ahead. "I have that kombucha you like."

"I'll have a glass of wine. I took an Uber. It's been a week." He slumped against the chair, exhaling with theatrical weariness.

"Busy at the gallery?" Dylan poured them both a glass of white wine.

"I can hardly complain but suddenly every up-and-coming artist wants space in my gallery. It's very much the Raffo-Shah effect."

Dylan handed him the wine and sat opposite her son at the kitchen table. He looked tired, his eyes small and his skin paler than usual.

"Maybe you should take a break. Go to the lake house with Murray."

"I can't take a break now, Mom. Work is nuts."

"That's precisely when you need one." Dylan didn't expect her son to take her advice, but it didn't stop her from giving it— she had learned this particular lesson the hard way many times over. "Even just for a few days."

"I might just hire a new co-worker instead."

"Really? That's great." Dylan bit back the words: if it's financially viable. She would have inquired about the gallery's finances without qualms before she'd lost half a million dollars, but she still didn't entirely feel as though she had the right to ask.

"Raffo's new pieces will easily fetch three times what her previous works sold for. Minimum."

Dylan couldn't possibly stop herself from asking the next question. "Which pieces are we talking about exactly?"

Connor chuckled. "We're calling it the 'I'm So In Love With My Best Friend's Mom Collection', so yeah, it's all you, Mom. You. And Raffo herself as well, surprisingly."

Raffo showed Dylan what she was working on all the time.

Dylan knew exactly what—and who—she was painting. It was an essential part of why they'd gotten so close so quickly in Big Bear and it continued to be the case in Los Angeles. But Dylan stayed out of the commercial aspect of Raffo's art. It wasn't her business.

Dylan didn't really know what to say to her son about that. Her stomach performed an unexpected somersault.

"Does it bother you?" she asked.

"Nah." Connor took a large sip of wine. "I'm still getting used to it but it helps that Raffo's so… Raffo, you know?"

Dylan knew exactly what Connor meant. She also beamed with pride a little.

"But she's *really* into you." Connor blew out some air, as though he still couldn't believe that his hot artist friend had feelings for his mom. Dylan understood—some days, she could hardly believe it herself. But there was no doubt about how much Raffo was *into her*. "If Mia ever sees this new work, she might never recover."

The mention of Mia's name didn't jolt Dylan that much. But it was a good enough segue into what Dylan wanted to talk about with her son.

"Speaking of Mia," she said a little clumsily, although Dylan mentioning Raffo's ex certainly seemed to capture Connor's full attention. "She and Raffo are selling their house and Raffo made me an offer."

Connor's eyes grew wide. "Please, tell me whatever you're going to say next doesn't include the words U-Haul and moving in together."

"What?" Dylan shook her head. "No, we're not moving in together, darling. That would be a bit soon."

"Phew." He pretended to wipe the sweat off his brow. "You never know with lesbians. They're very fast-moving that way."

Dylan waved off his comment and continued what she really wanted to say. "Raffo has offered to invest the money from the sale of her and Mia's house into my new agency."

"Ha," Connor said. "So you are U-Hauling, just not in the traditional way."

Dylan ignored his comment. "Before I make a decision, I wanted to get your input." Her son's opinion on this was important to her for many reasons. And she no longer wanted to hide anything significant from him.

"Raffo can do whatever she likes with her money." Connor stared into his wine glass.

"But do you think I can accept it? That I *should*?" Dylan's instantaneous 'no' had changed into a maybe over the past twenty-four hours. She had called Gustavo back and asked the agency for a few more days to decide. Dylan was fifty-fifty on whether she should let Raffo invest in her new business—hence her need for a second opinion. She traced the rim of her wine glass, remembering how Raffo had presented the idea—not with grand gestures or flowery words, but with that quiet intensity that made Dylan feel both seen and slightly unmoored. Like standing at the edge of something vast and promising.

"You're asking me?" Connor seemed a little taken aback.

"Yes." Dylan nodded.

"Why?"

"Because you're my son and I value your input on things, but also because I know you've been worried about me since my, um, disastrous investment and this doesn't feel like something I should do without consulting you." Dylan hadn't yet mentioned the obvious. "And because Raffo is your friend and, well, I want to make sure she's not just offering me the money because she's so… *into me*."

"She hasn't talked to me about it," Connor said. "She probably thinks it's between you and her."

"I'd just like to know what you think, darling."

"I think that Raffo is so in love with you, she would give everything she has to make you happy. I think that neither one of you are thinking very straight right now, but that doesn't necessarily have to be a bad thing." He sent her a soft smile that reminded Dylan of when he was the sweetest little boy. "If I've learned one thing from this whole debacle it's that it's okay to just go with the flow. I tried to resist you and Raffo being together and it didn't make anyone happier. I could advise you not to take Raffo's money, but to what end? You're both intelligent adults and I'm sure you would have the necessary paperwork drawn up to protect yourselves against whatever might happen in the future. But if you're going to be together, then why wouldn't you let her invest in your start-up? It's pretty obvious that you don't want to take another managing job."

Dylan absorbed her son's surprisingly mature advice. She took a sip of her wine, contemplating his words.

"I suppose this means you're officially more grown-up than I am. Should I start coming to you for life advice now?"

Connor snorted. "God no. I'm pretty sure giving your mom your blessing to date your best friend violates some universal law of nature."

"Ah, yes," Dylan deadpanned. "Newton's lesser-known fourth law of motion: A son shall not advise his mother on matters of the heart, especially not when it involves his best friend, lest the fabric of space-time unravel."

Connor grinned. "Exactly. I'm just trying to prevent the collapse of the universe. You're welcome."

Dylan smiled warmly at him. "My hero. Saving the world, one awkward mother-son conversation at a time."

"It's a tough job," Connor sighed dramatically, "but someone's got to do it."

They shared a look before breaking into quiet chuckles.

As their laughter subsided, Dylan reached across the table and squeezed her son's hand. "In all seriousness, thank you, Connor. Your support is so important to me."

Connor squeezed back. "Just don't make me regret it by walking in on you two making out on the couch or something."

Dylan rolled her eyes. "Please. We're grown women, not

teenagers. We have perfectly good bedrooms for that sort of thing."

"Mom!" Connor shouted, his face a mix of horror and amusement.

Dylan smirked. "What? I thought we were being straightforward with each other now."

Connor shook his head, laughing despite himself.

They clinked glasses, both smiling, comfortable in the knowledge that no matter how much things changed, their mother-son bond remained unbreakable.

CHAPTER 41

Although she loved every minute of it, Dylan was still adjusting to working again. She could ignore it all she wanted—as Raffo would deadpan—but you couldn't expect the same energy from your body and brain at the cusp of sixty that you had in your mid-thirties.

"It happens on a cellular level, babe," Raffo had said last week, when Dylan had fallen into bed next to her, too exhausted to enjoy Raffo's touch—a fact that had scandalized Dylan much more than it had Raffo. "Don't waste your precious energy fighting your own cells. It's futile."

Dylan's mad dash to the airport had ended predictably with a delayed flight to Chicago. Connor and Raffo had flown out a few days ago and despite being busier than ever before with her new ad agency, Dylan had missed Raffo as though she'd known nothing else in her life than Raffo by her side.

The sight of Murray waiting at O'Hare's taxi stand, fresh from his New York flight, lifted her spirits. She hadn't expected the wave of relief at seeing him, but there it was. Murray had become family in the most unexpected way—not just Connor's boyfriend, but the person who'd helped bridge the gap when everything had seemed impossible.

The flight delay had eliminated any chance of a hotel stop, but Murray—also her impromptu stylist—was already working his magic with her makeup in the taxi en route to Raffo's opening at the prestigious Dolores Flemming Gallery.

"Thanks for waiting," Dylan said as Murray tucked a final wayward strand into place. Her fingers brushed through her hair, deliberately tousling it. Raffo made no secret of loving her windswept look. "And for coming."

"Are you kidding me? Raffo's our girl."

Our girl. It was funny to hear Murray say it like that. As though it was the most ordinary thing in the world.

"Thanks for everything." Dylan knew very well that if it hadn't been for Murray, Connor would have taken much longer to come around and accept that his mother and his best friend had fallen in love. It might never have happened or it might have taken so long that Dylan and Raffo would have let the opportunity go by—although Dylan was pretty sure there wasn't much chance of that. Their feelings had been too strong.

"No thanks required. I was only telling it the way I saw it." Murray shot her a warm smile. "I don't know who he gets it from, but Connor can be a touch self-centered sometimes."

"*My* son?" Dylan pressed a hand to her chest in mock offense. "Never." Although they were joking, Dylan didn't think that Connor had been self-centered about her and Raffo being together at all. He'd only had a perfectly normal reaction to the news, but Murray had helped him to look at it in an extraordinary way.

"I'm nervous," Dylan admitted, her palms sweaty.

"It's only natural." Murray smiled warmly at her. "She's your girlfriend and, well, from what I've seen, you'll be on full display, Mama."

"It's not the work I'm worried about." Dylan could only feel honored about Raffo painting her so frequently. "It's how Raffo must be feeling right now."

"She's been here before and she's never been better," Murray said. "And she has her best friend and biggest ally by her side."

The taxi stopped. They had arrived at the gallery.

———

Dolores Flemming was a tall, stunning woman with an equally stunning but much younger woman as her wife. It startled Dylan because, despite her own relationship with Raffo, she hadn't expected that.

The opening reception was in full swing and Raffo, who looked absolutely scrumptious in a tuxedo and her hair swept back to reveal the sharp elegance of her cheekbones, was busy talking to everyone who wanted a piece of her.

"So, you're the inspiration behind all this," a rich voice murmured near her shoulder. Dylan turned to find Dolores studying her with warm curiosity. "Admittedly, when I booked Raffo for a show at my gallery, this was not the work I was expecting, but it's absolutely mind-blowing, so thank you." She shot Dylan a wink, as though they were somehow in this together.

"I really didn't do all that much."

Dolores snatched two glasses of champagne from a passing waiter's tray.

"I'm sure that's not true." She offered Dylan one of the glasses; Dylan gladly accepted.

Dylan could listen to people praise Raffo all night, but now that she had Dolores to herself, another thought pressed forward. She watched the way Dolores's fingers traced the stem of her champagne glass, remembering how she'd seen her do the same thing earlier with her wife's shoulder. The casual intimacy of it gave her courage.

"We don't know each other, but can I ask you something personal?" Dylan asked.

Dolores grinned at her. "After studying Raffo's work, I feel like I know you rather intimately, so it's only fair that you can ask me anything." Her smile was disarming and generous.

"How long have you and your wife been together?"

"It'll be eight years soon," Dolores said, her voice bursting with pride. "It was terribly complicated at the beginning, but here we are, so many years later." Dolores swallowed hard, as though the complications she just referred to made her emotional.

"Wow! Eight years." She and Raffo had discussed Dylan's age many more times than Raffo had wanted to. Because, according to Raffo, it wasn't an issue to be discussed. If anything, she liked that Dylan was older. That she'd lived a lot of life and was the wiser for it.

"How old are you, if I may be so bold to ask?" The politeness of her words didn't match the mischievous tone in Dolores's tone of voice.

"Sixty next month," Dylan said.

"Ah. Sixty is a tricky one. I had a melt down on my sixtieth. I wanted to break up with her even though my relationship with Sophie was the most beautiful thing about my life." She fixed her gaze on Dylan. "My advice is to not do anything outrageous or rash until the day is over. Although I fully sympathize with any doubts you may have." She gave a small nod. "It's not always a walk in the park, this difference in age, but, honestly, in the grand scheme of things, it's also no big deal." Dolores's smile was a lot less bright, as though a sad memory suddenly got hold of her. "You're joining us for lunch tomorrow, aren't you?" The brightness returned to her eyes. "Let's talk more then." She leaned in a little closer. "And congratulations. Raffo assured me that she couldn't have made any of this work without you. I mean, it's pretty obvious, but still." Dolores chuckled lightly. "I have to go do my thing, but we'll talk more soon."

Dylan watched Dolores disappear into the crowd, but even through the press of bodies, she caught the moment when

Dolores's eyes found her wife's—magnetic and inevitable—their shared smile as intimate as a touch.

———

Dylan's jaw slacked. Not because Raffo was stripping off that tuxedo she looked so dashing in, but because of the words that were coming out of her mouth.

"Sophie's boyfriend, who died, was Dolores's son, well step-son, really. Dolores's partner, Angela, died a long time ago, and Ian, Sophie's boyfriend, was Angela's son."

"You're making this up to—I don't know." Dylan shook her head. "Why are you making this up, babe?"

"It's true," Raffo said in her matter-of-fact way.

Dylan knew it must be true. It wasn't Raffo's style to come up with shocking tales like this. "Sophie was her daughter-in-law?" Her eyes grew wide.

"Well, not really," Raffo said. "But kind of, I guess." She grinned at Dylan as she unbuttoned her shirt. "See, there are much more, um, exotic pairings than us. My exact words to Connor after Sophie told us all about this last night."

"Jesus Christ." Dylan reached for Raffo. She hadn't seen nearly enough of her since arriving in Chicago.

"You'd better not be judging them," Raffo said, her voice all smiles.

"Who am I to judge?" Dylan found Raffo's dark gaze, and the world finally slowed to a perfect stillness.

"You're my old lady." Raffo couldn't even finish saying that without snickering.

"And you are something special." Dylan kissed Raffo on the lips.

"You know I don't think of myself that way," Raffo whispered.

"That doesn't make it any less so," Dylan said, meaning it from the bottom of her heart. "For someone who refuses to think of herself as special, you make some really special work."

"You're just saying that because you're in it." Raffo pulled back a little. She managed to keep a straight face.

Dylan couldn't help but chuckle. There were some things it was simply impossible to disagree with Raffo about. Although Raffo would probably disagree with what Dylan was about to say next.

"Dolores said something about turning sixty being really tricky. She freaked out on the—"

Before she could finish, Raffo placed a finger on Dylan's lips, gently silencing her. "The only thing tricky about your age is how it manages to make you even more captivating with each passing year."

It was unlike Raffo to say something so cheesy, but Dylan's cheeks flushed nonetheless.

"You're gorgeous when you talk nonsense like that," she mumbled against Raffo's finger.

As they leaned in for another kiss, Dylan couldn't help but think that just maybe, turning sixty wouldn't be so confrontational after all. Not with Raffo by her side, painting their love story one brushstroke at a time.

CHAPTER 42

"If the lesbians aren't doing it, it's almost certainly the invisible influence of the patriarchy," Alexis Dalton playing Justine Blackburn said on the screen.

Dylan chuckled so hard at that particular line of dialogue, she had to pause the movie—she didn't want to miss a second of *Gimme Shelter* now that they were finally watching it.

"If you keep pausing, we'll never get to the end." Raffo tightened her arm around Dylan, their bodies nestled into the couch. "You're sixty now. You'll probably fall asleep soon." Dylan's body shook along with Raffo's as she laughed at her own extremely lame joke.

"This Justine is just too much," Dylan said. "Did she really say that or was that something the scriptwriter came up with?"

"I'm not sure, but it sounds like vintage Justine." There was a reverence in her tone, a subtle softening that Dylan had learned to recognize whenever Raffo talked about Justine Blackburn.

"I'd love to meet her." Dylan shifted in Raffo's embrace, turning to catch her expression.

"Sure. I'll set it up. Maybe we can drop by the shelter next week." Raffo sat up straighter. "You know how I absolutely refuse to think of myself as special just because I have a talent for arranging paint on a canvas?"

Dylan wholly disagreed with this, but she knew how adamant Raffo was about this, so she nodded along.

"It's because of women like Justine." Raffo looked Dylan straight in the eye. "What Justine does *is* special." Raffo was far from the sentimental type, except when it came to the Rainbow Shelter and what it had meant to her. "She is how I measure being special. Compared to Justine, to what she does for unhoused kids, I'm nothing special."

Dylan knew not to argue against this. Instead, she simply settled back into Raffo's arms.

"We'd better keep watching, because I have one last birthday present for you today," Raffo said. "You'll get it after the movie is finished."

"What?" Dylan pulled back just enough to search Raffo's face. "You do?"

"Oh yes, and you might even say I saved the best for last." Raffo sat there beaming.

"How am I meant to enjoy the rest of the movie now?" Dylan tilted her head and pulled her lips into a seductive smile. "It's all I'll be able to think of now that you've said that." She blinked dramatically. "You should probably give it to me now."

Raffo shook her head, but she was smiling, her features softening—along with her resolve, Dylan hoped.

Then it dawned on Dylan that, perhaps, this last gift Raffo was referring to was something she could only give her when they were in bed together—even though they'd already spent plenty of time there today.

"Is it a gift of a sensual nature?" she asked, coyly.

"Hm." Raffo tapped her finger against her lips, as though she had to give that some serious thought. "Kind of, but not really," she said, finally—and infuriatingly.

Dylan made a show of checking her watch, startled to find it was already past eleven. Her sixtieth birthday had been a day full of celebration. First, Raffo had given her a brand-new paint-ing, for Dylan's eyes only. It was much more provocative than her other work and it was the most beautiful work of art Dylan had even seen, because it featured Raffo in all the glorious colors of the rainbow in a pose meant for the bedroom only.

Connor and Murray had cooked her an elaborate lunch and the four of them had had a wonderfully relaxed meal that had stretched long into the afternoon. Raffo couldn't possibly have saved the best present for last because spending time with her son and his boyfriend alongside Raffo as her partner was the best gift possible. For her and Con to be able to share a laugh about her relationship with his best friend, and even engage in a private eye roll—just between them—about Raffo's matter-of-fact tone when making a point, was all Dylan wanted.

Before they'd started watching *Gimme Shelter*, Dylan and Raffo had spent a few hours in bed, many of those with Dylan's hands pinned above her head.

On all fronts, emotionally, artistically, and physically, Dylan couldn't be more satiated, so what other gift could Raffo have for her? But that was the thing with Raffo. She always had one more trick up her sleeve.

"It's almost midnight," Dylan said. "My birthday's nearly over."

Raffo snickered, folding herself into a cross-legged position on the couch, and nodded at Dylan. "From that first day in Big Bear, it's been impossible for me to resist you," she said.

————

Celebrities had been flooding Raffo with commission requests, offering serious money for paintings of themselves or their families. Raffo's answer was always no. While she'd filled canvases with Dylan's image, she neither considered herself a portraitist nor enjoyed working on commission. Until someone very specific called.

Raffo pointed at the screen. She wasn't just going to come out and say it. She loved watching Dylan squirm too much for that.

"Do you know who wrote the screenplay for this movie?"

Dylan shook her head. "Is that something I should know?"

"No." Raffo was just stretching out this delicious moment. The whole day had been a string of beautiful moments. Even though it was Dylan's big birthday, it felt like Raffo's celebration too, that's how much she had enjoyed it. She couldn't get enough of the smile that kept appearing on Dylan's lips, and of how much she relished simply sitting at a table with her son, just chatting away, basking in all the love around her.

Because of her own unfortunate family history, Raffo had been so afraid of coming between Connor and his mother, perhaps because she'd never been taught that simply loving each other can make so much possible. That being part of a family is not conditional, like being part of Raffo's family had been after her mother's death. That Dylan and Connor's bond was strong because it was forged in the kind of unconditional love Raffo had gone without since the age of thirteen.

"*Gimme Shelter* was written by Charlie Cross, who is married to Ava Castaneda," Raffo said.

"I definitely know who Ava Castaneda is." Dylan's eyebrows danced suggestively. Every time they caught *Knives Out* on TV, they found themselves mesmerized by Ava's signature move—that slow, deliberate way she'd taste from a spoon. "And I surely also know who Charlie Cross is," Dylan said. "I had a few of her *Underground* books with me in Big Bear." She put a hand on Raffo's knee. "I only just finished the one I was in the middle of that night you so brazenly seduced me."

Raffo refused to take the bait. "Are you not really interested in this present? Is that why you're goading me?" She shrugged. "Okay. Fine. I'll go alone."

"Go alone where?" Dylan dug her fingertips into the flesh around Raffo's knee.

"Do you know who Ava's best friend is?"

Dylan shook her head again. "I'm too old to be abreast of all that." The grin on her face told a different story.

"Ava is best friends with Faye Fleming." Raffo wasn't one to waste time on celebrity friendships and affiliations, but after *Gimme Shelter* had come out, she and Min-ji and a few other people she'd been at the Rainbow Shelter with had mapped out the links from Justine to the biggest celebrity they could think of. Their own degrees of separation between the likes of Faye Fleming had vastly decreased because of the movie about Justine's life. That was Los Angeles for you.

Dylan's fingertips tapped an anxious rhythm against Raffo's knee. "Faye Fleming is married to the one and only Ida Burton," she breathed, her voice catching on each word.

The memory of that day in Big Bear still brought heat to Raffo's cheeks—Ida Burton's voice floating from the deck speakers, narrating that sultry sapphic story, revealing exactly what Dylan had been up to. So when Ida Burton's people had called to commission a portrait of her family, Raffo had said yes in a flash—on the condition that she could bring Dylan.

"Would you like to meet Ida Burton?" Raffo asked. It sounded as solemn and serious as she imagined a marriage proposal might sound.

Dylan's eyes grew to the size of saucers.

"I've agreed to paint her family portrait," Raffo said, edging closer. "We're meeting next week, and you're coming with me." She pressed her hand to Dylan's chest. "If your sixty-year-old heart can handle it."

"No way." Dylan leaned in, studying Raffo's face with laser focus, searching for any hint of teasing. "Are you messing with me?"

Raffo slowly shook her head. "I wouldn't mess with you about something as big as meeting Ida Burton, babe."

"Where are we meeting them?"

"At their house in Malibu. Connor has set it all up. I wasn't sure he'd manage not telling you. I owe him big time. I might have to paint Ida's gay ex-husband to pay him back." Raffo wasn't even kidding about that.

"Connor kept his mouth shut so you could surprise me?" Dylan's voice cracked with emotion.

"He sure did." Raffo should have known this tiny tidbit would get to Dylan the most. As a mother, she'd had to overcome quite a few things to get to this moment with Raffo. To have them celebrate her sixtieth together, as a couple. "Happy birthday, babe," Raffo said. She leaned in closer. "Sixty looks damn good on you." She kissed Dylan on the lips.

"What on earth am I going to get you for your birthday after you've given me all this?" She pulled her lips into one of her irresistible smiles.

"Don't worry about that for even one single second." Emotion roughened Raffo's voice. "You've already given me everything." She caught Dylan's inevitable protest with a kiss.

GET THREE E-BOOKS
FOR FREE

Building a relationship with my readers is the very best thing about writing. I occasionally send newsletters with details on new releases, special offers and giveaways.

And if you sign up to my mailing list I'll send you all this free stuff:

1. An e-book of *Few Hearts Survive*, a Pink Bean Series novella that is ONLY available to my mailing list subscribers.
2. A free e-book of *Hired Help*, my very first (and therefore very special to me) lesbian erotic romance story.
3. A free e-book of my first 'longer' work, my highly romantic novella *Summer's End,* set on an exotic beach in Thailand.

You can get *Few Hearts Survive* (a Pink Bean Series novella), *Hired Help* (a spicy F/F novelette) and *Summer's End* (a deeply romantic lesfic novella) **for free** by signing up at www.harperb liss.com/freebook/ or scanning the QR code below

GET THREE E-BOOKS FOR FREE

ABOUT THE AUTHOR

Harper Bliss is your go-to author for emotional and steamy sapphic romance, delivering stories that resonate with readers who crave love, passion, and a touch of drama.

Beloved series like French Kissing and Pink Bean have captivated fans around the globe with their unforgettable characters and heartfelt journeys.

Recently, Harper has been creating the BlissVerse—a universe of interconnected celebrity romance stories, all loosely set in the same world.

After years of adventure in Hong Kong and beyond, Harper now writes from Ghent, her favourite Belgian city, where she lives with her wife, Caroline, and their high-maintenance cat, Dolly Purrton.

Harper loves hearing from readers and you can reach her at the email address below.

www.harperbliss.com
harper@harperbliss.com

Printed in Great Britain
by Amazon